Eden Aflame

Philip Grimes

Contents

Neukölln, 1923

My name is Jophiel, with locks so fair and curly they trap sun like a jar. It was I, a female bailiff, who threw Adam and Eve from Paradise.

Somewhat moribund after this the Lord handed me a new century: the German twentieth.

'Go down from here prized Jophiel,' said my Lord. 'And, if you could, really rake it up.'

I was polishing my flaming sword at the time, trying not to singe my wrists. I said: 'Haven't they suffered enough? I mean... the burning fields of Europe.'

'Suffered enough?' My Lord looked surprised. 'They've only begun. They're just growing into themselves.'

~

The dressing room clock over a frosted window said ten minutes to showtime-- "Is there anything you need Missy?"

"No sweety pops. You run along."

I didn't. I stared - by the fire bucket missing its axe - as she smoothed her cropped black hair in a corset half-undone, her shoulders like prized cakes in muslin.

"What's up little fella?"

My gaze held. "Well if there's nothing I can do for you, is there anything you can do for me?"

She was smiling under her arm. Eyes weathering my stopped time, bringing the old and new from Mobile Bay - an ocean of heaped stockings and friendly light.

"Ah come here, Detty Boy."

I did.

"There are lines we shouldn't cross."

I nodded - wide lips of ultra-varnish.

"Sit."

I did with pleasure.

"Actually, get up a minute. There's something I can do."

She strode to the door and locked it, had me back on her thighs with the hot bulbs. All the girls here crop their hair divinely to the nape, scald it to submission with careful fingers. Her hand rummaged in my pants like a car footwell.

"Think I lost an earring down here."

...And tumescent me blinks, a mess of containment. The door sucks and her legs lever-arch the scarlet corridor, past a blurry pic of Marlene as a nipper, towards our auditorium. The Show. Bankers fidget in high collars, moustaches like foot-scrapers, wringing mirages over their sticky tickets... I uncrease the *Morgenpost.*

FURTWANGER PLEA

Look at this guy, Oskar Furtwanger-- I spoke to him in a sun-drenched lav on Friedrichstraße. Urinals are awkward enough without a sex killer in the next duchamp. I was struggling to go. He turned with a face that was shaved, but he'd missed a corner.

"Don't worry," he said. A faraway smile. "It'll come right soon enough."

If I wasn't worried, now I was: "I guess," the smile I returned was peeled.

"Just takes a bit of planning."

I watched him shake. Hammer enthusiast and fiddler. His shoes were cracked but conservative, as if memories no longer paid the bills (and it no longer mattered). Behind us, a carnivore vented in a cubicle - tumbling uranium. I didn't know how to reply to this molester without looking easy... or encouraging a stewed treatise on the decline of Prussia.

Maybe it wouldn't come right. Maybe, it was such chats as these turned things wrong.

But the echoing meat-eater was done, and Furtwanger's eyes slipped their cog. His soft scalp, full of pickelhaube yearning and boys' buttocks, clipped away on the rayed concourse. Moments later he led some curly kid off the platform. Auburn kid, all rubber-limbed with pamphlets. He was my age, fourteen or thereabouts, and communist.

I flap my Morgenpost: "Pressed for comment Furtwanger's estranged wife said, 'He'd taken to putting socks on before his underpants as he dressed. Something had flipped.'"

Estranged --yes, but alive! Oskar yanked his waifs cross-country too, Leipzig, Lübeck and Travemünde. I mean I'm Red, I turn the heads of spent men, I was in the lav - what if 'Wolfman' had nailed me? A mask to my face that is. "Highlighting the dual victimhood of Wilhelm's abdication." (Fine words.) "The homebound who can't dream, and those in the field dreaming for eternity".

But did curly kid escape? Well, he survived for rhinoplasty at the Charité and a rethink on Red Struggle. It was a debt collector stopped it.

A simple bailiff. Furtwanger was a year late with dry cleaning bills from Aachen, traced by Puppe Capital Services. The bailiff didn't want to appear in court, saying he was a humble employee making a living, for whom exposure - even in the public's interest - undermined his work.

The long arm of debt saved Pepin - a young Franconian progressive - debt and admin. He's very beautiful, or was, looks like a crown, not a mask, should be nailed forcefully to his head.

And Furtwanger himself? With the back parlour looking suspect to 'Gustl' - a teenager face down on a bench, his head at the end with a tin mask hanging off - the bailiff intervened between the hammer and last nail, flooring Furtwanger with a wrestling leap. Hannover precinct duly intervened with Edward Heinrich - a forensics man from America into ballistics and entomology. In this case, geology. Grains of sand all over Furtwanger's house linked to a trail of abductions on the Baltic coast.

So, if you want to frot teenagers and kill them, watch your debts. It's indicative though isn't it, the gall beneath...

She's back, unsoiled, flops in a chair and tosses me her cane. I watch her copper apples cross the room (around my paper).

"Security."

"What?" I put Furtwanger aside, dizzy with sensation.

"Did Albert ever book that firm? He talked about it. There's weirdos now."

"Which firm?"

She recakes. Crinoline is covering the dream; I listen to it rustle. "I've no idea Hon, I deal with erectile issues."

Flushed I get up and leave... Missy hums. ...meaning to cool off with Paps and his paperwork, but approaching the office there are voices.

"Your product doesn't exist. What do you do?"

"Keep the others at bay." Hahn voices - perhaps Missy meant this security firm.

"What others?"

"Exactly Pops."

"Aach, you talk in... *knots*! I won't have it until next week, we banked yesterday."

The unstable pregnancy of Hahn silence. I hear one shifting his weight like something down a warren. "There's a day."

Papa's breathing in his nose. "I can't pay without surplus. If I go under you've nothing at all."

And his logical head is visible in the gap, wondering what happened to rationalism, the war of words.

The air thrums, until Gerhard snaps it taut. "We're going to depreciate your assets."

"What?"

"Come on, Carlin. When you see your assets devalue, Brüning, you'll be up-front."

I run down the womb-red corridor to the dressing room, Papa's voice pursuing: "Let's pick it up when box office comes in. It's satire season!"

"Will do Pops."

I open the door a crack and watch. Missy says, "Whatch'y up to, Detty?"

I shush her, but the door crunches my head in the wall. "Evening. Just you tonight Missy Lehane?"

It's the elder Carlin, a big east-central man with remaining hair like sea foam. For something so featureless Carlin's head really strikes, like his chromosomes argued from the start. To

5

accuse or prohibit this head, you imagine a mere instant of liability in the eye before it's coming.

Missy doesn't recognise him at all. "Mm-hm."

He says nothing - a potato lost in a cupboard - and the door closes his curiosity.

"That firm?"

~

The auditorium hushes. The head of Missy's cane appears from a worn velvet curtain, then a boot that sparks like tourmaline - kicking a series of 'one night onlys' in her *Fleischer's Holeproofs*. The stage rises sheer for African legs, and the hand that plunged her crotch, manhandled the fruitless cane, now rubs the lobes of industrialists.

"Over here Missy, I've been to Brazil!" A breathless pear in a waistcoat mops his neck. I bounce eyes over the audience: no weirdos tonight. Prairie dogs eddying cigars of thin victory, she is untouchably theirs, but what? Possession, tourist; American Missy has one heel in the primal, the other way ahead.

Missy's lashes widen. She heads for the pear, dropping a glove at the feet of a front-row shadow. She leans to pick it up, overbiting with a chinned finger of apology. Cleaved brown squeezes like Madonna and child and our auditorium sighs, but the silhouette doesn't move, and Missy clips down the gummed floor to banana-boat man, who mostly cowers bar a straining twig. The spotlight unsticks an instant, holding only its copper buttock.

I've seen Missy out with her Mama, Davione, shopping in Wedding. You wouldn't believe she's a convulsing sex princess when you see them poking fruit. Looking skeptically at guajavas; they touch as they talk, darkly wintering, sending comfort through skin. Often stately (like a collonade), their heads soon hurl guffaws ...*But wait*, Missy's hand insists on Davione's arm, like the joke wasn't done and Mama laughed too soon. And she'll bend with a reluctant smile, like all the best joy.

I look at my trousers short in the ankle (the height of), and it feels like they're shrinking up. Captain Lehane honks from a scuffed Maybach on hawkers' corner; a family unit.

You are holding a child's homework really, given when this began. I sat with my tongue in my teeth last night - a herringbone bag at my shin - sketching Furtwanger. Sharonstraße blinks gauzy, wet and private below as Eden tilts.

To appreciate our city and times, you've to dig how death pursues us. If not Death, its receptionist. There's claspy handbags and feminism and shit, futuristic light bulbs, but really we're a stadium of crime - pro, field and amateur.

I should hand this journal to Inspektor Lange, but I won't. He's scratching his head with the press and a baying noose; his shipped microscopes from California - no, this'll go to grub Hartmann the publisher. He'll want something spattered on the front. And we'll need to discuss Mama - the first schism - but I can't, it's only been a year.

~

The poster pleads: 'Exclusive'. It's another one-night-only, but this time there's an upset - a maniac thought Missy's voice told him to strangle a baby. I heard the thump and echo of the seats as he launched. He was wrestled to the floor by other dreamers before he could grasp her breasts with trembling hands. Sometimes in these sojourns on the weary carpets, I see nerves in the scaffolding (and it's all scaffolding), as though to hold this ocean in symphony is no less a conductor's job, highwire.

And there's Hahn, look, filth-eyed in the footlights in black worsted - unaroused I assume. Skimming eaves not flesh. *Your dense energy, are you the bad guy Gerhard? Does your universe contract?* Sitting with a weight on your chest; ideas that don't pulse. He saw it all unfold.

Missy was in the wings later, knees in her arms. She'd got some notices in *Auto Magazin* and *Querkopf* for something fully-dressed, and her ornate eyes were glued to the boards, rendered huge in dimmer light.

"People say about stuff, it's my world. Don't they," Her broad voice clanged and she waved a heavy wrist. "Say it about a lover or the army, a career or whatever. But this *literally...*"

I followed her gaze to the roof, the tangled scenery broken rank in shadow; the fur-toothed auditorium. She smiled as her thoughts processed over my face.

"What'chya up to Detty Boy? Why don't you and me make the evening blurry. My shout."

"Could start in Paps' office, his distillery cabinet?"

"Don't be calling your Pops a lush," her head tilted. "He's good enough." Some affection must've risen with her name in print, poking out of the harsh white like a kodiak in spring.

And she went on to tell me about Spanish Fort and the piano missing keys. Great Uncle Beau who played side for Leroy Waltman but, returning with a little dough, his missus had shacked up with a minister. And cousin Maribelle, that was Aunt Bessie's daughter, could get her work up icy Boston as a shopgirl but she demured that. And I remember wondering why people voyage the planet to follow a light or run a bath they're comfortable in... and we never left Paps' office. I walked out with Missy a little fuzzed and tactile, the brush of her arm a fuse to ignite each dawn; busying my hand. And when I watched her the next evening, I felt the pressingness of time, how my New World could be broken by preening others, like I'd dreamt it. Yesterday's whisky might be tomorrow's curtness at the door, a stranger snapping braces on.

It bathed and tugged my heart;
the deep hungers, a needful
burning tinged with sadness. But
you know about these things, right?

~

Neukölln Palast owns a block of Sharonstraße, bow-cornered and shining in autumn rain. Each October Papa's *Rotbart* goes respectable inside. The expressionist Werner Vogel wrote 'The President's Heel' (satire), and the lobby glitters with maybe not the great and good, but those with millions of Papiermarks to flutter over deep sticky pile.

The foyer has two Dadaists, Voigt and Busch, propping a Doric column. The Hahns are still here - velvet-collared meteors with firearms, whom its said shot Akim the casino product, and cut a councillor's tongue so he struggled with decisions. There's Paps' financier Weiß reflecting the chandelier, and Hartmann - Plague Town - who bulk-sells pulp killings true and fantastic; he arrived in our armpit like a bubo at Mama's inquest. And there's Raymund, nephew to 'Holeproof King' *Fleischer* - feigning seventeen years of nonchalance at the bar, though I know his seismic eyes scout. I may have given an impression of innocence, but there's no innocence in what Raymund does to me.

Dimming hush-- A chalky, sweat-streaked face, cheeks rouged for the lights. The President's fatness is exaggerated, the actor in a bald hairpiece. The set is an elegant bed chamber of a remote, verdant-lawned palace, away from his marital home. Missy plays Martha Washington, whom we'll understand to be a negro of both street-smarts and victimhood.

I try to catch Raymund's seated eye, but he hasn't looked once since the foyer.

It's morning and the President stands at a huge painted window in little attire:

President
Look at the garden, all is sweet. The bees pollinate with their happy hum. Each flower cares not who pollinates, for without attention it would die.

Martha

And you will return to your wife.
All is sweet for you Mr. Bumble.
We are rooted in soil, whereas you
have bought the sky.

President

I'm in public office. How could it
be otherwise? Were I less
complicated, let's say a stage dancer,
the world would care less for my
private life.

Silence...

President

You must promise discretion
Martha. Otherwise...

Martha

What?

President

Well. You must promise discretion.

Thunderclap, drumming rain. It's maybe outside, or in
tandem to the production I don't know, but it's the interval.

I rolled over his arm. He'd deep green eyes in pearl skin. A mop overhung - habitually pushed back - but now Raymund's mouth was immobile red. I put my hand on his stomach, where muscle bunched like hard molluscs.

He sighed. "I expect we'll catch up at the weekend or some such?"

"The play's not finished."

"It is. All meaning was front-loaded."

"It's Vogel's latest work and I wanted to discuss it."

"Discuss Vogel." Raymund scoffed. "A fat President caked in paint having a colonial affair."

He got up roughly out of my hand and put on his shirt with the recklessness he'd dumped it. Stood by the chair. Thick wood crosshatched the loft and the moon was algae-filmed in the skylight. Raymund's expression only really softened in sleep.

"Come on. Guess."

"Eh?"

"What happens."

"I can't."

"All's beautiful in the world while the President slips his negro, but the fascists or something home in, and the liberal holiday's bust. The Prez betrays it all for career and national stability. Something like that... Probably a press smear."

"Why do you ruin it?"

"Honey, I see endings coming, you know?"

I was left in the loft, the clump of Raymund's boots on metal stairs, heading who knew where, my callous Attica. My warren of Corynthian pigment and tossed props.

I returned to the stalls between variously-sized backs. Depressingly, as chalk and grease actors played out Vogel's obvious masterpiece, Raymund was right.

Glasses twirled the lobby, their owners impressed how *The President's Heel* investigated Germany with sledgehammer realism.

"Hey Missy."

"Little man. My greatest fan."

It was so quiet back here, dark with bright corners as she unmade. She wasn't a networker.

"What did you think?"

I looked at my shoes a bit.

"What?" Her hand raised to her mouth. "What!"

Being cross-Atlantic, Missy's eyes that appear all surface don't judge much. Maybe a Yank's a friend for life but broadly; less intensely. Like you're a feature in their landscape.

Her world is all friendships. I once (I think) caught her masturbating, or working towards it. But even that seemed an act of generosity. Not child nor adult but between, her desires intact while demons press the house, nosing the open windows.

"You were the best."

"That's all I need to know," she sliced my affront.

I heard my voice. "You going somewhere?"

"Clärchens." She remained quiet and serene as the the stage-garb uncaked. "Honey. Come sit down."

I always did.

"I'm a little older. Maybe someday, if you promise to always hold me in regard, we'll sail away together. Will you hold me in your highest regard?"

I nodded. "Of course Missy."

So here's me in my attic, clueless amid wood. Where beams hold firm and history stops. Where sound thumps up from rehearsals each day, frozen in deco. Raymund seeks swift pleasure and benzedrine, Missy is at the ballroom and I'm not. Paps is oblivious. My cigarette pirouettes turquoise in the moon. Sometimes I wake from a dream of fire escapes with a flaming sword.

~

Mascara brushes fell in a dribble of wailing. The chorus line couldn't function. My father was trying to ascertain.

"She's in hospital getting stitched. Why would they do that?"

Papa was pale and shocked and distraught.

"She's our damn goddess!"

"Who's *they*?" asked Fuchsia White.

"Those two skulk round here once a month, sis, regular as my painters."

Paps had to say something, but instead fidgeted his felt hat. Eventually: "The police will find those responsible. Don't you girls fret. You're perfectly safe in this employ."

The sick world tilted; my chest all wire and choking cotton. I felt these forces of anxiety in the room - each girl had her own - and sharp, quivering breath. Missy had been carved. Affronted and agonised down some mean alley.

Hospital visiting hours were strict and the *Rotbart* line waited a respectful distance from Declan and Davione Lehane. Missy's parents left with Davione's arm across Cap Lehane's torso, inconsolable now Missy was out of sight. Declan showed nothing, but he'd the Somme-branded face of the Royal Ulster Rifles. Decommissioned, his body was still a mannequin for the uniform.

My clucking mamas now chained Missy's bed - and I hid in the toilet. At five when all were ushered away and a slopped supper due, I left the toilet for Missy's bed. She'd bandages on her cheeks but her mouth was free.

"You can't be here." She spoke in grit and wadding.

I slid an arm round her and put my head on her smock.

"If you're gonna cuddle for the whole world to see, swing that curtain."

I did and for thirty minutes lay on the edge.

I got shovelled out by a tray-wielding orderly and wandered home, imagining the knife sideways under bandages; the venal rebuke for some other's sin. Sat, my hands dangling. Aware now of the muscles in my cheeks, how they pushed and pulled and did everything, everything you needed.

~

The barge will shove brackets of wake down silver-green. I'll be on my cleat there by the schiffahrtskanal, as an owner's eyes pass, two-stroke puttering as his heart must. I'll look at the axe, down my flannels in view; its fire-red head blooded. And it's just meat isn't it, in the planet's eyes, meat with hands. But we won't be forgiven, only reprieved. With luck we start over in the wash. I feel as solemn as a church right now.

~

I first drew breath as Declan's lot were building the Titanic, 1909, on Jophiel's Day, September 29. I don't remember Papa leaving for Schlieffen's Plan, but I do his return. Summer 1918 - that dry June experts called our coffin lid. I was nine, clasped in Mama's floral thighs, her sand and kerosine fingers rasping my head under Potsdamer clocktower.

'Papa,' I swivelled.

For a moment my shapeless brown father disappeared behind a tram - my chest thumped oddly. When it had rumbled on he stood by a neon ad for Pernod I think, or Daimlers, or the carburetors they put in Daimlers.

"They missed." Mama's caress of his feldgrau sleeve - her sham ditz - seemed as undecorated as the sleeve itself.

"But I didn't." And Paps' hand slipped off my curls to a kit bag, wherein was the grainy, limbless reportage he'd sell back west.

Paps survived the Signal Corps - the Bertha craters of Champagne petalled with bone - a canny eye getting him to Wolff Telegraph Bureau where he wrote me cheerfully, Mama less so; like funny papers in the broadsheets. And trudged home with a helmet ill-fitting his Jewish head. It would be four years, between Paps' homecoming and Mama's vibrant slaughter.

If school broke early - a sick teacher or whatever - I'd feel headachey and adrift. We lived on the borders and I'd stop my friends from going home; eat wurst at a kiosk and throw stones at ducks. I didn't want to go home: Mama got up to stuff, while Paps worked late booking genius.

A keyed door and hasty upstairs rustle... The smell wafting down. Edsel Richter, a dour communist whom it was said behaved strangely - a couple of schizoid episodes at Zoologischer and Lunapark - would saunter down the stairs talking about materialism. Flushed Mama would say something like '...well that's enough about home furnishings, you must come by for dinner'.

But that day my headache of alienation made me dizzy. I remember no noise when I opened the door. Something was wrong in the house. The smell was different: like iron before snow. I walked slowly, deliberately, up the stairs and opened her boudoir door to witness a new kind of painting; a new kind of sculpture.

No cheap and vulgar rouge smudges my new mothers' cheeks, not even the black girls; this is the twentieth century. They're sharp, a gash of crimson for a mouth. Dressed as men their haughty sexuality's not sustainable - a violent sod may slap it out - but it's a suspended pose.

Weiß came by. I only know him as that, of *Weiß & Shackman*. He's nicely furnished with a compass-tache and collar pins; slim watch on a hairless wrist. But for all his chatter he's inscrutable, as if words are a screen.

He, like most who work in money, 'patronises' the arts, but Weiß and the Hahns don't know of each others' existence.

"The President's Heel was rather clever, Albert. But... I noticed the theatre was half-empty."

"Filthy evening. The weather kept them away. "

"Mmm."

Paps avoids difficult conversations by pretending he's looking for something, muttering *the hell did I leave it*. He employs this method without fail every time. I say 'without fail' but... Papa's not a shrewd or inventive man.

"You're a skilled impresario. I wouldn't patronise you by calling our arrangement charity. But I must get close to breaking even, you understand?"

Meaning he didn't mind the lost sheckles if new clients clocked the patronage; a Weiß long game.

"October run's on. The magnates replace the Hoi Polloi and prices go up. If the weather holds, I'll pay some interest."

"Albert, if you don't mind my saying, you have a hunted look."

"It's this schedule. And I do mind you saying. "

"You realise now is a bad time to be a creditor?"

Indeed, cash spirals like a vulture on an updraft. Loans are short and the streets - apparel, high-end design - go barren as manufacturers keep their own product for storage.

"Reviews were as you'd expect," Weiß said amiably. "The socialist press liked it."

"I don't read reviews. They make me bipolar."

"Good word yes, apt word," he nodded sagely. "Kurt Tucholsky of *Die Weltbhün* said *'it rummages in the unconscious mind of scared liberalism'*. The conservatives thought it childish clap-trap. *'An obvious utopian-dystopian skit where the central u-turn is the only drama, and the conclusion utter nonsense.'"*

"For god's sake Weiß! I said I avoid reviews, which includes having them read back."

Weiß became cold and straightened his silky tie. "Very well, I'll keep them to myself." He got up. "Bear in mind Albert, philanthropy isn't a statutory duty, it's merit-based."

With his hat he left like a Panamanian plantation owner.

~

I was in the dressing room. Missy put her wig from *Dr. Caligari the Musical* back on the bald white head (she plays 'angry mob'). Her scars were fierce; she had a sign-off for welfare but, given no speaking or singing role, she'd come back.

There was a hard knock on the door. I went to answer it and saw the rain-specked police macs and light-blot of Gründgens and Lange. "Brüning, we'd like a word with Fraulein Lehane."

I leant back. "How long till you're decent Missy? The Precinct are here. To the tune of two."

"Give me five."

I moved out of the way to let another girl out, in mufti and mac and slung handbag, giving the policemen a wary look as they moved aside.

They hung in the corridor, and as rain releases the smell of a dog, so it released the smell of police macs and whatever they'd eaten.

Eventually, Missy's head: "You can come in."

"This is Inspector Lange, my assistant."

"Pleased to aid this enquiry... your terrible experience, Ma'am."

Gründgens gave Lange a leathery look, made more flaming by the low bright light.

"So Fraulein Lehane. I need to check details. The man who attacked you wore a mask."

"Black balaclava yes, rib-knitted."

"Rib-knitted?"

"The weft."

"His face was unidentifiable."

Lange had wandered over to the chair I'd left. I hadn't quite left; in the doorway. Lange was staring at the fire equipment: the case where the axe should be, the shape of its dust-free zone.

"But his eyes were distinct," Missy countered, "Heavy orange bags. He was about six-four."

"The same height," I chipped in, "as Carlin Hahn who harassed Paps not five hours previously and came into the dress--"

"Why are you in here, Brüning. This is confidential."

"I'm a witness. Gerhard Hahn told Paps 'we'll devalue your assets'. Then Carlin came in here and said 'all alone tonight Missy?' Didn't say anything else, just left."

"I'm interviewing Fraulein Lehane. So, why are you here?"

"And why aren't you noting my statement?"

"When I'm good and ready. Get out."

"Before you do," Lange softly interjected. "Where's the fire axe?"

"No idea."

"You have any idea when it was removed?"

"I don't work for health and safety."

"OK. Get out."

I checked Missy's eyes. She tilted her head.

Paps is either a kind man, or he dresses up concession. He used to help out Missy with her rent, and since the Hahn carving has installed her in a flat on Gutschmidtstraße paying the lot. Ropey area, but I do wonder if something went on.

I spend my time at Missy's now, and often stay over because - as Weiß pointed out - Papa's such obvious quarry he doesn't give a shit.

"I've laid out your costume. Got rid of the dent in the top hat."

"Sweetheart. And I need my make-up bag."

"That's packed, paint and kohl, mascara and lipstick."

She sighed and said quietly, "I don't need lipstick."

She is recuperating, and in some small way she's lucky she's half-negro, as the shiny weals running into her cheeks aren't as distinct.

Paps commissioned two musicals for her, in which she will be heavily made-up with her glorious, contortionist dancing; still mesmerising the guppy-mouthed stalls. Both require her to paint her face like a necromancing skull, and the librettos and plots are frankly awful, hastily written in guilt. *The She Devil*, and *The Voodoo Queen*, but it's work, and like sun struggling through thunderclouds, it breaks her depression a little.

I lay in Sommerbad Kreuzberg park with Raymund in a rare stretch of October sunshine. We weren't in plain sight of the bigoted unwashed (cleaning in the lido) and our hands were on each other, faces in each others' necks. Wine was cheap, somehow beating cash in the downhill slalom, and we'd had two bottles.

"I'm sorry about my curtness the other night but... You see one day," he rolled his long-lashed eyes, "if you *ever* get round to reaching adulthood, we might spend who knows how long together. So I must spread my wings a little. You understand?"

"It's no more legal as an adult."

He pouted. "I'd feel happier if you were a few years older."

I nodded my chin into my chest. I was stripping grass with my fingers.

"You and I are different from the others Detlef. We must suck all we can out of life."

I lay back with my arms behind my head and that lazy, workshy sun warming my face. "You were right anyway."

"Eh?"

"The play, the second half. To save his career the President breaks off the affair and then implements a more militant, less tolerant society, which is what the silent majority wanted anyway, and it reinstates his reputation to a large degree."

"Oh, well..."

"That's why I need to discuss these things with you. I want to study theme and structure."

Raymund scoffed. "With a tailor's apprentice?"

"You have the quickest mind."

"I don't think you ought to study Vogel. Read Chekhov, Ibsen, Pirandello."

"How do you know all this Mr Tailor's Apprentice?"

"Because, Kaberet Kid, my mind is a rapier. It is mercury and quickly bored, seeking new stimuli as clock-hands seek more time."

He smiled, put a hand on my crotch. I felt woozy, dreamy and content. After a while we walked to a copse, found an airy glade and began the slow deeds.

I realised I'd be dashing to catch Missy pre-show. She insisted I wish her luck, feigning fury if I didn't appear in the dressing room. I left Raymund sauntering to the pool for a dip and trammed to Sharonstraße.

Backstage in the red corridor stood Gründgens, Chief of Neukölln, tapping his foot, his shako helmet clasped behind his back, awaiting Paps' return. He looked with disgust at the burlesque photos, as though he'd need a bath when he got home.

He wasn't squeamish with dead female flesh, just the live kind, such as Fuchsia and Gloria who now accompanied Papa along the corridor, peeling into the dressing room already wearing their cabaret tights and heels.

I should say I knew Gründgens from Mama's inquest. He'd been civil until he fished two facts: that Paps only shot a camera shutter in Willhelm's great Quantity Survey, and that we were partly Jewish; Gründgens suspected it from his looks and profession anyway. And having established these facts he stayed on the case - turning thin air mainly - because the prime suspect was a Commie. (That special back-room questioning where screams don't travel. Once Edsel Richter's alibi checked, Gründgens kept the case open as you might a window to air.) But the younger Lange took details.

"You've kept me waiting nearly an hour."

"I can't keep someone waiting if I don't know they're here. Is this about Missy?"

"Preliminary enquiries."

"I can answer all enquiries easily: Carlin and Gerhard Hahn."

"The Hahns run a security company, a civic service. Or do you believe glaziers pay bombers to gain business? I suppose you do, it's how your kind of mind works."

"Which *kind*?"

"The un-German, accounting kind."

"I'm Albert Brüning, born in Köln." Paps' stoop got prouder. "My father was a bacteriologist working for little pay and less credit. He wrote a biography of Telemann for less. Would you like to hear more about my un-German family?"

Gründgens smiled nastily, but said nothing. He'd never heard of Telemann.

"The Hahns were extorting protection money. They said they'd devalue my assets. I assumed they meant arson."

"It's my understanding you went to *them* for protection."

Papa smirked. "And you're a man of deep understanding."

"And you're a man with no leading lady."

"Not just the Hebrews then, eh, negroes too? Half the workers in this district think she's an angel. And she's mulatto anyway."

He snarled, "Which is far worse in many people's eyes."

So there it was: the man who should be studying crime-scenes, instead browsing eugenic pamphlets.

"She's the hardest working girl in this theatre."

"Well she'll have to work harder now."

"Good god, man, what happened to you as a child."

Gründgens cool broke in trembling rage. "You scheming Kike. There was a murder two days ago, not far from here. Similar scene to the one *you* know so well. An axe. And Edsel Richter has the strong alibi of being in a secure asylum with schizophrenia. It's bloody strange Brüning. I'll be all over your Rotbart..." he scoffed. "And as for clown-face Lehane, she can take a back seat. In the shadows where she can't be seen. Just her white monkey teeth in the black if anyone can ever make her laugh again."

Paps was disgusted and looking down the corridor caught me staring at the exchange. "Go help the girls Detlef. Go on."

I was fossilised in astonishment.

"Go on! Fuck off! The dressing room."

After a few days I mentioned Gründgens to Missy. I lay in her bed. She'd nestled under my shoulder, sticky on my chest, and I circled her nape.

"There won't be any justice Missy."

"For what. For me?"

"Yes."

"Oh I knew that. Reconciled, sweet thing. The Hahns got the police in their pockets."

"With money?"

She nodded silently.

"Hypocrite bastard."

"Why?"

"That Chief Gründgens, on your assault. He was also on Mama's murder and he called Paps a greedy Kike the other day. That shit takes his own pay offs."

"Honey, it's how the world turns. Don't get upset."

I looked into her raised laurels, to understand. Life spoiled by a split-second shunt of metal. *Don't get upset?*

"Why'd you say that anyway."

"What, justice?" I knew Gründgens leant his full Teuton pea-brain to the 'Jewish question', but in my familiar corridor new information was imparted; obvious stuff really. "It's not just Jews. Negroes too."

"Don't say that," she slapped me softly, tiredly. "I'm not, for one. I'm half Irish and half St. Vincentian. And two it's not nice."

"Sorry, it was his language," I lied.

"Mm. Just keep stroking my neck, dumbo."

"Yes Missy Lehane. And is there anything else you'll need this evening Ma'am, or may I retire."

She lifted her hand to gently slap me again but her voice was a murmur: "Was that the household help, or calling me a primadonna". Before I could answer her hovering hand draped across me and she was snoring.

Brassing it through the porterage, a clip of marble in slipstreamed fragrance. The suck of racing-green and no care in the world.

I fondle my old Beholla with the box magazine, a queasy dawn lighting my friend-vacuum and my piss bottles on the landlady's sill. I'm thinking: 'That totty goes in the Grand, her Schiaparelli wrap and powdered fotze, I could stop her, turn her inside out. I could spread her like rosewood-stain.'

Why? Why dismantle the lovely Schiaparelli girl?

Oranienstraße; nightmares of clutched breath...

Feeling her heartbeat and breath, I undraped her arm gently and found her tipple of choice: vodka with cloudy lemonade. I always read Missy's scripts and her jotted notes. It's maybe educational to read bad drama.

The She Devil concerns God revisiting earth as a female prostitute, to see to the needs of the languishing; the duty-strictured, the honour-bound, the spiritually and sexually empty. Those whom society thinks stable with their wives and lives, but actually fend off despair. She always refuses payment. The point being: what is true kindness? But the problem with hastily-written vehicles to keep people in work - in this instance - is that God's unlikely to turn up in gris-gris makeup with a Glasgow smile and top hat and tails, convulsing like a serpent on a gravestone.

Thin-fingered dawn had me nodding in the sheaf and Missy muttering as her arm reached for nobody in the sheets. It was the weekend so I could get by on false-fuel.

"Honey boy, come back in here. You can't live in melodrama all night, and you can't drink all my vodka."

I knew what had been a favour of relief for a needy teenager weeks before had changed. Missy needed me, however shameful it was for a girl turning eighteen taking steps into womanhood. She knew I adored her like the chorus line adored her: sister, mascot... angel. And for now at least she found warm proximity a kind of existential balm, leaving the physical aside.

I hadn't finished the script so tried to Raymundise, speculate like it was front-loaded. And of course I did as Missy bid because Missy is Missy; and what Missy wants she gets, clown-face or no.

I caught the tail of a conversation that made no sense in Paps' office. The Slav accent of the tiny Jewish man who eventually left was so thick.

"It's too much."

"Risk, my friend."

"The money I buy will devalue nightly."

"For me too, of course."

Why would you buy money? It's a promissory note. Surely money buys *things*. A teacher said these notes aren't backed by gold anymore. I was too young to understand speculation. I kind of got it that dollars were in demand because they were stable... because America was stable. That's as far as teenage economics went.

"It's not a good time Albert. And it's not my specialism. Passports, birth certificates."

"But at that cost, it's hardly worth the risk for either of us."

"If you could pay in dollars or whatever holds, I'd drop it."

I could hear, or sense, Paps shaking his head, spreading his hands. "Maybe I'll run it past Weiß," he murmured. "Dollar loans."

"Listen my friend. I feel for your predicament. You're a good man. An old friend. I want to help. But you got to remember there's set up costs."

"Which you can reuse."

The visitor's hands raised and shoulders shrugged. "But it's not something I'd pursue. I'm helping you."

"I know," Paps said quietly. "I know you are Balthazar. And I thank you."

"We must meet up soon, more auspiciously."

I sensed Paps' melancholy nod. Out of the door came bustling Balthazar, plainly dressed with a briefcase, waistcoat and watch chain. He stopped, squinting at me a while through wire-framed cheaters. "You must be Detlef. You're the spit."

I nodded. He tipped his hat. "A great pleasure. Almost a man and never have we met." He held out a hand and I shook it, warming to Balthazar instantly.

I mean how hard can it be,
and who'd care?

Missy made kartoffelsuppe and I headed for the phono shop now Berlin's sun was warm. Leaving Missy happy in her apartment singing unmolested.

Nurnberger Straße was pallid; biscuit tin buses and lamposts curling over themselves, our squat and heavy buildings, our geometric feats, as solid as Monument Valley.

Pushing the shop door I saw Ernst Bebel across the way in shade, trilbied and slender: *Mr. Watercolour*. Unlike his namesake (that Saxon claxon from the barracks) Ernst is vague and indistinct. His easy gate belies his rigid job. A mere impression of a man from afar, all created via pastel shades.

As a *Rottie* regular I tipped a hand in his direction: he was making it big on Gropius' coattails with curvy, functional shit. And lugging his son with the ugly chin - Günter I think. Dragging him like a reluctant dwarf (an eight-year-old face in its twenties). The child seemed not only revulsed, but angered by the streets. Like he'd been forced into the world without reasonable explanation. Watercolour Ernst always had time for me, I liked him. A Hamburger.

The rumour mill - by which I mean the lapping tide of the dressing room - had it Ernst got some rebel activist up the duff and was now concluding a messy divorce.

I don't get much allowance (as Paps sits head in hands), but I'm putting it aside for a phonograph. One day the owner'll stop eyeballing me, as I take my first record to the counter. So I slope to N, see if they have the New Orleans Rhythm Kings with Jelly Roll. They do. And *Congaine, China Boy, I Wish I Could Shimmy Like My Sister Kate...* it's all here. And for sympathy when Missy, or a languid Raymund or some ankle waifette visit my pad: *Sometimes I feel like a motherless child*. Dig?

She's in *The Voodoo Queen* now which, for fans of rushed, prejudicial bollocks, I should explain is about a New Orleans cult. Missy is Maman Babineaux, a wife who murders her bathtub gin-running husband and subsequently survives the town lynching her. She is shot and hung from a live oak's bough, but a week later is seen walking round town. They believe her the real goddess Maman Brigitte, a foul-mouthed Haitian deity who guards graves. It's a rip-off of Kipling's *Man Who Would Be King* except it's beyond racist (their accents and aspirations are slow and low) and inherently sexist. Unlike Kipling's Dravot, who bathed in adoration and treasure only, Maman Babineaux creates a tyranny that mirrors her own lynching; a cult of revenge. Female power, in Krause's play, seeks only misery and horror in others.

Still, Missy gets to bound around stage like a dead monkey, so I'm sure she's thrilled.

"That's pretty sweet, Bal. I wouldn't look twice."

"Forty six attempts. Taught me a lot. In fact it was my apprentice Mordy got it."

"For which I owe you more than money."

"Well, mainly money, but perhaps a meal at Josty's."

This was my second Balthazar eavesdrop (Bal and Al as they call each other) and it was my turn to press my face in my hands. I realised what was going on. This couldn't turn out well. If he paid the Hahns with them his life was on the line. And if it was for Weiß, the man's a fucking banker!

"Can you wait until the end of the week. It's our biggest run and most popular show."

"I know, I saw it on Sunday. Yes I can wait Al."

The burlesque girls fuss around Missy now like the Queen of Sheba. She truly is their totem. Her grace of movement on those tough brown pins guarantees a certain dignity even after the cutting.

The first payment was made. Gerhard on the premises alone, counting notes. I could imagine Paps petrified, glancing for ink traces rubbing off on his fingers.

"I don't get it Pops."

"What?"

"I was in the foyer Friday night. There weren't too many people. You gambling now? Getting lucky?"

"Latecomers. They don't drink at my bar. Load up at home on the cheap stuff and miss the first ten minutes. Annoys the performers but... yes, packed house."

"OK Brüning. Good for now."

"I have a proposition."

I heard the amused silence. "So?"

"You wouldn't slaughter the chicken that lays the egg, right?"

Another silence, like a shrug of disagreement on that point.

"Say we shift from a fixed sum to a percentage. The box office. When I win, you win. When I'm struggling, you cut some slack."

"Ahhhh.... that's easy to say in a goldrush. But if I ain't getting my dough most year round I get lax, and the others move in, and you've seen what they did to Missy Lehane. Those bastards."

I wanted to kill Gerhard Hahn then. To treat the crushed life of my queen as some deceitful piece of chit-chat. If I'd owned a useful weapon I'd have rushed him there and then. Probably been knocked to the floor with a single backhander, but at least I'd have defended. And maybe that's how people get on top, by not caring about people they don't care about.

The upshot?... Paps was getting away with it.

~

"Your margin notes. They're always motivation."

"Sure Hon. What else. Couple of markers for climaxes, but I ain't no intellectual. Gotta be credible. Angry when I'm angry."

"What about overarching structure and theme?"

Missy took a deep breath that was so tremulous it frightened me. I must have said something deeply stupid.

"What's up?"

It was a while before she turned back to me. "Honey, I know you want to write these damned things and you're full of curiosity, you're very young and its all ahead."

"So are you."

"In years."

"Which is the measure of age."

"Look at my face, Detty."

"You're busier than ever."

"Two plays. Charity. And then?"

I rolled into her and realised she was scared; perhaps not all the time, but with spasmodic frequency. It was a while before I could think what to say:

"You underestimate people. Your audience love you. Your mugshot was in the paper after you were cut and people saw.

Still they flock. I know those plays are shit, but you hear how loud they applaud? They're not clapping profoundness."

"You're a kind man, Detty. Will we sail away together?"

"That's the deal. I just keep holding you in high regard." I laid hands on her unblemished body.

I was in *Cafe Griechisch* with a strong coffee, poring over Ibsen's *Creditors* when a confluence of bad luck arrived.

I realised Weiß was in the booth behind, and then in walked Raymund with a boy on his arm. Younger than me with the face of a cherub and confidence I don't possess. They sat on a table four yards away. Raymund had taken to wearing round collars and striped slacks with gaiters. He rather liked his hair at the moment so wore no hat. But it was that thin spiv's tie gave away his intent - not an honest salt-of; more a chancer with a headful of illicit. Noone noticed me with my face in Ibsen (which I could no longer read) and my back to them, skewed to the window, dressed in black wool with a worker's cap and docker's boots, which I'd decided was my look.

Since Mama's death and Paps' hunted indifference, and since the formal letters from *Leibniz Gymnasium* sit unopened, I've turned education into a part-time activity. Three days a week, if that. And on Thursdays Raymund should be at Maria-Selleque Textile Technische but clearly isn't.

My ears flipped independently like chameleon pods.

"After Christmas I'm pulling the rug. He lives in a dreamworld."

"Well technically that's his job, he runs a theatre?"

"The man can't audit. Or cater to the mainstream, or compromise for the masses."

"His reputation is high."

"Like pie in the sky. The Palast proprietor is fed up. Give the people what they want or they'll stop you doing it altogether."

The other ear.

"It's coincidence Ferdie. You make me sound like I prey on youngsters."

"He's as young as me."

"He was just a fling."

An arrow pierced my heart. *Bugger you Raymund. You perverted old chorister.*

The Griechisch Cafe resides in the Palast complex, and Bohemian expressionists glide and confide here during the day. The inseparable Voigt and Busch; Ernst Bebel when free of Günter (word is he'll soon be freed forever; there's no custody battle). Tucholsky the satirist was in the other day.

Compared to Paris's cramped cliques and absinthe dreams, this place is an ocean liner; a gleaming vessel of chandeliers lined with a giant armadillo skin of mirrors. The boiler room that keeps it all moving is jazz with a dancefloor to frenetically foxtrot, and the huge first floor balcony curves like a sun-bleached whalebone.

It's also full of tourists but unlike sniffy Paris, Berliners love welcoming fat Americans and ramrod Brits, aloof Frenchies and bumpkin Slavs. Come see Brecht and Dix. Take in some cabaret. Saunter the walkways of Gropius' mind.

"You and I are different from the others Fernandas. We must suck all we can out of life."

Double bugger you.

*Unter-den-Linden, morning: note an underlying
pathology or malaise in the bright outlook*

~

So I'm forever in the Griechisch thinking of my future. One does, because there's so much of it. Roman has a dishcloth over his shoulder, and the floor-length windows give us a rain-grizzled hutzpah. Like we matter. Simple worshippers in the booze pews; salt pillars in the grey umbra. Many booths have lone customers; a troubling sign as society disagrees with itself and keeps private counsel. I chew my pen, look at the beginnings of a play. I feel compelled to write in the Greek Tragic style; bound to. I drink my muddy coffee.

Gründgens hurried over the bright marble, his slipstream bracketed in smoke. He wore gloves and carried a holdall; not attire I expected of Neukölln's Chief Bastard; he looked more like a cat burglar and entered the Rotbart, so I left my coffee and script.

There was nothing on this evening: the only people in there might be Paps and promotion staff. I went through the dead black auditorium and up the side stairs. In the corridor, the door of the women's dressing room was open. I boldly walked in and found Gründgens placing a fire axe in the case. Not, as it turned out, in benevolence. He jumped at the sound of my footpads but turning, had a satisfied air.

"Well well, Brüning Junior. Look!"

He pointed at the axe in its clasps.

I shook my head in puzzlement. He happily jutted his chin at the axe. Still no response from me. He nodded his head vigorously at it with wide eyes and brows.

"It's an axe," I said.

"Yes, it's the axe from the Oranienstraße. A perfect fit wouldn't you say?"

"Are you gifting it to us? Can you do that with evidence?"

He pulled the axe carefully back out. "And look. The shape of the handle and the head, both exactly align to the dust-free area."

"I think fire axes are a standard shape," I offered.

"I'm afraid they aren't, Brüning the Lesser. It will depend on the grain of the wood. And the heads vary. Some are more like machetes. Some like ice picks. This one, is like... your axe."

"Is there anything I can help you with? You're not actually supposed to just stroll in here unannounced. It's private property."

"Stroppy little Semite."

"Also, are you supposed to be taking evidence out of the station?"

It was hard to tell in this dim light but Gründgens seemed to be turning first ruddy, then drained. "Spare the bloody rod," he spat.

"So... if that'll be all?"   •

"As you rightly say evidence should be collated and kept at the station, so..." he turned to red cabinet, and with a hefty, angry yank pulled it off the wall.

"Hey!"

"Your pinchfist father can come and fill in the relevant forms. Out of my way."

"Hey!" I added, weakly to his back.

~

We stood in the station's yellow foyer. Behind a panelled counter, some youthful bureaucrat brought out forms and ink.

"Couldn't you have brought this to the theatre?" Paps said. "Do it all in one go?"

"I'm advised if fingerprinting remains incomplete, we will indeed visit the theatre for missing records."

"Yes but, couldn't you have done that in the first place. It's a waste of time."

"Not police time, sir. It optimises our time."

"*Our* time. A total waste of--"

"We'll be done very quickly, Herr Brüning. Here... and here."

Paps looked at the pile of forms paperclipped with photos, with a fingerprint box at the base.

I looked at Papa, then at Missy and Fuchsia and Gloria. And Cristoph and Hubert, respectively the stage and premises managers. The other girls and back-office would come when they were good and ready. Although there was no reason to suspect the lighting technician any less than the rest of us; he was a quiet sort: too quiet?

I found it ridiculous, frivolous, until Missy stepped forward and I saw the brown picture clipped to her form, her cheeks pristine and her eyes startlingly direct and hopeful. It had one of those US landscape backdrops; the pioneer kind. I made a strange noise, swallowed it, and wandered to the corner.

We left in a scrum of blue language.

We had flu when disaster struck. Missy had it bad so I was indoors mollycoddling. Then I got it and we were zombies for a week, though her fever passed and she just blew her nose at me while I sweated and shivered.

A crashing, persistent thump at the door at five on a Sunday morning. Missy answered it.

"Oh thank god. You'd both better come quick." It was Gloria Frank from the chorus line.

"What's happened? Detty's not well."

"Fire at the Rottie. Albert is mad with worry that Detlef's inside. And you Missy. He's not seen either of you for days."

Missy dressed quickly and me in a dizzy, stumbling haze; the three of us got to the Palast.

We became aware of the fire before we saw it. A few blocks away the sky was underlit by pumping clouds with orange undersides, some vast idling locomotive, swirling and specked with cinders. Then we saw the top of the flames lick the night like snakes tongues and then, turning the last corner onto Sonnenallee, the spitting white heart, beams of charcoal in its midst, the sparks and cinders like snow in reverse; snow's negative. The smell was awful: as if a gasoline station, a tannery and burnt coffee had collided, and the backs of onlookers were penumbra'd dummies.

The building's black skeleton was revealed like some demonic abode risen through the earth while opposite, the eerie glow was reflected off the Church of St. Fridolin of Säckingen, staring passively at hell.

Smeared firefighters were at work. More than usual maybe - two hoses - but others using buckets of sand and water as it seemed the mains firepoints weren't effectual. Half the fire had been doused, the other half more difficult to reach. One of the trucks unhooked and drove round the back for a better purchase on the last flames.

We were locked in disbelief, and I wondered if Gloria and Missy thought the same: all that past, now as pungent and irretrievable as Johannisnacht; all our futures hanging on cinders, no money, no work, no boards to creep, the smell and the memory that would remain and hang. They were searching the silhouettes for Albert, and periodically so was I. Eventually he came walking round the corner, face studying the ground, arms hanging loose and low like a neanderthal in a collarless shirt and brogues.

After twenty long minutes the fire was out leaving only smouldering black beams: a rebellion put down.

Misery and exhausted firefighters stood in Sharonstraße around the smoking corner. Maybe a quarter of the theatre in the middle of the complex had burned to charcoal - could fall in.

Before Missy or I could catch Paps' attention Gloria was hollering. "Albert. Albert!"

Finally he turned, saw the three of us and his upper body joined his arms in slumping, but in relief. He walked quickly over. "Where the *hell* were you? I was beside myself. Thought you were up in your loft hideaway, taking drugs with that bumboy..."

"Pardon?" said Missy. Two elements in that sentence alarmed her.

"Missy, dear Missy," Paps sighed. "I was worried sick, trying to account for everyone." He turned to Gloria. "Gloria, you're an angel."

A firefighter was hovering a few yards away, and as Paps looked at me, I looked at the fireman. Paps turned round and walked to him.

"You were lucky, the water mains are leaking and the pressure was low. You ought to come in and see something."

"What kind of thing?"

The firefighter looked sheepishly at the rest of us, then said quietly, "Before the police drag themselves out of bed."

As Paps went in through through the side door stage-end I followed quiet as a shadow. Once I'd got to grips with the state of the destroyed box office and facade and refocused on Paps and the firefighter, it all added up.

An open briefcase of fake money sat on the stage with a paper sign leant in its lid which simply read: "Ach je."

I tried to assimilate in a dark corner seat, shivering and pasty in the heat and pungent stink while Paps pointed, gesticulated and shrugged at the fireman.

If they'd left that as a message - *oh dear* - they couldn't have meant to burn the whole place down. I was getting up to sneak back out when Gründgens appeared. Paps kicked the briefcase lid shut with his toe and strode angrily towards him. "Now you believe the Hahns are reputable?" He snorted. "Bloody civic service."

"It was Gerhard Hahn," Gründgens said with level satisfaction, "who called the fire department. He was passing a few streets away."

"You *are* kidding me."

Gründgens shrugged. "As Schuster's leaseholder I expect he'll be glowing with self-congratulation he let Albert Brüning run his theatre."

Slipping out I knew Palast insurance would cover all this but... the box office? Continued lease, work, art, reputation, refurb, *money*? Hahn warning shots across the bows, it seems, splinter the prow.

These are good: *Butch Cassidy cleared a swathe with one of these*

The next day a strange sight greeted me. I went back to the stinking Rotbart more through habit than purpose. I wasn't the only one magnetised like grieving relatives to, essentially, an insentient building, an impersonal husk. Some of the chorus girls stood smoking, gazing, folding arms across their breasts as if that might scaffold them against facts. But in the midst of it, in a patch of unburnt cobbles, Günter sat, his hands flopped out front, palms skyward, his legs bracketing his sunken pear shape. He was wailing and sobbing.

I clambered over cinder-beams. "It's Günter isn't it? Ernst's son. What the hell are you doing here?"

"I'm sorry."

"We're all sorry Günter. It's a tragedy."

"Did anyone die?"

"No. No no, thankfully nobody died. Only our spirits."

"I'm so sorry."

"The show will go on."

"On what. You have no stage."

"The stage is fine. It's the doorway and box-office are ruined. Come on you can't sit here, it's probably toxic."

"I've got bad lungs."

"All the more reason." I tried to help him to his feet.

"No don't touch me." He got up of his own accord, and I felt abashed. It's funny, we must leave traces of ourselves, odour and memory, in buildings.

~

"What you reading?"

"That murder, at the Oranienstraße Grand."

I put the magazine down, eyed my underpants drying on the heater.

"Isn't there enough shit in the neighbourhood without digging out more grizzle."

She glanced frowning at the lowered magazine, *Forensics Quarterly*, and my nakedly crossed legs. I put my hand over. "What?"

"Shouldn't you be reading Shakespeare?"

It's true, I should-- "Yes."

"And don't just sit there in vest and socks, it's strange."

Paps often surprises my disdain. He's more resilient than I thought. Or braver or stupider. In a makeshift office on the first floor of the complex a regular visitor now is Ernst Bebel, with cardboard tubes and portfolios. Paps is well-liked and people go out of their way for him, with discounts and sometimes gratis.

They're redoing the facade in the latest style, from Schuster's insurance. (Paps wriggled in angst until that briefcase was out. Until Gründgens had left in emphatic boredom.)

Thing is... Paps' artistic reputation is sky high; he could cut away from the Palast, east Berlin even, and start anew.

Brave, stupid, resilient. All those.

On the strength of Ernst's credentials Paps got to stay on and refurb. And I got to know Günter, the ancient eight-year-old dwarf.

If Günter was in Paps' office he was oddly serene, his pained demeanour softer, a porcine finger tracing the lines of the Palast floorplan: the ballroom, *Cafe Griechisch,* the arcades of brass boutiques under their glass roof, the theatre (pre-charcoal), the minimal white art gallery at the rear with floor to ceiling light. In the middle of the marble atrium was a fountain by Alexander Archipenko, the whale vomiting out Jonah onto a beach with water spraying round him; though to me it looks like a cubist marionette balancing on a leaky pear.

But that's cool. Unlike Weiß, Herr Schuster has vision.

I stood a moment silent in the doorway, a lurking malevolence. "Can we chat?"

It was quiet. Ernst had left, and blind dusk groped the alley and hung in Paps' open window.

"Sure."

The only other light was a curved brass lamp on the leather desk like a banker's or croupier's. He wasn't in too bad of a mood. Schuster'd signed the plans; work started Monday and Ernst had recommended developers.

"Banknotes."

Paps looked up with a face suddenly sealing in surprise and annoyance.

"Don't do it. He's a banker. All he needs is a whiff and he'll check numbers with the mint."

Paps grinned with caustic amusement. "Really. Have you had dealings with German banks for long now, Dets?"

"Write it off."

He watched me a bit. I still hadn't entered the room. He frowned and gave a mild shake of the head.

"You can't pay the girls with them, that would be wrong. And you're on a tightrope with Schuster."

"You may have noticed I keep my nose out of your business." He picked up the unopened letters from Gymnasium, slapped them back down, pulled a reefer butt from his waste basket and threw it back in with contempt. "Particularly... where you stick your Johnson!"

"I don't want to fight Paps."

"Then keep your nose out of this office. Next time we chat, let's talk about your career."

"I'm worried. Far as I can see the Hahns, being the Hahns, let you off lightly. I mean, they've screwed Missy for life and it upsets me and grieves me raw, but..."

"It's all paid for."

I wasn't sure what that meant; a final gambit. "Just use it for sundry shit, far from here. I'll take it as pocket money. Let's not shit on our doorstep."

The simmering finally boiled over. "Don't tell me my business boy. You're not Gustav fucking Stresemann, you're a fourteen year old queer. Go learn something."

I left his chaos.

~

Papa's turn now. You may have seen there, he didn't enjoy our chat. Sent me to a psychiatrist, Dr. Winter. And by sent, I mean as near dragged me by the ear as a man can a teen as tall as him.

He'd found a proponent of Krafft-Ebing, the converter; the curer. I'm not gonna knock the old tit - as useful as a Mystic Madam - but he's otherwise liberal and sympathetic given he's Austrian.

VOLXI EDUCATIONAL

Dr. Winter's New Opinions

Introducing Dr. Everhard Winter's pioneering work with inverts

Registered Sexology Clinic

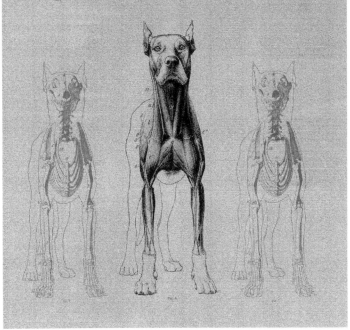

In the latest parlance Dr. Everhard Winter is a 'sexologist', a Rasputin of the cock, and rejects all but what chimes with his view that homosexuality can be unlearnt, born of insecurity, cultural deviance or warped domestic events. Or perhaps the lord Jesus flows through him.

"Your father says you have taken up with an older boy."

I sighed and shrugged.

"Be frank. That will be the only mention of your father in our sessions." He smiled. "These are confidential and they're about *your* wellbeing only."

"Well, taken up is incorrect. He likes to shop around."

"Ah. Which is not what you want."

"That's tricky."

Dr. Winter *doesn't* have snowy white hair nor a cold demeanour, just a temple-grey coiffure, zinging entropy and lots of pens.

"Please," he indicated I elaborate.

"I mainly shack up with an older girl, woman really, as of next month. Sex isn't that frequent, but she's my true love. ...I think."

Winter's eyebrows bunched. *Now you can see our expensive sessions running past the horizon, can't you Doc.*

~

Gymnasium-- Cold sun motes over gouged desks, screwed to iron frames. My hand shoots up.

"A castrated psyche, sir. Angry but robbed of its capacity for violence." I'm trying to ignore the kid Helmut behind, kicking the seat of my chair. "The epileptic fit at the end tuns Adolf's reprisal on himself, a masochism if you will." I pause, as cool winter coats my chin through the window. "I'm not sure if *Creditors* is misogynistic, or a critique of the male ego and its predilection for self-pity. One can never tell with Strindberg."

"Fotze," the kid behind muttered, with a terrific hoof that vibrated my arsehole. *He goes - I know where he lives.*

I figured the twin prongs of going back to school and an absence of Raymund might end the Winter Sessions, which Paps can ill-afford even with toy money. Paps has more to worry about than my dalliance with the wrong genitals. Besides, Raymund is managing my unconditional surrender to women well enough.

~

Missy clunked in a carpet bag. Her spare hand held a bottle of brandy. "Come on. Leipzig."

"It's ten in the morning."

"My day off."

"It's raining, and freezing."

"My fault?" Missy pulled out a thermos of coffee, the cognac's complement. "For an afternoon nip."

"It's two hours to Leipzig."

"What are you, a clock? Get your coat, I wanna see the whatsit."

Yes I am. Purveyor of temporal and seasonal facts.

Being cold November Missy hooked close on my Chesterfielded arm. We passed mausoleums to the untold from Leipzig station, through a tree parade of wet sun.

The 'whatsit' loomed over everything. Some Nordic cliff a bunch of Barbarossan masons had really gone to town on. Cullised and fluted, stain-arched and igneous; free of nonsense. You wouldn't have a beer with those stone fuckers: look at the size of their swords. Its vastness made the flat land flatter.

"Hon?" Missy murmured, sat by an ornamental lake watching the rain lance.

"No, they were fifth century."

"What?"

"Huns. I think my jaw's a third pole."

"No, *Hon*. You know I joked about high regard and such?"

"Mmm."

"Well you have. Did. You know."

"Of course." I watched her feet splay, glanced at the ring of clenched scabbards. "It's probably warmer in there."

In the crypt we steamed as foals on the steps with death masks and stone babes in arms. Tranquil emptiness, a throb of blood.

"Your gods won't mind a winter warmer," she pulled enamel mugs and brandy.

"Valhalla heaves with drunks."

As Missy fussed cups on marble I felt all this had departed. The same urgent vitality one feels by a grave.

She pecked me with fortified breath and I figured she was... making room; rearranging.

"D'you think we could--" her eyes scoured the imperious guards.

"I don't know."

"There's no-one here."

Dry leaves scuttled the Yank. It's good, French brandy...

~

The Hahns start their mornings out of Cafe *Wien* on misty, bin-heaped Sonnenallee; because lunkheads believe Austrians can cook. How do I know? I'm following Carlin.

It's plush enough; thin and secretive with frosted glass, heavy iron and tile tables and cane chairs. There's a back curtain that flips frequently and not for staff. The privvy's in front, so what's back there is illegit or there's a lot of broken-nosed chefs.

A certain number of people go in and don't reappear, then the Hahns get up leisurely after a coffee, slow breakfast and smoke, and amble on through.

Carlin is the brawn, the idiot, the lumbering lunk. He's got ten years on Gerhard, slower in all regard. Late forties easy. I'm profiling, see? How does his week shape. How much actual beef is needed as against the remembrance of beef past, his history of harm?

So I'm in my Swiss hat sipping miniature coffee. The comings and goings have trails on, like speed in slowness, like real time is too fast for life; or maybe life's in the trail. It's druggy, in truth. Motionless people blur. Cafe surfaces. Me also, but I'm not watching me, I'm transfixed by an old man at a table by the beads; the only substantial item in the cafe.

Face pink, sideburns joining his 'tache. His eyes are rheumy but hard. I imagine him pickelhaube'd in old sepia or photogravure; medals glinting brighter than his teeth.

I'm not fussed if Hahns see me at the *Wien*. It's a stone's throw from the *Palast* and I doubt I even register (beside fresh meat, rivals). Dicier is following Carlin into a tenement. The further away I'm clocked, the riskier for Detlef's sunny future and handsome face, cotton?

Sometimes I lose my quarry at an outer door - a communal - if I don't get in quick. And most of the time the angles of the corridors and walkways mean I have to stay out of sight or listen with my ear to a door. But once in November in a new modernist block, Carlin didn't close the apartment and in the angles I could see Carlin and the resident.

"My stuff?"

"Sure, in the safe. Two secs."

"Why didn't you get it out. You knew I was coming."

"Makes me nervous Mr. Hahn."

The habitee walks to the safe. Two seconds become ten, the metal door opens, Carlin opens his briefcase for Rentens, but instead pulls a *Mauser* and shoots him in the rear ribs.

"For valuing on the Ku'Damm you louse. You should've left."

He scoops all from the safe, doesn't care the apartment door's open and only the stone-deaf haven't heard, and heads my way. I've never been hotter on my feet in a stairwell.

My breathing slows sitting on a tram to Neukölln, while the crime ebbs. So Carlin kills. Competent and happy in his work (he was whistling *Charleston Dance*). Gerhard talked of 'escalation prevention'; now I know where the escalator stops. And I'll have a map.

~

Paps and Ernst bobbed around the long-johned contractors in November. Bucket chains and beams on hoists; dust only tamping when it rained.

They worked through Saturdays and I sat with Günter and my forensics magazine. He peered over my shoulder, reading the articles and breathing stertorously.

"Do you want this?"

"You're reading it."

"When I'm finished?"

Günter started pointing out what the builders were doing wrong. A tarpaulin covered half the work, which instead of building in layers, they were finishing and plastering crosswise.

"Schuster wants them all working. Time's a premium."

"Each job takes longer."

"They can't rely on the weather."

"It's inefficient. Haven't they heard of numerical prediction?"

"Uh?"

"Weather forecasts."

"Hence, this!" god he was frustrating. "Schuster's lost a--"

Günter looked at me. "What's he lost?"

I'd seen the Hahns through the hoarding door, leaning against mediaeval St. Fridolin's. Carlin's curled wursts held a cig. They murmured and their arms didn't move or gesticulate. Then Gerhard flicked his head and the pair sprung.

I whistled to Paps. He looked and I jabbed a finger at the oncoming bastards. Couldn't make much out, until Carlin's head ducked the hoarding and they beelined. Papa's adams apple went down and up.

"Morning Pops."

"Yes?"

"Expect you'll be wanting your money back after what those brutes did." Gerhard's head tilted one way, his brow the other, in significance. "A refund as such, seeing as we failed to stop them. But I did call the fire department so," he nodded at the pristine parts of the building, a little hot steam from his mouth, "I kind of helped there."

Paps didn't say anything. A long silence slithered the noise and dust.

"Well...' Gerhard pulled his cig case from the velvet collared coat. "Refunds can't happen I'm afraid, despite what you found on your stage. But I've been thinking about your proposal."

Paps' eyes widened.

"Forget the flat fee. Box office like you said. Shares."

"Hold on... of course I'm pleased, pleased that you're agreeable. But I never said shares."

"I did."

"Gus Schuster owns the theatre."

"And you own Brüning Theatrical Holdings."

Paps scratched his head, something occurring. "If we sank you'd lose it all. Let's do percentages and if it works, then shares. Maybe, six months."

Poor Papa, he planned for breathing space. What did he think would happen between now and then? The Hahn beam was on Papa and the Hahn beam wouldn't leave, whatever verbal trapezes went Paps' way. Günter droned like lido noise, punctured by the crash of masonry.

"Thirty three percent in Papiermarks."

"They're not legal."

"So change them at the bank."

Paps opened his mouth, then bravely went in. "Look I can't accept this. It's my livelihood and... I've accommod--"

A grinning finger wagged. "You nearly got us all in trouble, didn't you Pops."

His eyes lowered, wordless.

"Escalation prevention. What d'you expect next time?" Gerhard looked at the buckets and sweating menders. "Let's find somewhere quiet to talk. That cabin."

"What about?"

"I want an introduction. The man with the machine."

They crunched off, leaving me with Günter and noise. The wrench of scenery being shifted.

"Fuchsia's old man's fighting Saturday. Wants me to go."

Missy'd bustled in from rehearsals and dropped a bag of groceries on the spindly table. I pulled the top aside to nose it and got swatted.

"Where?"

"Halensee amusement park."

"Luna? Brutal. You going?"

"If some dashing fella escorts me."

"Man, that scene's rough. It's a different place at night. And it's not what it was. All but the gambling, revues and fighting long left the sun to bleach it."

"Look I didn't arrange the fight. Besides, dummkopf," she rolled her eyes. "We'll be with *Fuchsia*, and Fuchsia's fella is in the *ring*, being a middleweight fighter who *breaks jaws*?"

"Oh yeah." I acceded, but I wasn't such a dummkopf. The baying unwashed didn't worry me. It was the puppeteers, long risen over gloves to owning books. When something kicked off, it was owned by the owners themselves, or if not they weighed in quick. I stayed after dark once with a keg and a schoolmate: Sinti dog fight. And the knifings were so blitz you couldn't know if it was security - to pacify - or spraying so the dogs didn't return.

And the women, oh man - the kind that insist on a 'jolly day out' however many bodies line the path.

"Sounds like I'm going then," I smiled.

~

I sat in the *Griechisch*. The fire only mangled access to the gallery and vomiting whale. And being Doghouse Brüning's son, I'm still on free coffee.

I've started rescheduling (pushing away) my Winter Sessions, citing homework and prior engagements. I don't feel too bad given the payments aren't real. The fusty madman wouldn't check his own balance, let alone my banknotes. I'll summarise his theories?

A gay is cultural. (I lie on the duplicitous, chrome-legged couch.) There are three prongs to the deviant: a hatred of women installed by an unloving or disciplinary mother; thereby an inability to broadcast feelings to a female object; making instead a 'male confidant' in that journey the object itself; a proxy for what can't be had.

I think that's it. There's probably other ways to say it.

'Cept I see beauty everywhere. Sometimes while Raymund's achieving my mind's on Missy's hot prickle. Sometimes when Missy moves warm at night I think of the junky at the bar with raw pink lids blinking in boredom. Sometimes I see beauty in a cherry orchard or a stream (but however I manhandle these, they give nothing).

"Knock knock."

Paps looked up, dark-circled eyes unblinking. He'd softened since, well: since Raymund'd gone, my return to school, the

Winter Sessions but maybe most since I'd been nice to Günter the sociopath.

"Come in Detty. Drink or something?"

"What's on the menu?"

He looked at his watch, checking it was reasonable to ply me.

"Well, I'm whisky and soda."

"Same then."

He shunted ice and levered the bubbles, handed one. You'd never believe Paps was down the plughole if you scanned his office. Order reigned, like a demented tyrant cataloguing before a putsch.

"You hate me talking about your work I know, your... predicaments. But I was thinking."

Softly: "Any idea's becoming worthwhile, Detty." He cleared his throat, downed his drink. I could see his protruding lips and open yaw in the bevelled glass.

"You'll listen?"

He nodded. "Mano a mano."

"Don't drag Balthazar in. He's out of the country."

"No he isn't. He's in Mitte."

"*No*, he's in Poland or wherever. Tell him to lay low. Get hold of his printworks and show Gerhard. Tell him... tell him... when Balthazar's back he'll configure it for Rentens and hand it back. Angle for compensation for his outlay, but don't push hard. Just get you and Balthazar out."

Paps swirled empty ice. "And if the Hahns screw up?"

"How?"

"Spend in the wrong place."

"It's not your risk. You took your risks already and look what you got. If you do as they say, the savages won't touch you."

"Of course they will." After a good degree of staring without focus through the bottom of his glass, he hit the cabinet again for a bigger one. "And if they get their velvet collars felt my balls go in a vice, while the police trace the mint to Bal."

"Lay off the schnapps Paps."

"No," he snapped. "Not with things as they are. I couldn't have known, Detty. How could I have known?"

"It's just a fire," I said. "Schuster'll be over the moon when it's all done. ...Young Günter has approved the design." I smiled.

"I know you and Missy are close." Paps murmured. "I couldn't have known. How could I?"

Oh. That.

"Noone blames you." I took a draw on my tumbler, "Besides, you never asked for the Hahns to blot the sun."

He nodded absently. He was far away on a drink pillow, with Glasgow smiles, fire, Limited Companies and sodbusters.

~

The phonograph. Counterfeit paper. Toy Jew money. All very regrettable. And mean-spirited, no? ...One day I'll go back to Herr Dietrich and give him what's owed. So long as he whisks them lightly into the system nobody loses, except Herr Hyperinflation, but he's a giant so its a mere freckle.

The portable phonograph is beautiful. I keep it at Missy's: a Koffer-Grammophon *Decca Junior*. It's built into a leather-covered wooden case with a sound disc in the lid, and a Crescendo Junior soundbox. It's totally the height of. And it raised Dietrich's wiry brows not a little me pointing at it. After a while: "Paps' birthday." That didn't quite cut it: "Mama's cash," I added.

The shellac itself I bought with real Rentens; a point of pride as I stacked four records on *Geschichten*'s counter. (He couldn't make much of a living anyway.)

I shouldn't say this but Missy's face was more clownish than usual when I opened the case: shining unfettered joy, then suddenly dipping to a frown, and then her head tilted and deepened the frown. An entirely silent monologue: *Wow cool! Hang on how can you afford that? What's going on? ...Detle-eeeef?*

"Just a perk. All our other shit's belly up," I said.

"That explains nothing."

"No. But... I've also got these."

I dropped a leather travel bag on the rug, the flat back full of records, the front a buckled pouch holding vodka. I clunked the bottle on the table and revealed: Sidney Bechet's *Wild Cat Blues,* Abe Lyman's *I cried for you*, Arnold Johnson's *China boy* and The Creole Jazz Band's *Dippermouth Blues*. I stared at the last like a saphead and internally thumped my forehead: so insensitive.

"If you won't be needing my services this evening Ma'am, perhaps I could take the evening off? Shall I wind her up?"

"You wind, I'll uncork." She went for her mixer and vodka. For a couple of hours the clouds thinned; our thunderheads vamoosing to the sound of *China Boy*. Missy had no Oriental moves, so cobbled something like a frisky Cleopatra and a half-charmed snake: slowly undulating, pulsating, hands over her stomach and hips and neck lovingly, eyes closed in bliss, an occasional slow twirl. I looked down past my belt: oh dear.

By Sidney Bechet's fourth airing, Missy wore nothing but her hikers and stockings. I am a lucky boy.

In the morning I caught her in future-fear. Frozen. Anguish. Mouth downturned but open, eyes wide and staring in horror. She was sat up, her arms draped between her thighs.

"Hon?"

"I hate dreams."

"A nightmare?"

"The opposite. Happiness. Then I wake up."

In the quiet she must have realised such an all-encompassing misery included me. Silence thickened. Did she want me to feel as she felt?

"Come on babe," I reached a half-asleep arm for her stomach, "you're walking out with the hottest man in town, you're a star and we've got a phonogram. What's not to be happy?"

"I *am* glad you're here you know." She fell back on the pillow in a flop. "And not just because of this, or that." She pointed at her face, then down below at Mrs Fubbs' Parlor.

"I know."

After a while: "What was your Paps on about? Bumboys. Night of the fire."

"Oh," I tried to nuzzle in a bit, but that soft offstage stomach went high-kick hard. "He's actually a tailor but he knows about theatre. And shares his drugs. Paps assumes being pals with a queer, you know..."

"Mm-hm."

"He may fancy me, I've no idea."

"Tall kid about my age? You're with him in the foyer. Rayner."

"Raymund."

"He's a wreck. Beautiful but... You're not doing heavy shit are you?"

"God no. Do I look like him?"

"Mmm." *Off the hook.* The body unwound.

I kissed Missy and felt her miriad palaces.

"I bet he does fancy you."

"He's got a boyfriend," I sighed, and breathed hotly on her neck. Good morning Berlin!

~

Paps needed help wheeling something heavy from his canvas truck into the bank. Now you might think that's bullion or antiques for a deposit box or something, but no: it's the Papiermark payment for 33% of *Brüning Theatrical Holdings*.

Look at Paps in his waistcoat, turnup pleats and brogues, with the big-wheeled trolley from the *Palast* bay, ruddy-faced through exertion or shame, swearing up kerbs, me trotting beside like a nervous assistant, lunging to keep the paper vertical. It's embarrassing enough having Yanks stare as we shower stall-holders in monetary garbage, minted bollocks, or exchange a brick-like wad for an egg, but we have the special humiliation of this being a third of Paps' life. Foisted. Stolen. Carved in.

I mean, what would an alien think? These humans carry large barrows of paper, ever more desperate and territorial with each dawn. Children build kites and wendy houses with the stuff. What is this paper they worship? Their gods forsake them.

The bank foyer was full of money. Elegant columns supported stucco ceilings over shaded marble floors. Now, basically, a pulping warehouse.

The bank clerk - both he and his bow-tie drooping - saw us approach the glass. He waved us to a loading lift, but Paps was confused.

"I need to change it up."

"Look behind you. That's everyone else's needs changing up."

He handed Paps a docket. "Leave your pile, fill out the docket, and tape the stack to keep it all together. Tie the docket to it with the string provided, and come back in about forty eight hours. We may have got to yours."

Paps looked physically drained. "I just leave it here in the foyer, with a flimsy card with my name on it?"

The clerk shrugged, not unkindly, but in void helplessness.

"Won't it be worth a quarter in forty-eight hours?"

"No. That's the good news. Renten stabilises Papier, and exchange rate is now fixed by the central bank."

Paps nodded, stared mistily around. "So. Just... over there?"

The clerk nodded gently with a supportive smile.

~

All the fun of the fair! Saturday night. We blew the Stadtbahn at Fehrbelliner Platz. I'd've walked the rest but the girls had dolled. It's leafy here so you figure its going to be nicer.

Mmm. The girls bumped gums waiting for the omni. After the musical thrum of two mulattos Fuchsia must've nodded my way:

"Boss's progeny is deep in thought look."

"Hush woman. Lot on his mind, ain't that right Detty?"

"What?"

"See."

They thought none of my thoughts. The pair'd squiffed a few already but I was spirit fog. What did Missy think her cuts said? In her finery with vengeance written on her face, and with a teen? The wife of a sap? I couldn't be the reason for the cuts, nor her protector. So what was the signal? Steer clear or, are we perfect mugs?

Oh, and I *did* put a hammer in loops I'd sewn in my baggy striped pleats. Its shining head is denser than skull. Life is getting precarious, Berlin a questionable buddy.

It was Coney Island in winter, except this ailing, fading fun-land struggled on. All darkened, we passed the creaking rides, the Switchback Dipper - a huge undulating railtrack for thrill-seekers; the theatre of letch, the 'ethnological' human zoo, the Swivel-House on a piston, the water chutes (aka tart aquarium) and Head of Horrors, whose gaping mouth you entered through, screamed if you fancied, and departed from its ear. On a hill overlooking was the derelict palace which once brought finery from Charlottenburg; it now looked like a gawping deep-sea fossil, a boarded black silhouette on a moonlit night, frozen in horror like Missy had looked the morning recent.

The terrace was three-quarters full and the bookies never left their boards, tapping incessantly.

"Shall we check odds?"

Fuchsia shook her head.

"Full house. He must be good."

"Not putting money on my man. He ain't young."

"Mind if I do?"

An ambivalent shake of the head.

Pinocchio money in my pocket, it's dark, and the crowd must think it's evens or they wouldn't come. 8/11 against: winnings in the real stuff, losses in ringers. I sound a fool at the chalkboard (this foreign etiquette). "Herr Peters, yes er... Clarence Peters... the older chap..."

The bookie laughed. "Catch-all Clarence? Sure." He put my 100 Trillion on a weighing scales - he wasn't counting them; we now have eine milliarde mark notes - the fighters were in their corners and the trainers' faces jutting in their ears. "Living the dream, sonny?"

I shrugged. "I work hard."

"Don't piss it away."

I turned with my slip, but he added, "And if you got more, keep it hidden."

Back with the ladies it was taking a while and I got edgy. "Refreshments?"

The girls laughed. "Hon, I did say load up at home."

"I can see a bar."

"Yeah, four million for a beer."

"I'll get this. No refresher for the ladies?"

Fuchsia made a gurney face at Missy. "Any short, with lemonade. It's about to start."

"I'm sure it'll go the distance."

Soon as the bell rang, the bar cleared so I shoved through the backwash and got our drinks. Round one was over when I'd slopped them back. Clarence took an onslaught. I probed Missy for commentary but all she said was he'd defended his head.

I'd got a closer look at Clarence: in shape but... he really *wasn't* young, half a life hauling bricks and the last couple in a crane. Sweating already. I guessed he'd defend five or six, then counter in bursts.

The bell rang for Round Four, and 'Blitz' Burkhart came out in a flurry, most of which Clarence dodged on his back foot, or only glancing contact. He mistimed, or hadn't the purchase to dodge a jab that the Blitz followed from an innocuous miss, as Burkhart stepped into Clarence's space. He landed a heavy one cutting Clarence's eyebrow. A little seeping red began and Blitz got confident; went to town. Clarence was backed to the ropes and could only get off by obstruction, clamping Burkhart's arms and leaning onto his shoulder. The ref split them and Blitz Burkhart continued his jabathon *but*... it was slowing and Clarence noticed.

Though he was cut he'd spent no energy and decided to pay for an attack. Man, those were heavy swings. He received two full frontals for his troubles on the way, and then the hooks landed. A body blow almost lifted Burkhart off his feet, bringing his head into risk and a mammoth downward hook floored him. But he got straight up, shook it off and seemed to come back fifty percent faster. Clarence took a blizzard and the blood began to sheet. Bell. The crowd went mad, Missy'd squealed when Burkhart hit the canvas, and Fuchsia just coolly blinked like a cat. I looked around...

Come on Clarence. Get him out of steam with those silly little dances and flurries and then floor him again. I never wanna get old but show me what an old winner looks like.

Or... show me the back of Gerhard Hahn, talking heatedly with the barman holding notes in his hand. What the hell is he doing west? And with barmen looking subservient. If I'd known...

They're arguing, the barman's pointing, Gerhard's peering, the barman gesticulates, Hahn placates and holds a note up to the light.

"Ladies, we gotta go."

"What? Clarence is back. It'll be over by the seventh."

"I *know*. OK I gotta go and Missy too. Here, take this." I handed my slip to Fuchsia, and dragged Missy with more strength than usual.

"Hey!"

"Just move. He's coming our way."

"Who?"

"Hahn."

"What here?"

"Yeah."

"It's open range to the main gate, they'll nab us. Or shoot first. Here..."

"What? We haven't done anything."

"Slip in, you can squeeze through that gap."

"Look, whatever's going on we'd be sitting ducks in there."

It was the Swivel-House, edged with silver moonlight and at rest. Perhaps it hadn't moved in months.

"Not if they don't see us go in. So... hurry?"

We slipped through a hatch in the back wall, using its trailer mooring as a step, and found shadow behind cogs and pistons. Curled in tight with knees pulled to our chests we heard each other breathe. Three - I think it was three - voices came closer, talking about us. One split and was told to hold the main entrance. The other two came towards the swivel-house. Stopped outside but talked.

"There's nothing in there."

"There's a hatch."

"You think I'll get through that?"

A sigh and silence.

I eyeballed the interior feverishly, realising I'd had no reason to drag Missy along. Nothing suspicious in her and Fuchsia watching a fight. Just me and my fun money would get anyone shot; get *me* shot. Though if they recognised Missy's scars they'd be unhappy. Suppose Clarence won and Gerhard lost; might put Fuchsia and Clarence in shit anyway.

There was a hatch in the roof, which sloped to a copse, beyond which was the tart aquarium and terraces. I pointed it out to Missy. "Hurry," I whispered hoarsely. "In the trees run straight for the terraces. Get some shadow. If you're seen head for the palace. You can outrun those turtles."

"Can I?"

"Hurry."

"How?" she whispered.

I put my head in my hands. "Climb up the machinery."

Whether they could get through the hatch I don't know but noise rattled. Missy gingerly climbed and I followed; on the roof we slid into soft foliage, or Missy did, I landed in nettles and let out a little wail like a marmoset.

We ran the trees but they'd heard and a shot rang. Missy was dressed to sparkle in moonlight, not run, bar her elastic ballet shoes. In the terraces I turned to check the copse. The lighter, faster oaf crashed out the other side, metal in hand, and saw me.

"Head for Luna Palace."

Could I hack 'em with the claw hammer? Dark, surprise, all that.

Luna Palace was boarded, now a home for junkies and the legless. Covered in bad murals and slogans over wild grass running to Halensee. Out back there was an exit to the world.

We had to dash without cover past the fountain and I heard the gun fire, a bullet whoosh past my ear and ricochet off the far stalls; I fell in behind Missy to make a smaller target and cover her. Reaching the terraces felt like relief but it was a pitstop. We jumped from the far end into long grass and the hill up to the palace.

"My legs are jelly."

"We'll be OK in the palace. There'll be people."

There was a problem besides the goon: the only other black people in the grounds were a heavyweight man and his girl. And there weren't many in Berlin bar touring musicians and burlesques.

Lead goon had to stop to catch breath; during which he lined his Mauser and took a shot. It skimmed my shoulder and I yelled in a hot sting, but the bounce deflected it. Meant for my head.

A loose board on a window hung on a hinge of nails. I pulled it and Missy rolled in breathing heavily. I followed, into a forgotten ballroom of dust and maybe-human excrement.

Got to the far door and listened. Outside was nothing, inside the scuffling of animal or human life. Far away I could hear conversation and the odd splinter of laughter.

The hall was empty, its broken tiles treacherous and cracked mirrors dangling. Once ornate French tables lay on their side like they'd fainted. If we could just make a dash out the back grounds for lovely normal Berlin...

A passage to a kitchen, before which was a room of meat-hanger hooks with a gulley and drain, and a larder. I looked in the larder and in the gloom was sure I saw a brass knob at the end.

"Here. That might be another passage at the back."

"You're bleeding."

"Sit tight. Catch your breath. I'll check the back."

Missy hadn't complained or questioned, like trust was a simple bind. I must keep her ragged heart safe.

I tried the door at the end. More storage. Now it might be luck diced us.

The moment Missy's breath died down I opened the door a crack. Mauser goon was making his way across the tiles, but was heading for the human talk. Simpleton.

Surely a kitchen would have external access, deliveries and such. ...Once Gerhard's bastard was out of sight we slipped through the kitchen and found the back door was stuck, needing an almighty yank. I stuck a foot on the frame and tugged. Clatter but no movement. Too much noise. I leant in to the door, and pulled with all my strength. A little give, more clatter. Down the corridor the movement was returning.

"Get out the way."

Missy shoved me aside, grabbed the handle and did as I had. A blast of summer air hit us, the door was open but I could hear a gun reload. Outside was all overgrown hedges over passages. We ran for the first opening. *Don't be a maze, don't be a maze.*

I could see a batch of railings in the trees, two panels lying on the ground. The goon rustled behind but this was it, almost home and dry.

We sprinted for the rank of trees and over the flattened railing. In the street beyond were people. Normal people. Dog walkers. Youngsters hitting town. About fifty yards away Kurfurstendamm began. We ran way too close to an oncoming tram, and on the main thoroughfare slowed down. I looked back. Nothing. Like we'd hit daylight and Mauser goon was a vampire. We slowed to a walk and after five minutes, a more obliging tram arrived.

I'd have to tell Papa. We'd do well to lay low.

~

Raymund is teaching me a lesson for something. He's beyond reach looking wrecked: cocaine, opium, benzedrine. But it doesn't matter how clammy or verbose he gets, he's still magnetic. Some people are beautiful and reality shouldn't touch them, though they're doomed to live it. Does what he wants, provokes pain and studies it like on a zoologist's workbench. Or perhaps he has his guilts. I feel older than fourteen but, let's be clear, I *am*.

"Missy's not around this weekend, in the sticks with buddies."

"Why are you telling me." Raymund's eyebrows bunched. I was blocking the view of an arousing boy.

"You're like some filthy chorister. What's off limits."

"Well. My bed, and the bed of your curious starlet, which doesn't leave much except your grimy loft."

"Papa's away too. In Heidelberg."

Got his attention, perhaps it was the full pantry. The old house. I don't want to tell you about it, really, it's not my best side.

In our wrangled sheets he reclines like a swan of white moonstone, all heat gone. In this house of dark memory, he lies over last night's reckless venture. I believe him a child of Middle-Germany; landlocked and once obedient, or so charming in rebellion all censure lifts.

"You know where they'll lay this."

I bring his Benedictine eggs and he pushes the Morgenpost aside, looks at them.

"Who, lay what?"

"They have to lay it somewhere or it will run about. They'll lay it in our community, like a runover cat."

"Furtwanger?"

"It's boys, not girls. If he'd just defiled one mini Heidi..."

"Defaced."

"Not sexual?"

"Furtwanger's gone. It's the wolf of Hannover you should be worried about. He's very much at large."

"At *large*," Raymund scoffed, poking yolk. His caffeinated body had agreed to break for brunch. He scooped eggs moving dark tousle from his face. I'd eaten mine as I cooked, puffing cigarettes.

Perhaps all that activity in the night is erasure; shaking off. In the day stillness replaces it. Ray's ego settles, to contemplate. Sometimes I watch him think. I wouldn't include Missy here (and I won't be unkind to women) but I've only met two kinds. Those who in solitude ponder relative wealth, with eyes that tire themselves, and those who instead wonder ceaselessly why they're not happy. Any who fit neither of those camps are goddesses. I adore them, our spare ribs.

Perhaps if Missy ever found out I could explain it's mostly stillness. Perhaps she already knows and well, perhaps she--

"As if these monsters are bigger than the authorities."

"What?"

"*At large.*"

~

Missy slapped the money down, but did *not* look happy.

"He won?" I was surprised.

"Sure he won. Knockout in the eighth."

"These Rentens?"

"Yup."

"How do I work out if I've been stung?" Five thousand plus in bank-friendly Rentens. "Catch-All Clarence is a genius."

"Sure he's a genius. Fuchsia wouldn't let him compete unless he could win. Fuchsia wouldn't date him unless he was real and honest, and straight." She stared at me without blink.

"She's a nice girl."

Missy said nothing, just kept staring at my soul.

"Where you getting this sort of money?"

"Gift from Paps. Won a mint on the hinnies."

She stared at me. After a while she shook her head. "I ain't asking again."

"Alright alright. They're counterfeit. Or they were. I passed them at Luna, figuring if I lost it didn't matter. I shouldn't have, but it was dark and busy. The bartender got an inkling and Gerhard appeared out of nowhere. I'd agreed with Paps: if we spend it we avoid Neukölln. How was I to know the Hahns are balls-deep in Lunapark."

"And that?" She pointed at the player.

I nodded and turned to retrieve my cigarette.

"Look at me you bastard."

It was Missy so I did.

"You're a hypocrite. And what's worse," she flung her arms up, "what's worse," the fire was in her and a fingernail jabbed my chest painfully. "*You* can't claim ignorance. *You* know. You know when the shit returns, it doesn't return to sender."

"Missy!"

"Go home Detlef. Go home."

Let's say Missy was *really fucking angry*.

How she found out I don't know, but she distinctly had.

There's only one way you'd suspect Balthazar's work: by laying it next to the real stuff in artificial light. It was the till, the heavy iron till with the Siemens lamp. Sunk. But he'd not have known whose it was, just it was circling Luna. Ha, *listen* to me! Does Gerhard need proof to kneecap Paps?

Turfing the west end's worrying though. Neukölln's just head office.

Missy avoided me for almost three weeks. Ice. The steady clop and daily toil of the lone woman. I don't know if at the end it was an act while she thawed, but it gave me a chance to think; jot play notes (my rejected heart more lyric), and stalk Carlin.

"What were you thinking?" Missy wore a cloche hat with short jacket, and a silk blouse top-buttoned. Dignified. "In fact, what is your *Pops* thinking? I wear his mistakes, I still work for him, and he's paying those slashers with fakes?"

She had called me to peace talks at the *Griechisch*. The terms of the Lehane-Brüning Treaty were reasonable to both parties, neither demeaning nor wilful in glory. Sinewy mind.

"No no. He's not bright but he's not stupid. It was me screwed up. I didn't know they were west. You can keep your hate-beam fixed on me."

"Oh Honeyboy. You know it's not like that. It's just…"

"What?"

"…Everyone's so damned reckless these days."

"You could say entrepreneurial."

Missy snorted. And if she hadn't then thrown her head back, she'd be laughing in my face. "Detty, you ain't even left school."

"I have."

"I mean official. Legal."

"Well don't worry. I won't try that caper again. I'll release the phoneys in innocuous places. Jewellers, record stores."

"No Detty! Bin the damned things. And tell your Papa do the same. There's other ways to weather."

I nodded in remorse. Seems I was off the hook.

"And, do me a favour."

I became a question mark.

"Every time you get an idea, run it by me. I can advise or run for the hills."

I smiled. "Sure."

Familiar voices on the stairs. I slipped in the dressing room and sat by the fire kit, behind the wardrobe. Picked up the Morgenpost so's not to seem hiding. As the guttural murmur passed and faded, I crept out and along. I heard scuffling and groans. The door was half-closed leaving a gap by the hinges. I peered through.

"May seem strange to you, but I don't *like* wasting my day. Beating talk out of people."

Carlin had Paps over his desk with an arm up his back and his neck twisted awkwardly under the lamp, held in the gorilla's grip at the back.

"Whatever you think I've done, Gerhard, it's not me. I've been behaving since the fire."

"Lunapark."

"Eh? I don't go on fairground rides. I'm fifty two."

"Someone does. Someone who uses your mint."

"You have... interests there?"

"Well, that's my business."

"So there was counterfeit."

Gerhard nodded. "I want to like you Brüning, but you make it so hard. You know what I'm feeling? Spare the rod and spoil th..." This gave him pause. The silence started to tick and Gerhard paced, his brow dipping. "You've got a son."

My back slithered.

"Whoa! Hang on. I don't ply him with bent money if that's what you're thinking."

"Why not? Above it? Only good for scum like us?"

"Of course not. Anyway he was here Saturday night, up in the roof smoking joints. I know, because I was trying to catch him at it."

At the window Gerhard's head lowered, giving Paps a death's head stare. "I haven't said what night it was."

My heart sank. *Nice one Papa, grace under pressure.*

"Alright, hear me out, please. We discussed it and agreed never to spend in Neukölln. I'd no clue you run Lunapark, it's the other side of town. That's why I just asked."

"Well, in this case, you can buy your way out. Is he back in the country?"

"My forger?"

"His name."

"I can't give you that."

"His name."

"You don't need it."

Carlin had gone easy, now the grip tightened, turned, pushed up higher. Paps yelped and Carlin pushed his now slack mouth into the leather.

"Brüning. His fucking name."

"Look I said," Paps gasped, "when he's back he'll recalibrate the print and hand it over. Couple of days. All yours. Capital, dividends. Free money. Isn't that what you want? Me, I'm just trying to recoup on a loss, like always. You said yourself you don't enjoy beating talk out of people. Nobody does. Come on Gerhard, I'm doing all you ask. Obviously we'll stay away from Lunapark."

There was a thick, acrid silence but it did begin to thin. Gerhard turned towards the door and I stood stock still, unblinking. He tapped a cigarette and lit up.

"A week tomorrow. Set up and in my possession. You don't spend anywhere in Berlin, ever, clear? And tell your fotze son to go play in the park and empty his pockets in the river. Come on Carlin. Tomorrow week."

Paps was released.

"Unless you want your arse wiped by nurses."

Neukölln is complicated.

It's a workers' district and as such densely socialist. The NSDAP call it Rotkölln, Red Cologne, and mount the odd sortie, a ragbag militia of supporters led by wannabe *Shock Troop-Hitler* recruits with bats, knives and sometimes carbines. (Berlin's an arsenal of pilfered war-ware.) I say rare, but they're getting thicker.

This splits the police, who don't like National Socialism but also *love* National Socialism. (Unlike the military, who all think Hitler's a fotze and General Ludendorff a treacherous weasel). Which leaves much to the gangs, or gang singular, *Hahn Security GbR*, who pay the police - I learn - and don't care for the extreme right, but neither do they Reds. Except! Reds are their bread and butter. It's a polygon of anger, money and unstable compounds, where payments stop some violence in favour of other violence. You latching all this?

So it's the ideal spot for a theatre frequented by Commies, sensitive gay flowers, negroes and Jewish musicians.

There are a few places will serve me alcohol. The *Griechisch* of course, run without irony by a man called Roman, and *Blaues Hirschcafé*, a total dive, whose attitude to having their licence revoked is akin to a smackhead's having his furniture taken. The staff are almost as undead as the customers.

"Evening junior. How's trouble?"

"Staying out of it. You?"

"Hardly. It finds me," he looked mock-ominously round the dart-eyed, crepuscular vault. "Ear to the ground so to speak. Good steak here mind. And Mademoiselle Lehane! Never seen you in the Blue Stag before now. Are you keeping well?"

"Well now Mr. Hartmann, I'm in a run of *The Voodoo Queen* which is doing nicely, thank you for asking."

"Yeah, who wrote that? Alger something… Voight?"

"Oh dear, you're not going to poach him."

Missy was courteous, ditching all spontaneity with whitey; couldn't drop her manners even if those lilybutts were themselves trash. Me and Paps, privileged. Beyond she played a corset-stiff boulevardier with a parasol.

He grinned. "All's fair in print and drama."

"Archard Vogt. Do ensure nothing conflicts with his Rottie residency, or I may have to pay you a visit."

"The trough feeds many swine," he said, which must have reminded him his steak was getting cold.

Michael Hartmann the publisher. Probably discussing something lurid with his thin companion; booth-clad in the Rembrandt light of a tasselled shade. Hartmann has a partner Schwartz, maybe that was him, meaning their chatter'd be doubly blood-spattered.

"Listen Brüning Jr., I need a chat with you. Sooner the better."

"What about?"

"Oranienstraße."

"I smell 20 pfennig pulp. What's up, your authors' imaginations failing them?"

See, Germans are lately mad for the grotesque. Don't ask me why. (Maybe Winter knows, I'll ask him.) *Hartmann & Schwartz* are fiddling with capillaries and suddenly pop an artery: 'Lustmord', lust for death, but *Fritz* needs claret up the walls in spouts and gushes. That's the important bit. Poison, wire, decapitations, foaming mouths, desirous motive and psychotic envy. Serious. It's a genre.

Smoke billows from the thin man under the lamp, while Hartmann wrenches steak like he's gutting fish, talking with his mouth full.

Later, while Missy's powdering, a hand grasps my elbow. Hartmann'd stuck around.

"You should be in bed," he grinned. "School tomorrow."

"There's no point. I teach them."

"I'm sure you do," he nodded and scuffed his chaotic hair. "Yes I'm sure you do. So..."

"Oranienstraße."

"You must have read about it."

"Yeah. The Grand."

"And?"

"And?"

"And, notice anything?"

My eyes narrowed in the gloom. "Are you angling for similarities with my Mama?"

"Sure. First thing struck me."

"I noticed similarities with a bunch of murders from the previous century, Michael. When those so dazed and confused by the present knew what they were doing." (Yeah I was drunk, didn't want to chat murder with Hartmann.) "That's what axe murderers do. Find an axe, and being Krauts we have exacting standards. Precision. What d'you want me to say?"

"We?"

"Fritz, the Teuton."

"Odd use of we."

"Pull your neck in Michael. I know you've got a livelihood to feed. I respect that. But I've got a lot on my plate."

"All I wanted to check was... Your mother, the murder weapon, the axe, wasn't at the scene was it. I had a note and I've lost it."

I looked at him, studied him. "No," I said. It seemed the simplest way.

A heavy sickness in my skull as I stand faint, hand on the boudoir door's handle. My eyes land naturally on the matrimonial bed. Empty, and the sheets are soaked red. Scattered round the room's window-end are body parts. It's open and net curtain sifts inward, gently on a breeze. I run to the casement, convinced I must have disturbed the killer. Look up and down the street. Just strollers. Suddenly my chest heaves and sobs and I can't breathe. I run in, first reach out for one limb, then change my mind, reach for the now compacted torso, like a giant pulped butterbean in ragu. I can't see her head. I search frantically, feeling but not hearing my own screaming. Mama's head has rolled under the iron bedstead.

"Shouldn't you be in bed, Herr Hartmann." Missy'd returned. "You have work tomorrow."

"Life works me, not me it."

"Well," Missy countered, "Can we get you something before Detlef and I retire to some privacy?"

"Nah." Hartmann eyeballed my face, etching and playing it like a gramophone needle. "I'll get what I need."

I nodded slowly.

"There'll be a leader piece in *Berliner Tageblatt*. I'm gonna draw parallels between Oranienstraße and your mother's death. How Richter, presumed guilty, was in a secure wing at the time of the Grand. I wanted to warn you, just let you know. And at some point, when a few more bodies pile up, a book. That's the only reason," he fixed Missy cooly, "I disturbed your evening."

"Yeah thanks. Thanks Michael," I didn't bother unhunching from the bar.

"Good night to you both. Have a pleasant evening."

All I could think was he needed a toothpick or to eat more like a human. Hartmann was a komodo dragon, half-chewing what came his way and festering the rest.

Schule. Out front stood Herr Defeats, simulating his nickname with a stare broken - I suspected - as much by years of our disinterest as shrapnel and gas.

"So as we've seen, it was Moltke's successes against MacMahon and Bazain at Gravelotte and finally the Siege of

Paris which led, in a very real sense, to the unification of Germany."

Krämer, a jam-jar eyed aficionado shot his hand up. "Is it fair to say Moltke's victories in France contributed to the false confidence of the Schlieffen Plan? And ultimately our massive and disastrous defeat?"

I hid my grin in my forearm. Good work Krämer.

Herr Defeats slumped, withdrew a moment into himself, trying to rally a counter-offensive but he couldn't, didn't have it in him. Dear me. The nobility of German offensives, and he a scholar and all (but not a great one, a children's one). It was tempting to actually know something, just so each victory he illustrated, we could end with a declaration that Germany lost everything; the lot.

Yeah I'm back at school. Figured a retry at education might burnish my dirtying halo.

And I'm attending my Winter Sessions again. It has occurred to me I'm mad; on a spectrum of charts; that Dr. Winter should be more concerned about psychosis than where my groin points.

~

Amelie Bergmann *did* look like Mama, it's a Berlin type - the older set - wear veiled hats or coloured pillboxes, as if there's a jolly funeral just round the corner. Or did, Amelie and Mama. Which there was.

I've read that serial murder is a question of analogues. Where one cannot fit the world as presented, what's presented must be changed. You could say Furtwanger was an original voice in a cluttered market, but man, the derangement; poor Lange and Gründ...

The public have much on their minds: card-punches and tin baths. They sit under our canvas as ostrich heads bolt through and stay put. There was a tranny in the *Griechisch* the other day in lime taffeta. She'd slashed himself, shimmering like a nymph with a laddered forearm. Assaulting her own myth. What d'you make of that? Is she on Amelie killer's mind? Furtwanger's? Or doing a job for them in franchised self-service.

~

Late again, Missy's heels puncturing puddles and my wet trousers flapping my Wildsmiths. Downpour and Neokölln shines. I caught our reflection in a restaurant: a wet boy in a bow tie and a scarred mulatto shorter than him in heels.

And then through the revolving *Palast* door, whacked by warmth and clink and laughter. We passed to the rear of Weiß.

"I like Stresemann," said his mirror-image companion; another fastidious Rothschild. "Fellow's got a grip on the reins whereas Cuno's a fool. Printing money. To pay bloody strikers my dear!"

"Agreed," the back of Weiß's slippery head nodded. "But we *do* need Frenchie hands off the Ruhr." He tipped his cocktail at the magnate. "Take a guess at the most profitable business before Stresemann?"

"I expect Not Being German. Or protest placards."

"Minting, my dear boy. The people who print the damned stuff. The irony!"

Their laughter was jowly and clandestine.

Several goofs and swells blew kisses at me (must be me, not Missy). The queen herself was enamel-bright with Cheshire grin, her hand spasming as she waved frantically at friends. We crab-walked between feathered shoulders, trying not to get caught in the pearl ropes, for our free punch.

The fire'd pushed the October run to November, almost crashing the end of season party into Christmas, so the rear gallery was open, brilliant with ivy trails of light around Dada daubs and guest Cubists. It all spilled through the atrium where Jonah and whale had never been so popular. A drunk-too-early girl swayed dankly on the fountain's rim.

I didn't have a penguin suit, just a tweed jacket and the bow tie pinched from Paps.

Missy giggled at me, "What are you doing?"

I was making cat-faces in my punch cup, tongue rasping my palate. "This is revolting. Shall we get a real drink."

"Long as real money buys it," her eyebrow curled.

"Never gonna let me forget, are you."

"No," her chin tilted. "I don't believe I shall. Now, who shall we take to the bar with us."

"Me?"

"Detty, we can't ignore everyone. And where's Fuchsia and Gloria?"

"I can see Gloria through the--"

"Oh there's Matilda!" I was heading west but got rag-dolled east. "We simply must."

Matilda was a decent purebred. I mean a nice Teuton, come of age and working at the *Großes Schauspielhaus* up north as 'The Pony': out of time and last in line for comedy effect, then coming forward as the best double-jointed, technical dancer in the encore; The Schauspielhaus was an impressive cavern of stalactite ceilings and a rotating stage.

"Max saw *The Voodoo Queen*," Matilda began. "He might have an opening."

"Who's Max?" I chipped.

"Our impresario. Dreams big honey. You'd be a f--"

"I'm tied Matilda. I owe. I mean I ain't doing anything to jeopardise, is what I mean to say."

"Whoa Honey. You owe him? After *that*? I'll send you the script," Matilda squeezed her hand.

Why do women just *get on*? As we warmed up the rain started to steam off our shoulders, rising to the rafters. We must look like cattle in eveningwear. "Ladies, I've seen a sad-looking friend sloping about. Gonna catch up."

Missy gave me a weird look. "You don't have friends."

"Balls. It's Raymund. Repair some bridges we made into charcoal."

The look deepened.

"Forget it. If you're at the bar, mine's a sidecar."

Raymund stood in a state of peak bafflement. Perhaps he'd neglected his *actual* friends so long in 'spreading his wings' they wouldn't show themselves. Alone like a self-conscious, gay island: it didn't suit him. *Chrissake*, I murmured to my stupid self and walked over.

"How you doing Ray."

"Oh don't call me *Ray*," he replied ungratefully, but his eyes were relieved. "Sounds like I drive an omnibus."

Then I'll call you Ray all evening, I mentally straightened my bow tie with a smirk.

"Love the rig," he said. "I don't believe I've seen you so grown up."

"But that's not your thing now Ray. You like Fernandas to wear knee-pants."

He looked at me in total surprise and had to recompose. But I wasn't finished. "Oh Fernandas, you and I are different from the others. We must suck all we can out of life." I tilted my head and raised my eyebrows.

He flushed. I wished he'd squirmed a whole lot more but he was a quick batsman. "So, you're going to be a lemon-squeezer this evening. Sensitive young man."

"Spreading one's wings doesn't preclude coming home once in a while does it?"

"No my love," the eyes softened. "That's why I came tonight."

"Of course."

He tentatively slipped an arm into my elbow crook and I shook it clear, sure Missy'd be glancing over her shoulder.

"Incidentally, I looked up 'fling' in the dictionary to see how long one was. Didn't say."

"Alright I'm a pig. It's pure gratification with me. I'm trying, Dets, I really am."

Nein Schweine. These answers are weak; unspecific, chalk and dust. Sand blown from a dead desert. Remnants or borrowed memories of what it was like to feel. You sallow husk.

"I came over to say, Ray, don't come near me again, and stay out of the Palast. Tonight's your last shindig, OK?"

"How dare you... fucking ponce." He jabbed my chest but it was a weak double-jointed finger that bent on contact. Caused me a glance at Missy and Matilda mind, to check they were immersed. I locked eyes with my queen horribly; her suspected queer flimsily laying in. Onwards and upwards.

The girls converged on Fuchsia and Gloria, slipped through brass-glass doors and hunkered into a *Griechisch* table. A livid mural of insults followed me as I headed to join them.

"...a glint in Albert's eye and you own nothing. Heir to the Rotbart bankruptcy. Don't tell me where I can go."

"What?"

"I said," he sighed, worn out, "can't we just put everything behind us."

"You put everyone behind you."

"Stop with the--"

"Raymund! Don't come back. Enjoy your evening."

I walked feeling bitch-vengeance eyes but... my integrity was solid.

I went outside to smoke and dropped a capsule of ground mescaline and opium. I soon felt warm and open, the *Palast* crouching like an alien vessel visiting us to reveal its culture. Curved and splendid, wet like a newborn. Come see our alien ideas: sex and gender are immaterial for we are genderless. Art represents nothing but itself. Form is function and sedition and critique of our rulers is encouraged. Wealth is irrelevant because credit is infinite. Forget your earthly woes and gawp. Leave that filthy *real* crime, unemployment, murder and debt, for we have pushed it all onstage, siehst du? Komm und sieh.

Yeah, and wake up head smashing like a gavel in reality. My lovely Weimar, you will not last. Your painted skin is translucent showing brittle bones and rickets and tapeworms

and palsies; deliriums and indecisions. You send out your plump
rep and call him Stresemann. A prissy Frankenstein. Nothing
to see here. Everything's fine. Get out of the Ruhr, demob the
Rhineland, swap your useless Papiers for Rentens and get back
in the factories.

And the monster appears docile.

I squished my smoke under a loafer and slapped gecko-like
back through the revolving door, looking up and going round
twice before coming out in the street. Trying again I landed
head-first in a stomach, gripped the man's shoulders
apologetically, gazed into his pupils' universe until he
nervously wriggled free, and I moved away to the *Griechisch*.

Where Missy and the girls had been boothed was a vacuum;
chorusless. I narrowed my eyes. I may have been stood there a
while, slightly bent, thin-eyed, slowly rotating, looking round
the room like a mad detective. (Perhaps Chaplin works on this
gear; I felt like a silent movie, the intolerable world now
affably strange).

There she was, accusatory and stiff, her drink a barricade or
balustrade or whatever defensive people do.

"OK, alright, yes I had a fling with Raymund. He wasn't so
deep into drugs or himself back then, and you and me didn't
amount to much. But we broke up by mutual consent
because *he* wanted to play the field," I jabbed my thumb back
at wherever he'd last been, "and *I* wanted to be with you. You
can believe me or not. But I'm not going into all this again so
don't ask me again."

"I didn't."

"What?"

"I didn't ask you."

"What!"

"I asked if you wanted ice and lemon."

"Oh. Yes. Please..."

Jesus, how do Mexicans stay sane on this shit.

"It's OK honey. I believe you."

"Yeah?"

"Sure Hon. I wouldn't care if you slept with asses. So long as you're monogamous when you're with me. I need honesty in my life."

~

The sky fluffed, its sun peaking to remind us we adored it (*always leave them wanting*). Davione had made us a picnic with spiced meat and cane spirit; luxury Sunday.

"Take your hand off, you barbarian."

"Which hand?"

"We're in plain sight."

She removed my Shackleton hand from her blouse but didn't remove me.

"They're not interested in us. *Mixed* couples. Anyway half of them are black."

"What does that mean?"

"Eh?"

"What did that mean?"

"Well, I meant..."

"Spit it out."

"Well just..."

"I can't think of a way you meant it that can be a good way. What did you mean?"

I got up on my elbow. Walking along the path below was my history teacher.

"There's Herr Defeats. He's always good fun." I stood and called at him. He stopped, looked round, looked up at me again and hesitantly walked up the grassy bank.

"It's Brüning isn't it? Er..." he clicked his fingers softly. "Dieter."

"Detlef. How goes it with you sir? Strolling?"

A couple of nervous black guys had taken the same path as Defeats up to us and stood a respectful distance with arms behind their backs. Defeats turned a bit disconcerted, and returned to us.

"Beautiful day, thought I'd head to Lunapark's anthropology section. I find our colonial mandates fascinating, as I suppose do you Fraulein?..."

"It's Missy Lehane," I said. "The theatre actress. They should level those human zoos."

"Can I help you fellas?" Missy called at the men behind. One brought paper and the other a fountain pen, proffering them.

"Sure. Where you from?"

"Gabon. I'm Emmanuel and this is Jemuel." The blue glow of new arrivals had faded to grey in their alabaster shirts, shoulders rolled in. What pride they'd shipped was maybe crushed a bit under fallen dreams. "Emmanuel works harder, watches more shows than Jemuel. Can you make his name bigger?"

"All fans are equal." Missy kept her fixed ivory for punters - the more since smiling receded the scars - and handed their message without getting up. Emmanuel skipped and took the paper and pen, walked off jabbering and slapping backs, which relieved Defeats.

"They need a Davione supper," I suggested.

"Course, Hon. Tell Africa to stop by."

"I'm quite sure Fraulein Lehane would enjoy the exhibits at Lunapark." Defeats peered foggily; too long, too rude.

I'd felt her coiling and now she unwound. "I wouldn't. I'm half Ulsterwoman, which makes me English but less polite, half-Carribean, which makes me African but less polite. So no, I don't take much interest in anthology sections."

"~*Anthropology*~" I whispered and got a kick.

"Stresemann's turning things round isn't he," I stepped in, and calculated my next gambit. "Seems democracy's bedding in well."

And I waited for the fuse to burn down.

"I think you've attended too many illusionists' shows. Democracy can't bed in if it's not something Germany acquired."

And you've been reading Spengler.

"Yes, bedding in nicely. Welfare. Suffrage. Scientific breakthrough. A future of peace."

Defeats gave a sickly chuckle. "There's only one peace that lasts, strength in unity. Decisiveness. That's our nature. It's how Germany was born."

"Willhelm was decisive wasn't he."

"My dear boy, German annals--"

"Pardon?"

"German annals are littered with brief alliances stronger than her own. That is the battle, dear boy." But he was flushing.

"Yes sir, bedding in nicely."

He stomped off. Only anger could raise those beaten shoulders. "You'll see!" he shouted back and headed off to look at negros in a confined space.

"That was a laugh riot."

"I thought so."

"Caged natives and Kraut artillery. Why's he called Herr Defeats?"

"His life's a failure so he lives in cuckoo-land. The fun bit is saying we lost our biggest test and have been humiliated since."

"Unlike *your* life Honeypot. Just don't get too many glories down there, "and she crushed my genitals far too hard, laughed and ran down the slope. I followed and the closer I got the more the laughter became nervous squeals.

"I must take decisive action with you. No compromise." I held her arms behind her back and wouldn't let her go. Until her flutter-lashed snake routine softened me, she slithered round and we achieved union on the path.

I was in Wedding market looking for native crafts. I need masks that can pass for voodoo. I'm now a production manager because Paps knows Gym's a dead duck and I'm heading into his line. Grand, right? Except it's actually just traipsing Berlin for improbable props and getting told I'm a fotze if they don't exist. I jumped a double-decker to Tiergarten where I figured to snooze and walk back in December sun. But I passed a comic scene outside the *Institut für Sexualwissenschaft* (the progressive sex people).

The Sex Institute is rather beautiful, a roofless modern clinic sprung between classic German buildings, but at its entrance a motley assembly of outpatients were acting as security. Guess who they were manhandling off the premises? ...Dr. Winter. Ejaculating my psychiatrist. All sanctioned. These sapphics and Klinefelters and unhappy couples had their bouncer's mandate from a small, friendly-faced Hebrew with a moustache and cheerful eyes on the steps.

All Winter's finery was skewiff from being grabbed, and he'd tweeded up to look bookish, but they weren't opening their archives to him! (Not him. But they would - one day those archives'd be opened, and the meticulous lists of names, the stringent data collection, the recordings of all sources and findings... *sheesh*!)

Winter's last assault to get back in was met by a bisexual pincer movement led by General Hebrew and more persons of unknown persuasion attacking his flanks. Winter's tie was still functioning as a tie, but the shirt buttons beneath were open and wrankled. I was watching a pan-sexual brawl.

You see, the Confused have amassed against the Certain and drawn strength in this, plus a building in a nice part of town: the whole is happier, and bolder, than its parts. And I salute them of course, confronting their fear as pioneers. (Except there's a singular lack of butch women.)

In danger of getting spotted by Winter in retreat, I hurried in an arc of the garten. Man, I wasn't letting this slide. A wildcard if he aggravates me.

~

"So this is...." Dr. Winter looked at some notes or schedule of thoughts, "Our fifth session. Good Lord, time rushes us forward."

I nodded vaguely. He had a slight swelling under his ear, more of a raised chafing, and I had to keep a straight face.

"We talked in the last session about your domestic environment and the untimely death of your mother. That's where we stopped. Let's pick up."

I shrugged.

"So you experience a terrible bereavement around the same time as you begin puberty. This must have been an awful time. Conflicting thoughts, anger, desire, confusion, lust, etc. all tied up with shock and sadness."

"I don't think puberty had much affect. I was randy as hell long before."

He frowned and tilted his head. "Prior to puberty the sexual object is autonomous, it is you. During adolescence the sexual object is formed beyond one's self. That's why I'm dwelling on a period which may be painful for you. The formation of your sexual desires towards the outside word coincided with the death of your mother. And of course hormones, wreaking havoc without your knowledge."

His room was bound with books, including copies of his own: *Ego Disruption & the Re-Signposting of the Sexual Object*. Plus works by the exceedingly gay Magnus Hirschfield and the latest coded claptrap from Jung and Freud (close friends; too close?)

"So?"

"What?"

"Tell me about the feelings you experienced. Did you feel attracted to men before your mother's death?"

"Dr. Everhard, I think I'm cured."

He withdrew into his neck. "In what way?"

"I prefer women."

"I see," He jotted a note. "Preferring, but still yearning."

"Is this a romantic poets meeting?"

"I have a note about you in the Palast apparently having a tiff with a young man... Saturday just past."

"What?"

"You appeared to be acting out your own melodrama in the foyer."

"You can't do that! That's *way* beyond your remit."

"Don't be paranoid, Detlef. A friend happened to be at the show and said it was an eventful evening. We were chinwagging merely as friends, as citizens. He mentioned the proprietor's son, whom I'm afraid I know is you. I can't *unhear*, young man."

"Well don't bring it here then."

"A little decorum and we'll resume." He frosted over.

Wildcard? ...Street ejections? No, save it.

~

"You know someone will ask us where they can exchange items before we get out."

We were in Wertheim department store on Moritzplatz, as Missy wanted to get an evening dress for ...well I don't know what for, I'm not always privy to her nightlife.

"Pah! They might mistake you, retail boy, but they'd instantly recognise the glamorous Missy Lehane."

Outside, banners on its arched frontage declared 'extra prices' inside, like an alternative universe. ('Not happy with this cost? We can add a bit more.')

The shiny atrium had a statue of Heilige Leonie von Cologne, the German saint of well-organised browsing.

"Girl! Girly! Now, can you tell me where I go to refund clothes please?"

I had to pretend my laughter was a cough. It was a fat - polite enough - American woman whose large shapeless fifties required bustles and accessories.

"Ah, you probably didn't understand European sizing. The scale is much smaller over here." Missy replied.

Fatty's flicker of joy at hearing another Yank quickly darkened. Again I spluttered and cleared my throat and started furiously studying camiknickers.

"Is this gentleman your manager?"

How long, I wondered, before this spat took the gloves off.

"Floor below, at the back on the left. And in return do you know where ladies' evening wear is. I've seen a beautiful Anton Recherche Japanese print I want to buy but they've rearranged everything. You'd think they'd put the expensive stuff in plain sight!"

I sat slumped on a stool outside the changing room. Missy'd rustle behind the slat doors. Every five minutes I'd be called to zip or button her, then her head would poke round, and she'd pirouette out in the dress.

"Too clingy? It's a bitch to get on."

"I prefer it to that boxy thing."

"Yeah, I know which part of you prefers it."

"The boxy numbers aren't flattering."

"Darl, it's the height of. Don't you look around you?"

"Well *that's* my favourite." I nodded at her. "Besides, those women are pencils."

She frowned at that, and growled. "Few more yet."

As the door swung shut again I called: "If you didn't like it why did you try it on?"

"Just to see."

A woman left the next cubicle, glanced at me and then double-took, presumably at my youthful good looks.

"Hon, you've always shopped alone and you always look a million. I need to get to the barber."

"Useless!" she yelled.

"I'll meet you on Potsdamerplatz. Under the clocktower. Say, a quarter gone five?"

There was some kind of noise of assent, so I went to Herr Kühn's, looking like a dazed Lord Byron. He has the best clippers. All Heinrich Kühn knows is I live in a theatre and dress neat, which these follicle merchants appreciate.

"Not long till Christmas."

"Bärenjäger. Blazing rows. Lying on a cold stone floor."

"Is that what you do?"

(Excuse this. Renten levelled out at four to the dollar: Christmas *can* happen.)

"Only way to deflate," I said. "Cold floor."

I was fairly sure I could hear gunfire.

"I eat twice, first time leave room for schnaps, then back for seconds. It's not going anywhere. I insist the good woman leave it in the oven."

Kühn did hair by halves: one side sprucing nicely.

"Imagine if we had prohi--" I really could hear gunfire. "There's people shooting."

"Aach. Turf wars. They wouldn't know a self-loading from a semi."

Gunshots smashed the window to pieces and it fell in - sprinkling, glittering: the gold-lettered *Herr Kühn Barber & Grooming* slid to our feet like gilt-edged ice. Which made the erratic gunfire louder, echoing and bouncing off buildings.

"Holy cow," Kühn dropped the clippers still whirring, I leapt out of the chair and flung the apron. He stuck his head out the window.

"Herr Kühn!" I shouted, "Pull your bloody head in man."

He did, but he'd seen enough.

"I think it's those Kapuzes."

"How many?"

"Hard to say. From the noise, maybe ten?"

"What do they want with you?"

He laughed. "We're just in the crossfire, sonny."

I crawled to the window, raised my face more gingerly than veteran Heinrich. Bursts came from one end of Kochstraße, went dead, then bursts from the other end. Then silence and a change of position and the bursts resumed from new directions. I trusted Heinrich, he'd bored 'Great War' stories into me like wells: if he said ten it *was*.

Heavy shadows darted between parked cars. The docile, busy streets now emptied. Heinrich was beside me, craning upwards.

"What you doing?"

"Anyone with a roof position will end this."

"Is that the best place? Can you see who's shooting at the Kapuzes?"

"You take a look. I recognise the man behind the cream Duesenberg. Your district."

I pulled my arse through the broken glass to the end of the frame, and peaked above. Cream *Duesenberg*, windscreen out. No movement. All quiet on his western front. Those unable to get out - Mamas with kids or old limping blighters - sat in doorways encircling their loved ones or themselves.

And then the man behind the *Duesenberg* was way forward, level with us in clear sight. I sank, to let Heinrich know it was Lothar 'Let's Talk' (a Neukölln horror), but Heinrich had vanished, reappearing first as a double shining muzzle, then eye whites.

"What are you *doing*?"

"Defence."

He sat beside me with a shotgun across his thighs, under the window frame in the snicking glass. The butt of my hands was lacerated.

"Don't go all Iron Cro--"

A heavy shape jumped over our heads and landed, skidding in the splinters and landing on his arse with a Tommy aloft. Heinrich quickly trained the shotgun on him.

"Don't move, son. My gun's on you."

Let's Talk did move, to see, and his own gun limped to ground level, but he didn't let go.

"Don't move I said."

He leant on the elbow of the hand holding a *Saur & Sohn* sub. He grinned, and carried on slithering round to face Heinrich.

"OK. Move then."

Suddenly Heinrich's gun went off, flashing a pepper of shot in Lothar's face, and the *Sauer* started spasming bullets.

Bloodbath on Kochstraße

13 December, A quiet Tuesday afternoon in Kreuzberg and the turf war escalating behind Berlin's scenes broke onto the street, between what police believe were the Hahn and Kapuze brothers' gangs.

There were three fatalities, one a bystander, Heinrich Kühn, the proprietor of a barber shop. Ten were injured, three critically. Shoppers and pedestrians ran for cover as windows shattered and shots rang ceaselessly for twenty minutes, car windows frosted as the shooters sprung between parked cars, dipped into alleys, or fired Thompson 'Tommy' guns from rooves.

Both gangs are notorious. The Hahns are the most provocative force in Neukölln district, whereas the Kapuze brothers run its north neighbour Friedrichshain. But proximity, rivalry and the sibling control of these districts are where any similarity ends.

The Kapuzes - gangsters no doubt - are well-liked by the predominantly poor residents of F. Undertaking daring bank robberies, they are known to distribute a percentage of each haul to struggling Friedrichshainers.

The Hahns, conversely, are feared in Neukölln for frequent revenge killings, unpredictable psychosis and their distribution of nothing beyond the gang.

Of the two gang-member fatalities, both were from the Hahn Gang. It is believed the turf war erupted over expansion into the west of the city, specifically the Lunapark.

Christmas '23

Yeah, you get your own newspapers, such is the ghetto of Yanks and Engländers sprechening Englisch on our straßen. But I like you coming.

Heinrich died of blood loss, riddled in his midriff. He was scared of nothing: life, death, Heaven's gavel-whackers, nothing swayed his constitution. I caught Lothar's last lead in my hip - where god only put coiled gut - but Lothar looked in such awful pain it was definitely all over in Kühn's salon. He'd dropped his gun to clutch his face and bled through his hands; red spider's legs between fingers and thumbs. The shootout clattered east in a crouch, with jump-shadowed rooftops, pushed by the blind aggression of the Hahn clan though they'd lost two. After a burst of fire, the last thing I'd hear was a ricochet like a question mark.

The clippers whirred, jigging in broken glass and hair. I glanced in the mirror: half my hair cut. When the window smashed Kühn had harvested a line over my crown. Heinrich and *Let's Talk* died in hospital.

I unplugged the clippers and bagged them. Limped to *Hospital Am Urban* almost in a faint - a dizzy kaleidoscope - as blood turned my trousers sticky burgundy. Once A&E knew I was a Kreuzberg victim I got a bed. To the blue-smocked woman - the lovely Krankenschwester - we're all deserving.

"What'chya reading Hon?"

"Friedrichshain local." I looked up with my shaven head. I'd had to strip the lot and looked like a virulent nationalist or XY lesbo.

"Turf war?"

"The longer it lasts and the more fatalities - I mean gang fatalities - the easier for Paps I figure."

"Mmm." It was thoughtful agreement.

Her gown drip-drying, Missy was in a coat with nothing underneath, her widened mouth like Anita Berber's black negative.

How did it start, or end? ...Me, I was sideshow; I'll be following the column inches like everybody. Lunapark was mentioned; that chimes. The spoofed-up testosterone and zinging lead moved north east, so I got a copy of *Friedrichshain Vorhut*, a local rag backing the Kapuzes: *...ambushed in Alt-Treptow... protecting the people of A-T... ...doing what the police are afraid to... etc.*

Seems the street melee splintered at Puschkinallee and Treptower Park, with pursuits into the markets and murky streets, the various parks, of Alt-Treptow and Friedrichshain.

Ten to midnight I'd had the bullet out under local anaesthetic. I watched the oversize tweezers, pointy forceps or whatever poke through swamped, congealing blood; the eyes of the surgeon rolling ceilingward, aiming for anything hard that moved. Stirring half-baked excreta. (Is it OK for that to get in your blood?) A dink on a platter, and after I'd been sterilised and stitched I was told I could leave. Return for blood tests in a week. (No, it isn't OK to have shit in your blood).

"Anya, Varya, Yasha, Dunyasha. They all sound the same."

"There's a character list in the programme."

"Fat use. The men are dark and intense and the women are dark and intense. Everyone looks the same."

"Racist. The Cherry Orchard is his masterpiece."

"It ain't news to me aristocrats can't change with the times and they go broke. White noise."

"I thought you'd like an evening out." I was hurt; wanted to be her sugar-beau for just one evening.

"Aw, Hon, I do. I did. I mean I am," she dug an arm into mine. "Let's go backstage. But if you see Max keep your mouth shut. You ain't selling me to the opposition. Like some flouncy slave trader." She laughed loud at herself. Sometimes Missy's laugh was a bellows, a vast hoot.

"Flouncy?" I was less troubled by slave trader.

She cocked an eyebrow at me. Then she saw Mahatma (or whatever) and trotted into her arms. They bounced cheeks and squealed. I stood like a shadow stage-left while destitute Russian aristocrats de-powdered and hugged. 'A bravura performance Hugo'... 'a triumph sir'. *What's wrong with white noise.*

"My favourite show-stopper!" Max appeared with raised arms and his impresario's girth. "Missy Lehane gracing us for Chekhov!"

"How the other half live."

"Now don't shoot off before we've had a drink. I'm excited. Promise."

Missy made faces and squirmed. I poked my nose in the prop shop. Wandered through to the delivery bay, went up flimsy metal more a ladder than stairs and found myself in the roof joists. I scampered back down.

"Come with me."

"What?" Missy was holding two drinks, possibly one on Matilda's behalf, but seemed to be drinking both.

"Upstairs."

"What for?"

"Some flouncing."

Max was walking over again, having left two actors who looked the same to look at their reflections. Missy ducked into my shoulder and we scooted to the rickety ladder up.

We were greeted by a grinning clown's head caught in skylight. Beyond it was a museum of oversize heads, uniforms and bustiers and guns and petticoats, fake knives, bottles of makeup and poison, potted trees, desks and dramatic living rooms, mantelpieces and masks, moth-eaten underwear and mannequins. All the way back into darkness among the beams.

"It's some awful joke shop."

"Nonsense. Go find somewhere cosy, I'll grab supplies."

"What for?"

"Sleepover. Must be vodka and pastry around. They're partying."

"Honey, don't leave me up here."

I reached in my pocket and tossed her a sloshing flask. "Drink the magic potion. I won't be long."

"Want to switch?"

She laughed between shunts. "No. I'm good."

"You're doing all the work."

"You're complaining?"

"Hmmf."

"I can't switch, there's a clown staring at me," Missy giggled. "I can feel eyes on my back."

"Oh."

After a while, the pair of us sheened and glossy on a decorators' sheet, I gave up.

"What you doing?"

"I'm too drunk."

"Longest you've lasted." Missy's mouth glittered and her eyes sparked mischief; the shadows were soft on her hand-sculpted face.

"Yeah but--"

"You brought me up here. Ain't leaving till I get satisfaction."

3am, I must have dozed and woken. She was draped and slumbering. Every time she twitched her fingers caressed. Female satisfaction sure gets you the prize. The heaviness of her body felt new, like only now was gravity including her. I mean we'd done it before, but not like this. Her closeness would stop me sleeping but I didn't mind, the breath and the hot hearth cooling, the razored moon.

~

"My colleague Kriminalinspektor Lange."

"We've met."

"He's helping me collate."

Paps and I sat in the police station across a table from Lange and Kriminalhauptkommissar Gründgens.

Gründgens leant in. "Greed. Money. Counterfeiting. Murder."

"You talking about the Hahns or the Jews? If it's the first you seem able to tolerate it, if monthly deposits at the National Bank of KriPo are any indicator."

"Quite an accusation, Brüning." Gründgens curdled. "You've heard of a newly published book, *Axt der Lust*?"

"It's a pun," Lange chipped in. "Acts and axe, you see?"

"Yes I can see that." Paps said.

I murmured, "I knew it was published."

"By your friend Michael Hartmann."

"I don't begrudge anyone a living. Not even you."

Gründgens raised his eyebrows at Papa. "Stroppy, queer little fellow he's become. Perhaps we'll conduct the interviews separately."

"Interviews?" Paps asked.

"Chats. Lange, why don't you take Detlef next door so he can focus on assisting us."

"Wait," Paps was firm, "He's not going anywhere until I know what we're assisting, and what Lange will ask. He's a minor."

"He seems capable."

"Don't blur lines Gründgens. I can make complaints as a citizen. What do you want?"

"Where to start." He pulled his chair to the table, hunkering in with Lange, and breathing in our space. "Arson, witness to two murders... one unsolved, one at the scene of Herr Kuhn's murder..."

"Which unsolved murder?" I said.

"Your mother's. You recall your mother? Last year."

"Mm."

"...fitting the description of a teenager fleeing the scene of a murder in a Kreuzburg barber shop."

"Who?" Paps asked.

Gründgens dipped his chin in surprise, then nodded at me.

"...Underage gambling and drinking and suspected passing of counterfeit banknotes."

"What? Who are you talking about. What's the basis for all this."

"I'm nearly finished, may I? ...Homosexual activity," he fished in his bag, "which is illegal even at *my* age and imprisonable at Raymund Vormelker's age. And all this, before I even get to the parallels made in *Axt der Lust*."

"Such as."

"Oh we can get to that some time. Let's focus on your present entanglements for now. See if we can get you in here for a longer spell..."

Meaning he hadn't finished the book (running his finger under the words, tongue poking out in intense concentration). And he had it in for us.

~

Christmas at home. Not my old home in south Neukölln ('Blutbad Haus'), the home I'd recently vacated for Missy, northside: now enslaved in tinsel and guarded by angels. The tree smelled of sap and leant sparkling in its creped bucket as if forcibly dressed in drag.

"What would grand Paps have thought?" I said, gazing through my cigarette at the despondent fir.

"If Hertzl can, I can."

"Who?"

"Father of Zionism."

"Oh."

"Will you ever take an interest?"

"It's because of Mama, isn't it."

"I'm not breaking with tradition," Paps snapped.

Missy sat on the sofa awkwardly drinking sherry. Each time she sipped, her eyeballs and eyelids swapped places.

"You don't have to drink it, Hon. I'll get Missy something a bit glitzier. Martinis all round?"

Weiß was here looking stratospherically queer. I think he moved in Connecticut circles less stylish than Europe so felt the need to compensate, *or*, people are so stylish in his circle that to prove his exquisite taste and peacock his targets, he overdoes it in general.

I went to the refrigerator for pre-chilled glasses. 2:1 gin:vermouth plus an olive. Received wisdom, but I like glacé cherries so bollocks to received wisdom.

While I mixed I thought about Lange's words. Gods of the street. It may have been true once, the wiseguys and their pocketed green men; still true in our wet metropolis but not so true elsewhere. Take Munich, land of beer halls, rebirth and

Volkskörper: now subject to unusual cycles and uprisings. A confusion injected into Fritz's arm. German hotheads usually swing molotovs, bats and knives at our useless leaders and their barricades; not so in Munich. A militia with guns.

The main hothead is a relic of last century's foggy glories (his invented uniforms no more stylish than the LaPos they clash with.) He tried to seize power inspired by Mussolini's March on Rome. Get a foothold in Munich and then do the same to dusty Berlin. Well you can *fuck off pal!*

He got five in the caboose. Should put an end to his brand of weasel shit.

Our goose was nearly cooked, wafting blanketed in special dumplings. I chinked through with my alcohol cones. Papa's not a bad cook; when Mama was alive he took over at Christmas anyway bar the goose itself. (And he's not deprived of his Hanukkah. Lights his candles and stuffs us with latke and sufganiyot. If the feasts collide so do the candles, eyeing each other suspiciously across the room.)

Missy cleared her throat through a silent interlude. "Keep an eye on Archard, Herr Brüning. I do believe he's being poached."

"Call me Albert for heaven's sake."

"Then you must call me Egmont," said Weiß. I stifled a laugh.

"OK Albert," Missy nodded courteously at Egmont. "But if Archard goes, who will write my plays?" Her face dipped in her drink but her eyes watched carefully.

"Vogel, Krüger, they're ten-a-penny," Paps waved her fears away. "Is Archard going up in the world? Don't tell me, Großes Schauspielhaus."

"Down," I offered. "Hartmann and Schwartz."

"Up financially then," Weiß smiled, and Paps fixed him with ill-humour.

Christmas Dinner was awkward. I'd had to persuade Missy - self-conscious of eating publicly - that Paps and Weiß would be thinking only of their stomachs. And in hindsight, Weiß was insultingly chipper considering what was to follow. There was a brand new twitch in his face mind.

"Albert, I didn't want to ruin Christmas Day, so I've waited until now to bring this up."

I'm listening outside Paps' tiny library. Though the house can't afford such space, Paps stubbornly believes in its prestige. Paps' looking wary and gimlet-eyed at Weiß I think.

"Go on."

"Well you know I like to do my bit for the arts. We're not beasts and we need culture, to reflect upon ourselves. In spirit I support you wholeheartedly."

"You're pulling the finance."

Weiß cleared his throat, spluttering a bit. He found Paps' directness poor etiquette.

"Not me," Weiß said. "A major shareholder is over, looking at our German portfolio. One Robert Shackman."

"Shackman pulled it for you."

"Robert hit the roof when he saw the Rotbart books. There was no logical way of stopping him."

"We just reopened, revamped, we're a glitzy new Schauspielhaus."

"And there's another small matter."

"There is?"

"It's rather delicate."

"Small *and* delicate, what could it be? Some kind of glass bird?"

"Criminal operations. Dubious interests. I'm not blind, Albert."

"It was hardly going to break the German economy!"

"What wasn't?" Weiß sounded confused.

"What?"

"What wasn't going to break the German economy?"

Paps seemed embarrassed and a little angry. "Just spit out the small and delicate matter please Weiß... er, Egmont."

"The reason, perhaps the whole reason, my investment is scuppered," Weiß said, feeling he'd neatly encapsulated.

"Just say it!"

"Certain brothers."

"Say it," Paps was quieter.

"The Hahn brothers."

Paps didn't respond.

"They *are* getting rather a grip on you, aren't they. We cannot invest now that the rot's set in, in all conscience."

"Alright. I don't want to talk about this. I accept your withdrawal Egmont. Thanks for the memories. Let's get a top up."

I hoofed away from the library and sat with Missy, made some cognac-slur for a bit, and then she asked if I'd walk her home. With which Weiß agreed, about to drive squiffed. He offered us a lift, and I figured he couldn't do much damage on Christmas night except to lamp posts. He dropped us at Buckower Damm and Gutschmidtstraße.

"You know what?" We walked arms enchained, the clip of heels bouncing off frozen surfaces. "Take your friend's offer up. Marika is it?"

"Matilda! Why?"

It was a clear frosty night, lit gibbously by the moon.

"It's not playwrights you should worry about. It's the whole damned charade."

"In what way?"

"Finance. Extortion. Stock. It's all carving the innards from Papa. I reckon by spring he's under. Get in the *Große*. Before fashion changes."

She stopped me and turned me. "What does that mean?"

"It means what it means," I stalled. "You're well-loved right now and you can charm anyone. Couple that with current tastes you're a dream ticket. Peak Lehane. But what if this gris-gris voodoo shit gets replaced. You'd be living on charm alone." I looked glassy and skewiff at her. "Is what I mean."

"I don't know how to take that," she huffed. "I'm halfway between kicking you and kissing you."

"Just do it. Sound out that Max fella. See what he'll offer. I'm being disloyal to Paps but you're the least of his problems."

"I'll think about it."

"Not for too long."

We'd reached her tenement and she fished for keys. "I'll see you in a while." I kissed her on the mouth, and was turning.

"You're not actually going home?"

"No. Something I need to do."

"It's two in the morning, on Christmas night!"

"What better time," I smiled, and clipped into the frost.

I walked up the alley behind *Cafe Wien* on Sharonstraße in no-man's night between Christmas and Boxing Day.

I put the couple of tea towels against the dirty pane, and struck it with my elbow. Then went round the frame knocking out the rest. Slipped in.

I trod carefully - my martinis and cognacs also to negotiate - searching the stepping stones of light for spots to put my feet, smacked my knee on a desk, and slid my hands around the wall where the door was for a switch: let there be light. Good god.

You couldn't have asked for a room more direct in its intent. A gloomy, dangerous affluence. Studded leather everything bar the wall, which was red-burgundy with some velvety curls in the paper. The studded leather benches fixed to both walls were like a parliament or court. Cabinets along the back: I guessed what they held. And lifting a lurid painting of a Bavarian castle, a safe set deep in the alcove. There wasn't much on the desk. A sheaf of dull papers, bills and dry cleaning. Presumably the interesting stuff was locked up. Still...

I rattled the drawers of the desk. Locked. I pulled a claw-hammer from my waistband and crawled under, levered the thin pliable underside of the drawer-chests, grabbed the bottom draw at the back and yanked. A creak. With more purchase fully horizontal, I gave a proper yank and the runners splintered off, bashing myself in the face with the teak facade of the falling drawer.

I rummaged in it on the desktop. Not much sense in the papers here. Unknown people dated long ago. I repeated with the remaining drawers. Three more to go.

What's this then. A statement or balance sheet. Dated this year or what remained. Names, credits and deficits, plusses and minuses. The grid was a stamp, and the figures within a toddler's writing. Legible, but only through tongue-out-of-mouth concentration. I knew one name, Alexei Yahontov who owned *Kletski*, a brasserie on Boxi Square, and the name below his was struck through with a 'D' in the margin. That'll do. I pocketed the sheet and left the room in disarray, splintered firewood in the otherwise robust Hahn nerve-centre. I knew what I had. What I'd come for.

Life's changing from events beyond, and faster than I can handle. Papa was a hard-working German and my folks loved me; their friends said I was adorable when I danced. At Grundschule the girls brought me gifts, and it was only seeing *me* took the creases out of Mama's face. Only something Detlef-shaped in the ether that webbed our Great War separation.

But then stuff starts changing. My world has people entering, once peripheral, now too close, *behaving*, doing stuff, turning things round.

The heavy air when Paps returns from work. The realisation our savings are worthless, our income plummeting. Less food on the table. There's a man in my Paps-less house during the day who talks of chilly Soviets and how *they* do things. His eyes flash with politics; my mother's flash with something quite different and more intrusive of his clothes. The opportunist Hahn brothers, their scarry mugs peering into our theatre.

It's all wrong, you see? I haven't known anything else, so don't bring 'anything else' in.

I lay my coat, boots and trousers quietly on the chair and slip in beside Missy snoring. The room is cold, the panes crystallising on the inside.

"Baby Man," she murmurs, "finished your night chores?" Her arm is warm, the sheets soft.

"Let's go somewhere tomorrow. Do the things couples do."

"Sure."

She stiffens. "Aaee! Get those icicles off."

I huff warm air on my hands and put them back. Slide them round her stomach.

"What do couples do?"

"Dunno. Walk on riverbanks? Eat lunch? See a movie."

"You're still freezing."

I put my icicles on her baggy cotton bed pants. She accepts them.

So we walked the crisp towpath beside the Dahme river through Karolinenhof, gloved, her collar up to the bottom of her ear-flapped hat.

"It's nice out here," Missy decided. We were sat on some kind of fishing or boarding jetty into the wide slow river. The sky was kipper, a watery sun in fillet cloud. A little fog hugged frosty dips.

"Turn up the heating fifteen degrees, I could be home."

"Which one?"

"Our little place across the Mobile Bay."

She took her hat off and smoothed her hair.

"Do you get homesick?"

"I can always get there. This is the modern world."

I was gonna say I'd take a trip there, but her head violently shot forward, she yelped, and a rough stone span into my lap. The sharp edge was bloody. After a moment, she fell sideways and was rolling off the jetty, I tried to grab her but it was a stalemate, gravity and purchase only holding her flimsily against the boards. The side I wasn't holding, against the jetty slipped and she fell in the water. Another stone, bigger hit my collar bone. Searing.

I looked at them. Three young men in braces or dungarees, with bloody great stones at their feet.

Missy was in shallows and mud but face down. I jumped in and turned her. She spluttered and was groaning, her eyes not opening. Blood seemed to be staining the muddy water but it was hard to tell. I guessed she was safe and sploshed out.

Since the clawhammer was a snug fit, I'd taken to just leaving it in the back of my high-rise trousers when I dressed. I pulled it out and started towards the attackers, dodging stones easily until I was close, so I ran at the one on the edge and slugged him with the hammer side of the metal head. That seemed to do the trick. Slumped, not moving. The other two started furiously pelting me and I ran into the stones with my arms crossed over my head, getting knocked back by a couple, except they weren't so sure of themselves. I swivelled the hammer and hit the nearest in the temple with the claw - not realising it wouldn't be easy to pull out. I left it there and went for the last but he saw the hammer sticking out of the temple and backed off, turning to run. He shouted over his shoulder: "Fucking nigger lover! Murdering nigger lover!"

I unhitched the hammer from the boy's head and went back to Missy. She was talking, but incoherent. Muttering at the clouds. I pulled her gently over the reeds to the grass and felt the back of her head. My hand came back caked in bloody mud. Christ. Tried to lift her. Managed about thirty paces before I collapsed.

"Missy! Missy. Sweetheart," I said.

"Blue crabs," she replied. She was babbling but conscious.

"Can you hold on round my neck if I carry you on my back?"

"No catfish tonight for Uncle Leroy."

"Missy!"

She managed to hold on round my neck, murmuring as we got back to the relative civilisation of Grünau's steam tram. I'd not checked whether I'd killed them. Most likely hammer-blow would survive, maybe not temple-claw. The bumpkin who ran was younger. Probably for the best. Look upon my work and consider his future.

What
are
you
up
to
Detlef?

I won't build shrines for the dead. The dead are extreme, they've outlived rationality. The dead, in some corner of their Norse genes, were always asking for it.

I'm outside *Bistro Karamazov* in January, stamping and flapping to keep warm. KPD meeting shortly, replete with militia. Yeah, I'm joining up!

I'll explain German Socialism while I wait. See, the SPD was our pre-war Marxist party but got all reformist and 'warry', so Rosa Luxembourg formed the Spartacists and USPD. Got bored with them and while noone was looking (1918 revolution) formed the Soviet-backed KPD (then got bludgeoned to death). The KPD's paramilitary wing are now the RFB. They *were* the PH, but the PH got banned last year. Those lefter than the KPD split into the KAPD, who in turn just WEREN'T LEFTY ENOUGH! So they split into the Essen Faction and the Berlin Faction, possibly over childcare and travel arrangements. It seems you can't be too left for the left.

Anyway, equality needs a boost. A rocket up its arse and the support of lowly Berliners. *Rotfrontkämpferbund*.

I'm in a loose street-knot in my docker boots and shaved head. Nestled in my pit is Trotsky's *Between Red and White*, and the scarlet mist pours out of my ears. There *is* no room for fascism, see? Not the bald Italian nor the tufty Austrian. Can't you detect the powder keg deep within us?

"Name?" The KPD man is pear-shaped behind his membership table, with those clips you use to hold sleeves up. Hardly modelled on Trotsky. His face sports no roaring tache nor Satanic goatee. Sheesh. I pump the air with my fist: 'Red Front!'

He looks at me blandly. 'Name?"

"Detlef."

"Full name?"

"Brüning."

He raises a brow, his mincy mouth disapproving of my ribboned fedora with the mottled feather (what would he know?).

"How old are you?"

"Eighteen."

"No," he said simply. "You'll have to join the Roter Jungsturm."

"That's a kid's party."

"...Where you can learn the tenets of the Communist Party and provide valuable support."

"I know the tenets of Communism backwards."

"Can you visit Halle in two weeks time?"

"Where's that?"

"A few miles west of Leipzig."

"What for?"

"A rally." He stamps me a crappy Roter Jungsturm card. "Swell numbers."

"Rally in Halle. Sure man."

At what point did Willhelm not think, 'Shit this is huge. I'm way out of my depth. The whole northern hemisphere?' And why don't the *Freikorps* accept we're to blame? A bloodbath dragging in two extra continents and their commonwealth?

But try discussing Schlieffen's Disappointing Holiday over a krug on a sticky table, and you're treasonous.

Why does our democracy allow militias? Because our democracy has no backing. The *Reichswehr* declared - shortly before being castrated to 100,000 troops by international accord - that they were independent and would obey nobody.

That should work. That'll be fine.

There's a power vacuum. Stresemann tinkers under the bonnet, but we're queuing for groceries while brains putrify in Ruralia, Styxburg, Moronic Munchen; even Berlin's suburbs host right-leaning meetings. You'll see.

We need a Ministry of Facts, to correct this spit-flecked rabble. Each beer hall needs a knowledgeable petty bureaucrat in the corner wearing sleeve clips, truth-checking what the pinhead shouts and interrupting when a lie's uttered.

So I killed a teenager with a hammer; what right do I have to wax. Well, eyes are eyes and teeth are teeth. If you seek conflict you'll find it, and if you don't you might anyway. If I hadn't hopped in the river Missy might be done for. (She's doing fine, thanks for asking, the burble about blue crabs and catfish receded.) I went too far, but I can't wear a rosette saying 'Beware: red mist descending'. Just don't throw rocks at us.

~

Three seconds before the outer door swings shut. Once inside, wait another four seconds until footsteps can't be heard from the second flight, now move. Floor three. Walk thirty yards to where the corridor bends for the last two apartments, including Yahontov's. Stay at the corner. Is the door open? Is Carlin now inside? Door open or closed behind him? Check.

Move to the rubbish chute two metres from the door; inset. Await the conclusion of Carlin's activities. Repayment or gunfire, neither matters. Door opens, gun now concealed on Carlin's person. Move quietly and swiftly, ensure the blade goes cleanly into the side of the neck. Out of action. Drag body back into room...

~

So I knew what was coming and fished in my own bag. He slapped down *Axt der Lust* on the table, which he'd tabbed with paperclipped notes.

And I slapped down *Traits, Characteristics & Crime Scenes of Federal Germany: 1871-1918.* Which I'd tabbed with notes.

Well it wrong-footed Gründgens but he quickly remobbed.

"What's this?" He picked the book up between finger and thumb. "You want to be a policeman, Detlef? There are plenty of opportunities in the Landespolizei."

"Just say what you'll say," I sighed.

Lange had called us to the station again. And on Paps' blower he'd said quietly, 'Get your facts, dates and times straight. The Chief's finished the book'. He wouldn't say any more.

Gründgens looked cautious now, flipping open his bedtime joy, clearing his throat. "The similarities are remarkable, and baffling given the man serving time for the murder of Zelda Brüning is in Wittenau Asylum's high security wing. It is possible - with press coverage - that another unhinged meesogine--..... misogynist took up an axe after reading the story, but unlikely. Criminologists believe that perpetrators of sexual murder, Lustmord, leave a signature. Something to mark it as unique. Or risk dying in prison anonymously if caught, and if not, living in another's shadow as a gory pretender: protege to a bloody Michaelangelo, copying spattered Sistine cherubs. I am convinced the murder of Z is linked to Amelie Bergmann's death at the Grand: the same signature - severed head, hands and feet - while the separation of body parts mirrored almost to their placement the death of Zelda Brüning."

The room was silent.

Uncomfortable.

Lange frowned and zoned out. Probably to behave as a genuine officer of the law. I looked at Papa: morose, punctured. Hard to believe he'd built an entertainment empire with the world now wanting our guts for garters.

"My turn?"

Nobody spoke. I leafed to a page.

"A spate of killings in 1878 coincided with a period of liberal governance, relative wealth, and the commencement of a welfare state lifting the most hard-hit from poverty. Prior to Bismark's program, investigation of Germany's most heinous crimes had always begun in nearby workers' districts - the poor and allegedly dissolute - in the belief poverty drove people to madness and crimes of passion. With the working classes attaining citizen status, such easy conclusions could no longer be justified, prompting a public outcry over unsolved cases, so-called 'cold cases', and a revolution in investigative techniques.

"Moreover, it was March 1879 that the Konigsberg constabulary announced that a man of good standing had been sentenced for a chain of thirteen axe-murders..." I looked up. "Ready?"

Sour faces.

"...Where the body was dismembered and the parts littered in the room. The head was not found with the body, necessitating a two day search to discover it in a coal scuttle, dust caking any putrefaction."

"Jesus," Paps muttered under his breath.

Another silence. Gründgens patted himself down for something under a gathering thunderhead and sprung up, out of the room.

After a while, Lange: "My Chief is concerned for your safety as much as closing off your late wife and mother's death."

Paps snorted.

"You're in over your head with certain people."

"While *your* arrangement is backed by..." Paps flicked his finger at the warren of the station, "an arsenal and your preferred magistrates. Don't tell me Gründgens cares for my wellbeing."

"I'll speak for myself only." Lange stiffened. "Ignore that Hartmann pulp, I'm worried a killer is at large, more worried than I am for your wellbeing. But…"

I looked up from my slump.

"You think the Chief knows your movements just from officers working their beat?"

Paps exhaled and pushed his eye sockets. "I didn't know we were of interest."

"When you're about your business you ignore the women window-shopping, the tabloid readers on street corners, couples studying menus in restaurants. Citizens they may be… but that's only half their use. You get me? There's two gods on the street, us and the Hahns."

"All seeing."

"Yes."

"Omnipotent."

"Probably."

"Can we leave?"

"I guess."

I got up, gathered my crap and aimed for the door.

"We work on leads Herr Brüning. If we have none we work on motive. And if we have no motive, we look at previous. Suspicious previous behaviour. How else would we go about it?"

"I don't know. And I've nothing against you, Inspector Lange."

"Where are *they* going?!" Gründgens strode back with a cigarette trailing smoke in his slipstream.

"We're finished Sir?"

"No we're not."

"We are," Paps said. "You've no reason to keep us here. I'm finished. Dets?"

I nodded and we shouldered past Gründgens. I prickled waiting for him to react.

He was livid and should've kept his powder dry. "If you don't know who killed your mother, why the hell would you derail our enquiries!"

It echoed around the corridor. A little plaintive. Very angry. Perhaps true. Maybe a human lived in there after all.

"I missed."

"Babe?"

"Didn't connect."

Missy was draped on me. "You're a lake of sweat. What are you dreaming about. You're frightening me."

"What?" I was gradually coming round in the grainy darkness. "Sorry," I groaned. "The riverbank. I don't know what's worse, my dreams or your burble."

"They didn't care about me. You don't have to care about them."

"Well I didn't, did I. I killed Lorenz Beck."

"Protecting us."

"Honey," I tried to stroke her side, but she was clammy too. "If you'd seen it, maybe you wouldn't feel protected. I wasn't pretty."

"I ain't pretty with my face buried in mud, bleeding and drowning in the Havel River."

"OK. I'll stop dreaming about it. Be gone!" I snapped my fingers, smiled faintly in darkness. Missy wasn't happy. Something perturbed her, maybe what I'd gibbered in sleep.

"Baby man?"

"Yes?"

"I think I might go home."

I said nothing, just watched the ceiling.

Eventually: "What about your mama?"

"She's ugly enough to look after herself. And she'll pay for my ticket. She's been terrified for me since I got sliced."

"Why does she stay?"

"Paps used to be stationed at Cologne. British Army of the Rhine."

I nodded, wondering where diverging fates might lead; she with the clown mouth and no contacts in America, me with my increasing criminal history and father in a vice.

"You can't go."

"Not for ever."

"No, I mean you won't float. You'll sink."

"Thanks for the confidence."

"I'm not saying it for selfish reasons. Your savings will last you weeks, you'll audition in New York or wherever. You'll be back in a cotton field, your life ebbing away, your confidence shrivelling. The next time I saw you, you'd say 'Yas'sum,' and 'Master Brüning'. Do the right thing. Stay where people love you."

"I can't breathe. There's too much pressure."

"You mean prejudice."

"It amounts to the same thing."

"Whereas Alabama is just itching to help negroes get rich."

"This country's changing."

"Maybe America is."

"But I remember its fields. The sunset beyond the bay up the Blakely."

I turned away, angry she didn't want my fields and sunsets. "It's your choice. But you're insane. A couple of cross-eyed farmer's sons throw stones and you think it's worse than slavery?"

"Now you're being ignorant. Slavery's been gone sixty years."

"Has it."

"You must have thought it was bad, you hammered his face."

"Was I right or wrong?" I turned back and knew how my eyes looked. "Decide Missy, because I can't."

Night thickened as she didn't answer. I felt sleep overcome again.

"Well," a murmur brushed the dark, "it was decisive."

I started laughing and Missy wasn't sure what it was, bent over to look. Saw it was laughter.

"Yes," I wheezed. "Indecision won't sink Detlef Brüning."

~

Furtwanger glares out of *Tageblatt* again. Seems it was more than masks and rape. Decapitation, then masks, then banditry and death. Post-rape's not ruled out.

Look at his swarthy face all scooped like a mollusc. Doctorate in Political Science from Heidelberg. Anyone studying political science should be buried on arrival, to avoid further complications.

He was, anyway, a child rapist. Didn't knobble the 'statutory' thing (as opposed to himself being a stiff-membered toddler). But this husk's decorated with the Iron Cross! Suppose such crosses and thesi allow him to the Reichstag - the Mendelsohnns' family home. It's not implausible he could sweep unconsenting sex under that threadbare moustache - hairless as his victims. Prisons you see, are not the blotted copybook they were.

Ugh, I shudder. What troubles me is, something's beginning. There is an ugliness rising: we didn't finish the antibiotics.

"Antibiotics?" Missy was shaking me. I had *Tageblatt* across my lap.

Don't go to the countryside. Man. I went to the Rally in Halle-on-Saale.

Or rather, counter-rally, which I learned on the train from a zealot already on the sauce at 11am. It was a military parade led by Ludendorff's Steel Helmets, so the police were coopted to keep Reds away from the bigwigs. In pointy-hat pomp they unveiled a new statue of General Moltke, which hotheads had blown up the prior year.

Old tortoise-face was erect in the countryside again, much to the chagrin of useless democrats.

Now I'm mopping a deep, stinging gouge on my nose, dizzy, my shirt blooming a carnation and my sleeve ripped up my arm, hanging like some Shakespearean blouse. Dust hangs in my throat. I can hear the barricaded shouts through a stone arch - those not hiding or charging - on this bubbling wind.

I lean on the bridge staunching my nose, my silhouette is sluggish in dark green water below. Berliners are used to gunfire now; infrequent, distant.

Returning through the arch, young fascists suddenly run the street at us in false uniform, sleeves branded *Sturmabteilung* and *Stalhelm,* beige street dust under heavy boots. The less nimble follow. Landespolizei sit on horseback rooted on tight rein; hooves fidget and shiny flanks flex in anticipation.

It's like fucking Russia.

And indicative of what the Generals see as glory years: that the mounted sit in *front* of automobiles. But the LaPo are stuck in entropy for a reason. Inside they coil. The spring must be tense and chamber loaded. Then.

With huddles of DNVP and NSDAP almost upon us, we flee the barricade, deflected through an alley into Ammendorf, where a second prong of police open fire. One Red with a gun under a Balkan coat brings it out and returns; others create makeshift obstacles from upturned carts and signs. We're trapped, have to scramble each other over a wall, tumbling into open park, breaking for trees. I feel the weight of my hammer leave, and stopping to retrieve it I get yanked by a comrade away.

In a copse we lean trunks, or bend over, hands on knees as the gunfire pockets, revealing distant laughter and birdsong.

I got the train back to Berlin in misery, my cheek sliding down my palm, watching the sponge-topped hillocks. I'd seen a few nicks and blood-sprays and a couple fall (dragged on), but I'd learn tomorrow a KPD was dead, six injured.

The green and grey of sky and field mesh so easily in their drizzle camouflage; only to suddenly clarify and Germany reveal her contours. It's then people want to know: what is Germany's limit?

For a long time the carriage was quiet, until some bright thicko fired up the Ernst Thalmann Song and I sang.

We pulled into Lehrter, where the sky through station glass was spooky tangerine. Something was off. Young drunk men staggered around commuters, who dodged them in wary disapproval.

I pulled my cap peak down, shoved hands in my pockets and set my jaw. Must've been a convention in Moabit. The streets were no less pent-up and drunk: our red k✮llectiv off the train hugged a little tighter on the concourse.

I leant to a fellow next to me: "Nationalists?"

"My guess," he said through barely moving lips. "Eyes front," he advised.

"Anyone heading east?" I said to all within earshot.

I stood waiting for a tram. Night fell. A man from a group fell into me and I flexed like India rubber, gently ensuring he stayed on his feet. They carried on oblivious. "But he has a block foot," I heard one of them mutter, and the others laugh. I exhaled as a tram pulled up.

The streets got Jewisher. I sat gazing and there, trotting diagonally, like an apparition or old newsprint, was a farmhand I recognised. *Shit*. He wasn't alone and was angling for this tram. His companion was too stubbly tensile to be less than majority. Looked useful in a fight. I averted my face. Once they were beside us, I glanced at the step up entry, and on they both got. (Shit, shit, shit!)

Cap down, fixation on shop facades. I felt my left shoulder wilfully slide down the backrest as they took the seats behind.

The bigger, tastier fascist said to Helmut (the surviving farmboy): "There's something you need to know now you're carrying the card."

Helmut didn't reply. So the back of my neck decided the dungsniffer must be nodding.

"Don't resist. Don't assault the LaPo. Go quietly and don't panic."

"What if they've got dirt on me... witnesses, like, for whatever I've done? I ain't going to jail. We're just getting started. Germany's just getting started."

"Which is what I'm about to tell you," Elder said calmly. "You won't *go* to jail. Unless maybe you kill someone. Rioting, a bit of assault, blood on the pavement... nah, the courts are different. See the police are confused. As such they're puppets, letter of the law. So you spend a few nights in a cell, but once you're in court, *Bam!*, you might as well be at a supporters' rally."

"What the chief wigs?"

"Sure man."

They were talking pretty loud for public transport, carefree and unfettered. I sat as still as concrete, wondering if my rear view gave much away. I'd almost arranged to meet Missy at Lehrter station but she was diverted to a rehearsal this morning. She could easily have been sitting beside me.

"Just make it plain anything you're charged with was anti-Red. That's all they need to know. It's Commies go inside not patriots. In fact, kid, you'd be doing a service if you let those scum assault *you*, send a few down."

Thanks for the info. The seat creaked as I rearranged my buttocks. I needed to cough. We were passing through Scheunenviertel, where the density of Jewishness was critical.

"Look at those white golliwogs. Those sideburned rats, have you ever smelt them?"

"Never notice them." Helmut replied, in hushed awe. "Not seen so many."

I needed to get off, and with that, my sphincter tightened. I got up face averted, holding the bar, then ducked my head as though I'd spotted something the other side of the tram, in the street. I walked the aisle, still twitching my head out the far window and jumped off. But standing in the steel-slit street, I couldn't help looking back. Helmut's eyes met mine briefly, narrowed, and were gone.

I watched dishevelled Magyars and Croats about their business. Every so often someone too sharp and spruce would part the grubby sea - a civil servant maybe - who had risen sparkling from his slum of a morning. The true melting pot, or cooking pot.

Nobody knows what they want. Or what they should have, or can have, are entitled to, not entitled to, who's wrong, who's nailed it, where to put the borders, what constitutes a population, what's an ethnicity, is a large ethnicity in the wrong place grounds to take that place. If you take it, doesn't that leave another ethnicity in the wrong place? Who's got the mandate on this?

Man, we threw Europe on the ground and it splintered. Sure, they smelted the Balkans back into Yugoslavia, but did you know Poland vanished for a hundred and twenty three years?

How does that work for mapmakers? He holds up his work. ...*No, you'll have to redo it, Poland's disappeared*. He groans. By the time he's redone it, Monte has split with Negro, creating two herb gardens. Romania's best buddies with Bulgaria, forming the People's Republic of Rogaria. This enrages the Sofian Popular Army who blow stuff up in Budapest, then Poland reappears and the mapmaker flings his pens on the floor. Subject to bloody change.

~

"Couple of minutes of your time."

"Sure. How can I help you."

"A few particulars have come to light."

"I thought you'd left her case for dead."

"When it was your mother yes."

"Charming."

"Lange tells me your prints are on the axe."

"I spent my days in the girls' dressing room where it's kept."

"Really."

"Lange probably found a dozen other prints on it."

"Couple of minutes of your time, very quick."

"A few oddities about the Dahme riverbank murder."

"Manslaughter, no?"

"There was nobody else, and Lorenz and Kurt and Helmut had been friends since childhood."

"Why on *earth* are you asking me about this?"

"Logistics."

"You've traced a homicidal angst over farmers to me? I live in Berlin, so that narrows the suspect list I suppose. Maybe I coveted my neighbours' ox? I

"Yes, largely obscured by the most recent user."

"You can't do this, I'm a minor. There should be an adult."

"We'd like you to come to the station, Yiddisha boy. We have something interesting to show you. In return, you may have something interesting to tell us."

"I've said, there has to be an adult. Are you deaf and anti-Semitic?"

"Bring your father. Or any adult who consents to carrying out the duties of an appropriate guardian."

"What are you showing me?"

"Photomicrographs. Please don't skip town."

"Is... this... a formal request?"

"What do you want, a fucking letter?"

"Does... what you have to show me make me a witness?"

"Get over here."

"So... you want me to come to the station to show me particulars about a case you're working on?"

"No. Just that the claw hammer in your flat, Missy's flat, matches the gauge of the indent, first thought to be a crowbar, and a Negerin with scars on her cheeks was verified in Grünau shortly before."

"You raided our flat?"

"Missy's flat yes."

"And you're suggesting Missy Lehane, star of the Berlin stage, likes to hunt farmers at the weekend?"

"No. Nor, tempting though it is, am I saying you do Detlef. But you were there. And something happened."

"Well then, I'll shop you for breaking and entering."

"Or you could help. I'd not want to see an innocent man guilty from lack of cooperation."

"How heartfelt."

"How about it also matching the Wien Cafe break-in? I'm not the only one who breaks and enters, am I?"

Bastard. For a man who looks like an exploding blood-vessel

"Yes."

"Want me to do your job for you?"

The suddenly muffled phone had a background of expletives.

he gets around.

~~~

No, the Hahns weren't pleased about their trashed office, but being pea-brained they linked it to the Kapuzes. Then set fire to a restaurant on Warschauer Straße, maiming the owner and ensuring conflict reescalation. I should be a military strategist!

The problem is Hartmann. I believe that beneath his grubbing and constant threats he's humane; he wouldn't inform the Hahns because he knows they'd kill me - if they believed him. Still, a risk.

But I do wonder, are the Hahns above getting their pocketed men in green to dust the office? Just enough leeway for the KriPo to signpost a culprit.

~

Luisenstadt Cemetary

"I have something may be of interest to you."

Michael Hartmann landed at the bar, picked up a mat and started ripping the edges.

"You do? What."

"Oh well, you know I'm a keen amateur photographer."

"No I didn't."

"Cafe on Hermannstraße."

"OK."

"Well I'd bought this new Leica 35," Hartmann pulled a compact, concertina-lensed camera from his satchel. "I took to carrying it around. Couldn't believe Gründgens and Hahn at the same restaurant table. But I wasn't quick enough. What my eyes saw pass across the table the *Leica* missed, buried in my bag."

"Good work."

"So I wondered if it was a regular payment, made a note of the date and came back around that date the following month, and sure enough... Snap, snap, snap."

"How long have you had 'em?"

Hartmann puffed out his lower lip and looked innocently at the ceiling. "About three months."

"You bastard. That's... obstructing justice." But I didn't sound too sure.

"Or... it's having the wits to sniff a good photo."

"What were you going to do? Sell them? Blackmail Gründgens? Publish a book on corruption in the Berlin Police?"

Hartmann looked at me calmly. "None of those things have happened, have they. Anyway, it came to my notice our friend Lange is a fan of... internal enquiries?"

I considered for a moment. Corruption, Gründgens, his unhappy face in clink.

"So, would they be enough?"

"For relief of duties?"

"For whatever Lange needs.

"I don't know. It could be. At least enough to suspend him while looking at his bank accounts."

"What's the quality like?"

"Dunno. Got to finish the roll, film's not cheap. But I'm quietly confident."

"Yeah yeah. I'll believe it when I see them." He knew he'd got my attention. I thought he was about to state the obvious, as his mouth kept opening and shutting: like how Gründgens had his sights on me and he might look better his face pressed against bars. But I said:

"So what do you want?"

"Oh," Hartmann grinned. "Nothing too arduous."

Dr. Winter Sessions Volume VII, he's calmly listening:

"...So in short Doctor, all homose... homoerotic thoughts are gone. I see no attraction in men. Beastly gender. I live with my girlfriend and we've never been happier."

He nodded with a faint smile: *you prattle on for a while.*

"It's my belief Doc, that my sexuality was subsumed. Or the opposite: it became warped and tangled; studying boys with an eye to how I myself developed. This became obsessive, due to an ambivalent distrust of women. I believe it's common for the romantic rival to become the object of desire, once one's eye is off the prize."

"Do you."

"Certainly."

"Your father's happy for you to live with your 'girlfriend' at fifteen?"

"I thought we wouldn't mention my father."

"Yes but, is he?"

"It's not formal, I sleep over. You were young once."

"How old is she?"

"Missy? Just turned eighteen."

He looked up. "Missy... Lehane?"

I looked puzzled and probably angry. "I don't think that's relevant to our discussions, do you?"

"The scarred burlesque dancer?"

"For chrissake yes!"

He made some notes. As slowly as he could, leaving me dangling as to the contents of his brain.

Watch your step Winter. You're this close to a Sexology Clinic chat.

"Considerably older. Do you enjoy the company of older women?"

"Sure," I shrugged.

"Is it necessary to you?"

"Gym girls are dim. I've always been around older women. I live in a theatre."

"Which you stopped attending months ago."

"Eh?"

"Your schule."

"Yeah. I'm training as a production assistant."

"Out of schule, a minor living with a consenting adult. Your fa--"

"Uh-uh! Don't say it. Besides, Paps' paying you and he knows my leisure pursuits."

He wriggled somewhat. "I'm going to suggest we keep our sessions going for a while. I'd like to try some stimulus-response tests."

Would you now. I got up from the couch. "OK Doc."

~

"Detlef. Detlef!"

I appeared at the metal door. Paps was in his canvas-topped truck honking in the Palast delivery entrance.

"Come on."

The rear suspension was low in the yard. I climbed onto a bouncy seat.

"Don't draw attention right? Stare out the window. Or tell jokes."

"Sure Pops."

"Don't call me Pops, ever again." Paps glared at me.

"I'm in character."

Paps throttled under hulking shadow into Berlin, heading for Sharonstraße; the *Wien*. "We can't lift it on our own," I said, "So why am I needed?"

Ushered through the restaurant's curtain we clipped down the corridor and were seated. I looked around.

"You'll need four men to bring it in."

Gerhard looked at us. "I thought you'd carry it in, surprise me."

"It's heavy. Four men."

"I'm kidding. They're doing it now. All geared up, ready to run?"

"As agreed."

"Good. Good man, Albert."

"Look, there's my contact's investment to consider. This was a big capital outlay. He's lost out."

"Mm."

Paps didn't enter the silence.

"So this is your son. Giving me all sorts of grief out west."

I looked at Papa, his gaze low and immobile.

"What you got to say for yourself, son?"

I looked around innocently. "I like what you've done with the place. That desk, the windows, the whole decor. Is it new?"

Gerhard's eyes thinned. He stared at me for a long period, reflexively pulling his cigarette case and tapping one on the tin.

"You should do your office like this Paps. I suppose security's important?"

After a prolonged and troubled stare, Gerhard turned back to Papa. "If I'd met him we might have done a deal. But I didn't. And you owed me. So we're done."

"You'll make more than any recompense. It's Rentens."

"Don't haggle after the fact. He relinquished his capital to save a Kike's arse. His business. Your business."

A lunk poked his head in. "It's in the utility thing," he sweated.

"Run me through it," Gerhard ushered Paps into the corridor. "Stuff it might pay me to know."

To Papa, winter light had never been brighter leaving *Cafe Wein*'s padded cell. Me I felt noonday dark, a brassy blackness as Paps drove the unladen truck north in sunshine, whistling. If I moved my head quickly the black periphery moved with my eyes. Fucking *Gerhard*. You may be brighter than Carlin, but it's not adding to the genepool.

I went with Missy to retrieve tickets from her mother. First time I'd spoken to Declan and Davione.

They'd met, conceived and married within forty-eight hours in Belfast, a whirlwind, after the *Norddeutscher* liner Davione travelled on hit a north sea storm and had to dock. Declan went to war with the Ulster Rifles, fought at Marne and Messines with a rapidly dying division, and survived the Somme. He stayed in Cologne with the Rhineland occupation and decommissioned last spring.

They were doing alright, with two large broke-through reception rooms and a reasonable stash of chintz, silver and linen.

"Where's this from, Mrs Lehane, it's delicious."

I held a fork up, something between potato and banana, oil-fried, crisp and mushy.

"Wedding market. And call me Davione."

"Sure Davione, what is it?"

"Spiced plantain," she smiled.

Lehane himself was quiet in his place setting. I wouldn't call him placid exactly, just... *ready*.

"Wedding. That's the African quarter, right?"

She laughed. "That's a bit grand honey. Let's call it the district where the chains are loosened."

She smiled like cynicism didn't actually gnaw at her much.

"I thought... because of the street names."

"They don't glorify Africans my love. They glorify their owners' exploits and discoveries. When Europe stopped exhibiting us, the cages were opened and the zoo keepers coughed in embarrassment. Wedding is the closest to an African plain."

I forked other stuff, coconut-laced and I thought maybe piment also. "I'm a bit ignorant of all that history, Ma'am."

Ma'am? Ma'am? What the hell was that? Herr Lehane politely covered his amusement with his fork hand.

"Why shouldn't you be ignorant? Good German boy like you."

Lehane Sr. straightened out again. "Don't rib the boy." He cleared his throat, as though in an unusual venture into conversation. "Missy says you're a Leftist."

Missy clattered her cutlery. "You can't ask him that! He's in theatre. What do you expect?"

"Tough enough as it is Missy, wouldn't you say? Throw in politics..."

"Yes?"

Lehane Sr. just circled his fork and pulled some wine.

"Yes," I plucked up a little defence. "This country doesn't know where it's going. We should step back from internationalism and focus on ourselves. Except the ones who do are racist bigots. So. I'm OK with Karl Marx, yes."

Lehane nodded. "You's think the Soviet Union cares for blacks, Jews and queers?"

My hairline must have shot back at *queers*.

"With respect I didn't mention the Soviet Union. You did."

He bent his head over last forks of rice. "That's true enough," he said, and a Belfast twang floated over the table.

Missy hurled tears in the kitchen with Davione, thumbing steamer pouches for the twentieth time. And as the weirpool filled the sploshes deepened. Declan's outstretched hand moved me to reclining chairs, and we sat apart.

"I know a little about your father."

"I suppose, because Missy is--"

"Got himself in a load of trouble." He brought a cognac over.

"That's his evening job."

"Only queer thing is you."

Some people just say what they say and you remain firmly at attention.

"My daughter is very discreet." He sighed. "But when times are rough..."

I blinked.

"I believe you's've been instrumental in her wellbeing. We... let her make her own mistakes, and more fool us in this unpredictable country, she's going home. But there is a man, Lange, who thinks you're dangerous."

I looked incredulous. Lange? Some kind of Unionist vibe?

"The Hahn break in. Steering your father's royal mint out of trouble. The Havel River, Lorenz Beck. More backstage than front of house, no?"

What do I say?

"What would you do for her?"

For Missy?

"Well sir. If you mean what I think you mean, it's not really would, it's... happening."

"Keep on."

"I mapped a route round Neukölln. Marked one of their cards."

"Which one?"

"The older."

"And you'll serve it up?"

"I think so. If not for her..."

Lehane kept staring. I didn't want to get too deep in those tiger-stripe irises.

"I trust you Detlef. But keep an eye out. I'll also be busy."

~

Missy's last play at the Rottie would be Vogel's most banal work, *A Latin Swansong*.

In the steamy green South American country of Cunozuela the Social Democrats and Communists have joined forces

(SDC) for a coup against the old military ruling junta of General Otero, who themselves have enlisted a far-right militia as urban defence of oil refineries and other oligarchical assets.

Missy plays the SDC activist Rossi Amaral who is discredited and detained for not having a Cunozuelan passport, and expelled, leaving the socio-communists with no popular figurehead. Trumped up charges against the SCP for undeclared funding renders the party illegal. A new conniving leader takes over - manipulative and pragmatic - and the cycle starts again. Only this time the SCP cosy up to industrialists and promise a mixed economy, with low taxation and welfare for all. They also promise to sell off oil and gas. When SCP are victorious they erect statues of Missy's character Rossi in lost adoration.

But the violent cycle continues with statues of Missy hauled down leaving ornate plinths in the classical fluted style.

~

Paps told me to take Günter for a milkshake or whatever; he'd a meeting with Ernst and the builders over defects. We sat in the noisy morning *Griechisch* and with no sign of milkshakes I handed Günter a lemonade.

"This murder is nothing *like* the Oranienstraße."

I was reading Ernst Toller, forcing myself really, knowing I'd got behind. "What?" I murmured.

Günter pointed at the article he was reading. "This."

"What is it?"

"Man arrested at Haffen Hold in Bremen. He'd thrown a sack with the lower part of a woman in it, a pair of legs. They held him and searched his flat, found the upper half."

"Doesn't sound like Oranienstraße. There are loads of psychopaths in Germany. That's what I keep telling Gründgens and Lange."

"Who are they?"

"Policemen."

Günter gave me his tilt-back head; the eyes myopic and chin jutting. Like his focus didn't latch unless he harnessed it to his nose. He reminded me of a Toby jug or gourd. He nodded. Silence fell as Günter read on, then: "Why do you tell Grudgings and Lodge that?"

"Gründgens and Lange. Because they keep linking Oranienstraße and my Mama."

Günter looked through his misty glasses. " Paps told me not to mention Muttis. He didn't have to. Why would I talk about *Muttis*?"

"He probably thought I'd be sensitive."

Günter pointed at the article.

"What?"

"Like that?"

"Yes. Last year."

"Oh." Presently: "One less woman in the world I suppose."

I spluttered into my coffee, which eventually gave way to laughter. "You'll have to explain what you mean Günter."

"Well," again the head elevated, peering down his own nose. "All they seem to do is tell you what to do, or ask stupid questions they know the answer to. Silly."

I stared at Günter for a while, but he was grappling with something.

"To which."

"Uh?"

"Questions to which they know the answer. Bad grammar."

"You reckon it's OK to snuff them out?"

He became grave. "Certainly not. It's illegal."

"I see."

The eyes dived back in to the magazine.

"So why'd you mention Oranienstraße."

"Because they say it has a "hallmark" - what's that? - the same as Oranienstraße."

"It's a stamp of authenticity in precious metal. Like a manufacturers' signature."

Günter snorted in derision.

"Spill your thoughts Günter."

"Well, unless there's a lot of you doing a murder, you can't carry the body alone if you're a weakling."

"Can't you?"

"Not in this one."

"Why?"

"He's only five-foot-two and she's big."

"Right."

"So you cut them in half."

"OK."

"But the Oranienstraße murder removed head, feet and hands first, took them out of the apartment."

"Same as my Mama, except, the hands, feet and head were still in the room."

Günter looked at me, his eight year old brain ticking. It was a while.

"Disturbed?"

"I guess so. But why would you take the head, body and hands first? Why not just cut in half and do two journeys?"

I opened out my palms and shook my head.

"Identification."

"Right. Like, identify the victim's face. Or fingerprints."

"Except he's stupid because she's in her own house, and prints are useless if you can't match them to something."

My eyes were widening. "Who's stupid?"

"Oranienstraße man. The first trip is dumb. And in this case," he flapped the magazine dismissively, "he just cut the body in half to carry it. That's common."

"In whose world?"

Günter rolled his eyes. "The world of murder, stupid."

I leant on the glass table with the previous couple's dirties stacked by the window, my play now forgotten. "You're a brainy kid."

He frowned and eye-rolled. "I'm nearly nine."

"I'll tell you something funny about Mama's death, shall I?"

Günter looked at his shoes, a bit embarrassed.

"Shall I?"

Continued shoe-gaze. "I don't want you to think. Well... what I said. One less woman. I know... well, I'm sure it wasn't very nice."

"So shall I tell you?"

He nodded, peeking up.

"Her hands and feet and head were no longer attached. He'd sawn the body in half. He abandoned it then."

Günter shrugged and gave a head-shake.

"There was blood all over the bedroom. You have to imagine, a ton of blood, right?"

He nodded.

"But, the body was still flushed and pink with life."

"Explain."

"Well, you'd expect it to be... Here, pass me that magazine."

Günter handed it and I flipped through.

"Look, look at all these people. Bodies losing blood go white, or grey or whatever."

"Mmm," said Günter. He pulled the magazine back off me.

"It's strange, to lose all your blood and still be full of blood, right?"

"Mm," Günter added, totally absorbed, my presence evaporating.

~

Missy's crates went on ahead for storage with one Aunt Bess in Hattiesburg Mississippi. The apartment got a bit spartan so I put books in to humanise it: Shaw and Chekhov; Gramsci and Lukács. Hauled old props and posters from the theatre to cover the emptiness. Missy played *Tin Roof Blues* on the phonogram and sat maudlin in the evenings.

"I'm scared Detty."

"So stay." I stood looking onto Gutschmidtstraße feeling void. I didn't want to plead. "It's white struggle everywhere. Scary here and scary there. Your family's in Berlin, the real one and the adopted one."

"I'm too small for this bloody world."

I breathed deep the open window. "Paps' letting me keep your apartment, so you come back when you miss me. Just visiting or your grand homecoming, I don't care. You come back."

We were morose on the train, in awe of time opening. A taxi from Hamburg station dropped us on the oily docks where everything shined. In the mist of Veddel Island Missy's *Cunard* lay still in the green Elbe, the sharp prow and black and red funnels ghosted by the odd night gull. *RMS Berengaria*, mist scarved. Her wet gangway was down and, with moon and stars hidden behind German wool, it seemed America may not be so far away after all; a few tossed and clanging sleeps on the ugly deeps.

We walked slowly, Missy in taut black with a pillbox tipped on her forehead, jauntier than I felt. Her pointed shoes looked odd on the cobbled jetties.

"You've got to come back. I'll kidnap your mother."

"Paps might have something to say."

"I like Declan."

"Sure. You can take the man out of the army."

I shrugged.

"Maybe things will change. You'll get what you want."

"Meaning?" I frowned.

"Socialism, dummy. And with it a respect for the working negro."

"You're not negro, you're mulatto via Ireland and St. Lucia. And besides it's not a nice word."

"St Vincent and Grenadines."

"All the same."

"Spread your wings my love." She walked to the gangway. "She'll feed you."

"Who?"

"Mama. Just turn up, can't help herself."

"Write me your addresses. Or telegram."

She nodded, brimmed a tear which breached at the Glasgow scar. Lifted a hand laden with a suitcase and hatbox and blew her kiss. Off she went into the fog like a viking for burial, 'cept her injuries were living and she'd alight in the steaming south. *Too small for this bloody world*.

My lackadaisical, kick-back Weimar; this tea party in a hyena enclosure. Missy was right. As she'd packed for shipment I glowered in my corner. My country. No: it belongs to the slink-shouldered and piebald. The iron-toothed. The night cacklers.

Money-Mad Lustmord Art Kill Kid

~

Right you fuckers, to work. You own the departure of my sweetheart, and debts will be repaid.

7:15am on Wildenbruch and Karl-Kunger. Linden trees shade the battenberg welfares and white deco. Neukölln, meet Alt-Treptow. Carlin's doing a casino and bar-owner before Yahontov. So I wait, his schedule out of sight until he enters; my soon-cordoned scene.

There's a leafy square opposite. I go sit on a bench and open *What is to be done?*. One thing Lenin got right was that rampant capitalism can morph into far worse.

Here he comes, bent-eared, tucking his shirt in like a late schoolboy, flapping his coat back in place with a shoulder roll. Looks up at the apartment, the open casements, the bell pushes. Gets no response on presumably Alexei's bell, so starts bashing every one in the block. Eventually, a gowned tenant pulls the door open and Carlin backs him in gesticulating.

Bourgeois societies are not "too immature to adopt Communism", just too segregated. Where there's ownership there is loss. Where there's value there's security. Where there is nothing, there must have been robbery.

I walk across the road in my postman's uniform from a Brüning production (*Don't Shoot the Messenger*), with a package wrapping a book from 'a secret admirer' of Tomas Lehrer of 3b, Rosenthaler Mansions. I bell him. He answers, and I hand him the thick package.

"Got a few more in here," I say, waving at the shady staircase. The door swings back and Lehrer shuffles bewildered to his apartment. I climb the stairs.

Where there's inequality, don't let the Reds in with placards. If they won they'd only usurp our corruption. And what were *they* doing while I sucked the Caspian dry, shipped slaves, perfected dynamite and mislaid Africans in quarries? Whose fortune *is* this? I'll leave it to an orphanage when I die, so fuck off.

The door is open. Yahontov, not answering his bell, must have been disconcerted hearing Carlin' bratwurst knock on his sanctum. What to do? Let your persecutor in without fuss, or hope the racket of a splintering door brings a neighbour?

The door frame's intact.

"Dear me, Yahontov, that's loyalty, that's nice. That's very nice."

"You're out of your area, Mr. Hahn."

"What are you explaining to me, Alexei? My districts? Where I operate? Next you'll say you're in the Kapuze Club."

Silence. Yahontov creaks on the accusation. He must have. I move to the inset disposal chute, a bronze plate with a door that rotates. Nice. I take off my postman's cap and listen.

"See your Kapuzes do half a job. Offer their half-baked product to your cafe. Your *brass*erie. Might scatter a bit of bounty on the bereft and broken. But it ends there. Where are they now? I'd say you're in need of their services right now."

"Mr Hahn, they may not be preserving me at this moment, but they will protect their interests and reputation. Whatever you're planning to do with me it will return and bite you, so why don't we sit down amicably. What can I offer you to drink?"

"Yeah. A drink. That'd be nice."

I hear clinking, soda spray, then a shriek and broken glass.

"Fucking shareholder's club? Robin Hood's merry men? You're in a warzone, son. The switched get stitched."

"Carlin please. As you say I'm in an awkward position. We'll wor--"

A thump and slump. Something groaning and heavy hits the floor. Two shots, thin and snappy and jarring, causing little flashes to come out the door. A growing shadow and Carlin is in the corridor.

One cannot see the past as an inevitable progression towards the present, or raise it thus like *translatio imperii*; rather the present is an outcome of time's arbitrary flux (which one might mistakenly call 'history').

I walk quickly on the carpet. The clawhammer lands in his neck with a gravelly 'chok' like steak. The frosted deco corridor lights are pleasant, shining up their muslin glow like an Atlantic liner. I'd not expected to hit an artery but the gush looks promising as his hands rise. I yank the claws out which pulls flesh too, hanging on a skin-hinge as he gasps and stumbles. Is that the rim of an artery I see, sopping and geysering in putty hands? He mustn't fall. I can't leave him in the corridor.

Carlin was swaying, his eyeballs quivering, so I used his own upright, failing coordination to push him gently back to the apartment. He was trying to get his gun but wasn't really managing. He staggered, put a foot out to stop himself falling. I went round ninety degrees and shoved him through the door. Closed it behind us.

Hegel and Darwin are at odds here, and Marx corrects Hegel. A teleology drawn back from the present makes as much sense as the divine right of kings. Rather, take Darwinian mutability which is insentient and uncaring, knowing not where it's headed, and we may appreciate the random beauty of the future.

So I put down the claw hammer on an ornate half-table with a satin lamp against the wall and rest my hands on my hips. Huff and walk over to Alexei: quite dead.

Carlin groans and shifts on the floor like a terminal patient seeking palliative respite - in his death rattle.

I pull the axe from my coat and study him. Out of his misery? I wanted to leave a Glasgow smile like a 'fuck you' for Missy, but that's just a stupid Hansel and Gretel signature isn't it.

Annoyed by indecision, I hack at his leg below the knee. Martin Heidegger believes we can only understand being through our interaction with objects and people and the world. The shinbone is hard work. I've severed the leg, with a few ligaments and rubbery arteries still complaining and attached. He's still alive but won't be long.

Finally, sweating now, I pull the limb clear and throw it in the corner, where the bloody shin-end hits the wall, the leg wobbles and then remains upright on its boot, the trouser leg wrinkled round the shoe as though on the toilet. I pull out Paps' boxy *Eastman* to photograph it.

Whereas, Kracauer - though ambivalent to our new republic, its pace and production - believes we can understand modern existence through the surfaces and actions of others alone. The shutter clicks. By merely perceiving it: as a flaneur walking at half the speed of the masses.

I wonder what it would be like to drop an axe through a ribcage, so I lift it over my head. Smash his sternum, sink into flesh and bubbles, and watch the blood rise like blackberry sauce through crumble. I should get going. Too much more and I might come across as psychotic.

Consider that events of historical proportion are more complex in recipe than outcome. To arrive at a moment where some decision affects humankind - ascribed to the actions of a handful of men - an infinite billion prior circumstances shaped it. In fact we, as perpetrators, could even be called innocent.

I get rid of the blood - just a scum on my wrists - and open the door, glance around the soft-lit corridor; the walnut panels and discreet, unmoving doors. I reach the end and break into a bounce on the stairs. A woman with a trembly dog jumps in fright as I burst onto Karl-Kunger Straße. The trembly dog's wet hair round its mouth vibrates. We look at each other a moment. I head.

I suppose Kracauer is Marxist and I lean there. We die alone, no longer of the mass spectacle, knowing nothing but our own memory. If we sit in a chair doing bugger all our whole lives but gaze out a window, then what we see is meaning, just as if we participate in the aggressive production, this dictates the illusory degree to which we might claim understanding. So. Bollocks to Heidegger.

Bourgeois society is past mature; it's an ancient miser behind a wall hoping the carbine-toting don't get in.

Neukölln gang boss found dead

Carlin Hahn, elder of two siblings alleged to run the Neukölln district, was found dead yesterday afternoon alongside local restaurantaur Alexei Yahontov in Alt-Treptow.

The scene at Rosenthaler Mansions was undisturbed when police arrived, following a report of gunfire in the building. Surprisingly, no neighbour had investigated. Details released by the Kriminalpolizei are guarded, but Hauptkommisar Gründgens' statement reveals they:

"...believe a third protagonist is at large. Herr Yahontov was shot twice, his injuries consistent with fatal point-blank wounds. Herr Hahn's body, however, requires a post-mortem due to irregular wounds, excavations and imprints around his body. If anyone has information we would ask them to come forward. Nothing further to share at this time."

Nobody will mourn the passing of a notorious racketeer and mobster, but feelings and tensions are high in the community, following a bloody turf war that recently spilled into central Berlin. The people would like answers, and assurances of security in their daily lives.

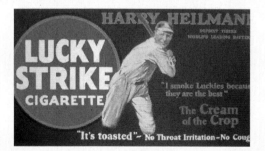
167

~

She'll be home now, in a flowery dress walking up some dusty path with bullfrogs, a wobbly orange sun in the treetops; racists gambolling and splashing in the creek.

She'll be the same girl that left, bar a slashed face and two years of adoration and noise.

Uncle Leroy is playing a guitar with only three strings, on his porch that creeks in the breeze, as does the shack and mosquito door. He's singing an old song about having sexual relations with his niece. At his flapping boot sits a porcelain jug of homebrew folks say makes you blind. Locals wave a cheery 'hello' to each other on rutted tracks, heading for KKK meetings.

Fuck's sake.

I place *Old Southern Jug Band* on the phonogram and the soft clack is broken by banjo and sax.

Why do I live in the imprint of her absence? The sunspot of her departure. Are us Fritzes really so bad? Her Mama doesn't think so. But her Mama wasn't made a black clown, and is protected by a Northern Irish squaddie.

The crackly shellac plays *Hatchet Head Blues*, with the missing trumpet ably replaced by... a jug. It reminds me of Sundays, with church over and the congregation dissolving, the rest of Sunday your own to celebrate and, perhaps butcher a chicken.

I lean on the sill. Berlin is quiet and black bar the new electric ads. Out there, men cackle like half-domestic hyenas drowning in guilt and sweating closely, schnapps-fumed or dulled by slumber where the guilts don't reach.

I saw Raymund in *Cafe Griechisch* the other day bracketing a lover; or client or dealer or whatever he needed and the mug indulged. He did *not* look good: thin as a reed; sunk as a galleon. The only thing holding him up was decent bones. Still handsome even as a desperado: inhabiting a space between last-ditch junky and perennial tramp. I missed him. Not *this* thing, what he was. (Yeah I know, he was an asshole, but an insightful and capable one.)

And something gnawed. I missed his mind more than his chalk-down behind. I didn't feel good about this, but Missy didn't care for Chekhov while Raymund *did*, if he could pull himself out of his opiate haze and fallout.

I used to lie on the warm spontaneous flesh of Missy Lehane, feel the hefty sleep of her innocence on my chest. But could I read *Easter Night* to her and see her clasp-handed in awe?

Raymund, get your act together. Our abominable worlds might collide again.

And the eyes slit-shift round the hall lest a better mug is on offer, passing me without recognition and moving on. I stand in the high whalebone gallery, hand on rim. His return scan passes but then slips back to my hooked eyes and skinhead (I've taken to total shearing: nobody knows what it represents; the ultra-fascists prefer a side parting). A smile of recognition, he puts a hand on his punter's arm with polite words, and heads for the base of the stairs into the whalebone.

He shouldn't even be here; I barred him.

Detty lover,

Trip was calm, relaxing even. It pains me, you know I'm pig-headed, but maybe your discouragement wasn't so mean after all. (Fatal maybe!) New York. Six auditions.

'We might give you a call.' …'I don't have a number.'… 'Staying in town?' …'For a while. The Edison.' (I write the number) 'Thanks for your time.'

So I look hopefully at the desk clerk five times a day in passing… Money's low. I'll head to Bessie's Wednesday. Send me photos of you. The one I brought is battered and scratched. Send a few. Get your gay friend Ray to snap some, all arty!

There's concrete canyons all round me - noise like you wouldn't believe (peaceful Berliner), and the sun is a rare visitor - I'm stuck between two homes, I don't know anyone and this place is energy, fizz, neon, sleet, dirt, bouncing off rejection and following a dollar. It's like someone took Berlin, stretched it, rammed more people in, and flooded it with murky water.

Tell me something. Write me. I've printed a few cards to hand out with Bessie's address, in case Broadway needs me.

Write often, and send those photos to Bessie's address,
Love & exhaustion,
✗ Missy losing faith

"You're a bastard Raymund."

"If you're going to save me from myself," He sat on the side of the bath drying his toes, shouting through the door. "I won't be able to stand a foghorn of recriminations."

"It's the price of your bed and board, shitsack."

"And I'm rather hoping, that is demanding, you don't interfere with my routine."

I looked up from *Forensics Quarterly*. "Your chemical routine?"

He nodded, but his words didn't match his pleading eyes.

"I'll stay out, but we meet halfway, right?"

He nodded again, and my eyes left his privacy. A while later he appeared in a towel, a malnourished rat with clean hair and a couple of scabs.

"Halfway?"

"Yeah, you can cook, inject, inhale. But there's a but."

Tilted head.

"Behave like a normal human being."

"Oh!" Raymund grinned broadly. "How boring." He paced over and lifted the cover of my reading. "What's this? Have you joined the KriPo? Am I under surveillance?"

"No, and yes."

He looked around Missy's ex apartment. "Can I make eggs?"

"Then we're going out."

"I'd rather hoped--"

"We are *going out*. And we're taking in a show."

"I'll need a fix. What show?"

"Whatever you need to do. Just attend, show up, it's half the battle."

Raymund looked at me curiously, not unaffectionately. "Archangel Brüning."

"Show some humility."

"No Gabriel."

He swished away over the carpet, his hollowness echoed by the floor. "And by the way, you have a loose floorboard." He stamped a foot on the carpet to illustrate.

"Leave that."

"What?"

"It's hardly life-threatening."

"I might do myself an injury. Puncture my foot on a nail."

"Leave that," I said, firmly.

Raymund sleeps his damned sleep, his coastal face more lapping Med than raging North Sea. Of course he's jacked up, and I insist he keeps his paraphernalia in a tin. Syringes and pipes, and the latest 'must have' fad: rubber tubing. The flat's clean, the moon shines, Raymund sleeps and I sit awake. As is my wont. I'll have the eye gouges of my father soon.

I was curious - nervous - as to what Gründgens and Lange wanted me for, so left my 'appropriate adult' at home as I walked up the station steps.

"Thought you'd be halfway to Timbuktu."

"Why?"

"No matter. Where's your father?"

"Can't make it. D'you just want to show me whatever it is and I'll get on?"

"Glad you could come." There was a familiarity in Gründgens' voice, or relief, as we walked the corridor past carbolic cells. "Owing to new techniques and Lange's diligent work, work he carried out after hours far beyond his duties, we are able to say with some authority, an authority hitherto unavailable to the Kriminalpolizei, that without further evidence to the contrary--"

Christ, spill it! What is this, a sudden pride in his work?

"--the axe used to kill Zelda Brüning, is the same used at the Oranienstraße Grand on Amelie Bergmann."

Believe it or not, this was news. "So... you're saying nutter Richter might be innocent?"

"Definitely. I'll leave you in Lange's capable hands. He has the evidence."

Lange sat with many papers splayed on a wood-topped desk with an ultra-modern magnetic tape recording machine. He liked tech.

"It upsets me to keep returning to you for enquiries, Detlef. Being a grieving minor and all. It's disheartening."

"Mm."

"As I've said, we follow what we know."

"Regarding which case? Seems all Germany's up for a killing spree, of some stripe."

"Stripe?"

"Political or monetary." I served him a significant eyebrow, lost in his focus.

"I want to eliminate you from our enquiries. Basically, leave you alone."

"For which you've dragged me here."

Lange's face pinched and he got up. "While you're here we're searching your apartment."

"You can't do that."

"We can."

"You can't."

"We expected you to arrive with an adult, whereupon your rights would be read and the warrant issued. You didn't. Our officers are executing the search. What should I do?"

"Call off your dogs."

"It'll take a while. They'll have finished."

"On what grounds?"

"The murder weapon of Lorenz Beck is a claw-hammer. Matching the gauge and weight of that killing Carlin Hahn, and similar in size to the marks under Gerhard's desk. Cafe Wien."

"With you so far. 'Cept... how are you ascribing hammer murders to me?"

"Missy Lehane was seen in Grünau shortly before Lorenz' death. And we have a witness statement."

"Do you," I was disgruntled. Lange wasn't using the language of being charged or arrested. It just felt like a conversation weighted in his favour.

"Let's just wait. Hope the boys turn nothing up." Lange had decided to let nothing more out, illustrated by a mouth opening, then shutting. He got up. Wandered the room.

The air was heavy - I liked Lange, just not under these conditions - and it was a relief when two uniformed LaPo or

KriPo - I don't know how they work things - called Lange out. Didn't quite close the door, and the remonstrations were equally sided between them.

Lange returned. "We're done."

"Wha'd'ya get?"

Lange said: "Just one item. But you're free to leave for now."

"No, I want to know what you found in my flat. And as my property, sign it back out."

"Just go."

"With my possessions."

"A play! You can have the stupid thing." Lange strode back out and shouted. He came back with my magnum opus for the theatre.

"Thanks," I said magnanimously. "My ticket to higher life forms."

Are we weak, realising our own exhaustion? I only saw the Great Extinction through a child's visions - bolstered by fake reported glories - but it rubs off.

Decades hence, my sons will stroll Prague and comment the place is confusing. Half, the old half, is monochrome and dour, reconciled to austere hunger and Soviet truths. The other half, like a dimension overlaid, has shiny hair and glowing *l'Oreal* skin and smiles; they touch cheeks in sunglasses and svelte clothing.

And such are we, forgetting the past though it appears in our faces, hands outstretched, begging.

Or maybe we're weak because the world demands nothing. Not right now. Just don't cause trouble.

"Oh, but you didn't mention that did you."

"What?"

"The Volkspolizei might ransack us while you're out."

"I didn't know."

"They took your play."

"Better that."

"Than?"

"None of your concern."

Raymund huffed.

"Ray. Can you put it away. I'm knackered."

My Primadonna,

I'm so sorry about New York... Of course I didn't want to discourage you. You're my soaring Aphrodite, and the Berlin punters were the luckiest. (Remember, you're probably as close to Berlin as you are to Mississippi right now? I'm not pleading.)

Ray and I no longer speak and I've barred him from the Palast. So enclosed are just some old photos; haven't changed much, right?

I guess you're relaxing on a stoop, eating from a vat with the sun on your face. (OK it's January). I miss you: Berlin is a shade greyer, the drizzle heavier, the electric signs dimmed in mourning. Matilda asked after you and almost lifted me off my feet demanding your address. (Expect a double-pronged flanking manoeuvre from us!)

Oh and Paps sends his regards and wishes you good luck, for what that's worth.

What I say now, you'll have to decipher: your laundry has been done. A kind of justice was delivered.

When you grow tired of wide rivers and beautiful skies, I await you in the damp iron streets, your one true audience.

Always,

Detlef.

𝒳

~

Paps slapped it down on his desk; where his face was once forced. I looked at the five inch card.

"Is it a joke?"

"I don't know."

"Yeah but... Does he think you're his pal? Part of the Hahn clan?"

"Who knows what that scum thinks."

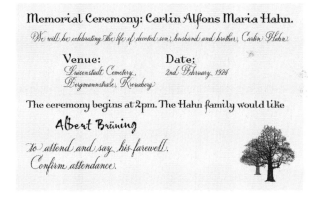

Memorial Ceremony: Carlin Alfons Maria Hahn.

We will be celebrating the life of devoted son, husband and brother, Carlin Hahn.

Venue: Luisenstadt Cemetery, Bergmannstraße, Kreuzberg

Date: 2nd February, 1924

The ceremony begins at 2pm. The Hahn family would like

Albert Brüning

To attend and say his farewell. Confirm attendance.

Luisenstadt Cemetery

And now...

...CLUES WILL BE LEFT

...LIVELIHOODS WILL BECOME EGGSHELLS

Physical Specimens

Clarence 'Catch-all' Peters

Eggshell

VIOLENCE PROCREATES!

THERE'S A CROWD SCENE...

AND THE DEATH OF...

Luisenstadt '24

I clamber cemetery railings, jacket double-folded on the spikes, landing in pine needles. Under velour fir I crouch at the last rhododendron before sun-licked lawn.

What does a Hahn burial look like? Well there's a collonade lining a gravel lane. Edging forward is a black convoy of Merc *770 Grands*, mudguards quivering. One's a hearse carrying about seven-eighths of Carlin (don't know if the leg's in) to a glorified bin, where an unhappy priest nods.

The undertaker's courtage-usherers look like sombre burlesque. Clench-fronted hands show respect under thin collars and ties. Hard skin and mouths that frown at an angle, muscle-fat coats, bodies lined with subcutaneous comfort food. Man these accomplices, these *henchmen*. Their seams must groan every morning when each potato gets in. What's it like to live a life largely in silence? Eat, frighten, collect.

And there's Paps treading carefully, dressed astute, as unreadable as his situation. Sunlight renders what I thought a coiffure just a thin netting over his nut.

I hear a crack twenty yards off and see Michael Hartmann crouched - much as I am - behind his own shrub. I poke my head out a little, and on the immediate lawn in front is a Hahn goon - some perimeter expert with security stance.

I weigh a rotting branch and throw it at Hartmann. It lands near him in a batch of bramble making a racket. The goon turns, stares, then heads to investigate. Hartmann fatly moves to re-hide, but he's made more noise than the log. The goon's now in the ferns barking "Halt!" pointing his stumpy *Mauser*. Hartmann chucks something shiny, turns and raises his hands. Once level with his interceptor, his arm is shoved up his back and he's bounced over the lawn far from the ceremony and ejected. I titter in the leaf litter.

What had he thrown? I make my way over. Took a while, but there it was: the Leica camera. Might it still contain the Gründgens roll? I bagged it, knowing Hartmann would be back as soon as he could.

Need to get closer; hear. See what passes between Gerhard and Paps.

There's other pulpheads; the press are easy to spot via bent hats, tieless check, bulging and scruffy shirts and bad diet. *Examiner*, *Morgenpost* and *Tagesspiegel*. I look at Gerhard. He's stomaching the press for legend, I guess.

Then there's unconvincing 'wives', their kids alternately bored or tearaway on the clipped lawn. And *there* is Gründgens, begloved and slab-faced. How would a legitimate KriPo explain his presence at a Hahn interment?

He wouldn't, because he's now feeling the grimy collars of grub street, leaning in to warn them. He is a tall man and blots the sun. I don't need ears to hear what he whispers: *Keep that camera and notebook away from me, or you'll feel the pain of existence.*

The pallbearers slowly remove the coffin and carry it to the grave, where men stand with leather straps. The coffin is laid quite gently given Carlin's weight, and he's lowered a metre or so closer to Hell.

I see Gerhard gulp. Is it sorrow? Fear? Emotion? How sweet.

I'm down Züllichauer Straße end in cedar. Pink mausoleums with sorrowful angels. Seated thinkers in lavatory-style ponder; cherubim bursting from laurel and ivy; phallic monuments with ferny bases. If you add up the magnates and manipulators buried through time, they could populate the earth.

...gathered to honour Carlin Hahn, who joined the Catholic Church in matrimony to his beloved Adalaide. Herr Hahn will be remembered foremost...

Need to get closer. The breeze is blustering only bits of eulogy my way.

...And his generous private donations to the Charité Hospital and Weissensee Children's Hospital, neither of which were through the family's concern...

Gerhard looked at (I guessed) Carlin's wife Adalaide, who clenched her jaw as response and remonstration. Her face was hard but pretty like a cactus. Gerhard looked away.

...killed in cold blood while running his daily errands...

Gerhard'd grown tired and walked to Papa. Pulled his elbow away from the homily. Halfway towards a Merc, Paps shrugged Gerhard off, shook his head and his hand. *No way*, he seemed to say. Gerhard grasped his elbow again and pointed a finger, then from a knuckle, flicked out one, two, ultimately six fingers. Paps shook his head again. Gerhard smiled; his hands seemed to placate. He nodded a few times. Expansively gestured and pointed at Papa with a smile. Paps lowered his head. Gerhard watched him. Eventually, Paps nodded.

They reached the Merc bonnet where a goon clasped papers, and brought them. Gerhard produced a pen, and splayed the papers on the bonnet. Paps was hunched - the worst version of Paps - and asked some silent questions. Gerhard pointed. Paps scrawled. After a while, Gerhard was happy. He shuffled it all together and handed it to the goon.

The homily'd finished. The congregation - wives hired and real, put-upon priest, Gründgens, dislodged press - melted to the industrial red building which was part-crematorium, part-reception up the gravel path. Gerhard gestured. The pair turned and walked slowly in conversation back to the grave. All the goons had gone bar a couple of perimeter experts.

Gerhard shot Paps in the side of the head. Paps' body lurched left and crumpled on the grave's rim. Gerhard used his shoe to push him in and signalled the goons fill up. As they started to shovel, Gerhard's gloved hand gave a dismissive wave at the new body - actually not dismissive, more effeminate - and he strode off.

I ran from the cemetery wide-eyed with terror, stumbling, faltering, the deathly ring still bouncing in my skull; cold with sweat, my hands numb. The earth and the filth. The engraved and greening stone.

~

You don't know loss until the second one goes. You think you might but you don't. People field-dress this emptiness with their own family; kids and so forth. But that's just morphine.

Only drink and Ray's tranquilisers could dull my vertigo and palpitations. He watched me scatter his tin, crush a pill with my glass and scoop it in my whiskey; watched with open, territorial concern.

"Can I do anything?"

I shook my head fiercely.

"I want to help."

"Can you resurrect? Or does necromancy elude you."

I'd not thought Paps in *danger*. Losing control for sure. It made me shudder. *The coldness. The certainty and suddenness...*

"This must be horrible, Baby."

...a rubbish puppeteer pulling strings unaware his own hand, indeed world, is on strings...

I'd tranq'd enough to look at Raymund with a semblance. "I'm a fucking orphan Ray." I headed for a chair, rocking it slightly before sinking in. "Two are required. I've lost the requisite two. And my main Mama's in Mississippi."

"Main Mama? Oh... I see."

"I'll sweep chimneys when I get out of social care."

"Mm."

Even in my bereavement, Raymund's eyes betrayed. He steered carefully, like a cat needing but no longer trusting its master. There *was* pity: a fragile and rarely used pity like the crystal decanter for guests. His nervous eyes said he now knew my basic surface hid nasty, possibly gore-laced business. *What will you do with that, Ray?*

Then I realised the weighty trivia which was encroaching was not trivia at all. I couldn't execute Paps' affairs being a minor, and for some power of attorney to be appointed, he'd have to be certified dead. If I reported Paps dead (requesting his disinterment from Carlin's embrace), I would be put immediately into care; which by no means put me out of the reach of Gerhard. If I reported him as missing, I would go into temporary care until they found him; which they wouldn't.

One morning Ray cleared his throat for longer than usual: "Is this flat registered to Brüning Holdings or privately owned?"

"I can't believe you'd ask."

"I'm concerned."

"I bet you are."

I'd have to visit the bank and obtain Paps' affairs. But until the police issue a death certificate, Paps' still alive. 'Cept I know he's dead, Gerhard knows he's dead, a handful of grave-diggers know he's dead. Do Gründgens and the priest know he's dead? Hell, I'm so off-map.

Gerhard's nugget brain would surely assign Carlin's death to the Kapuzes. Though Paps must've signed full or greater ownership of Brüning Holdings, thus outliving his use. It's too excessive. Missy's phrase often turned in my head before sleep. '*You can't claim ignorance. You know when the shit returns, it doesn't return to sender.*' That's a founding principle of terrorism.

The circuitry of my life is worn and familiar. Haunts and places of duty and refuge; summons and interview. 'Cept now, the things that sit behind are gone. Harnesses loosed. Making me some kind of floating, inflatable vagrant, occasionally pulled down by constabulary or turf war, infatuation and politics.

"I need to report a missing person."

The desk paperclip finally looked up. He'd been ignoring my presence and increasingly extrovert breathing, so I pushed a hand into his view.

"Right. Yes." He put down his pen like the docket he'd just filled was the Magna Carta. "What can I do for you?"

"I said. Missing person."

"Ok. Name?"

"His or mine? Well they're the same actually. Brüning."

"Which Brüning are *you*?"

"Detlef. You should know. We've met three times."

"Mm."

He walked to his personal Nirvana, a wall-mounted pouch of forms, and returned.

"We doing it out here?"

"Yes." The paperclip's brow bent. "There's nobody else out here."

"It's not very respectful."

"Are we speaking of the dead? As you say, we've met several times."

"What's that mean? I'm a suspect or a waste of time?"

"I'll take what details I need. If I have further queries, I'm sure I'll see you around the place."

He gave me a look less paperclip more... Satan's lovechild.

While Docket-Face got what he needed I just dealt with my palpitations.

I went to Haus Vaterland for a drink: The *Wild West Bar*. Before you slander me as a native tourist, there's a reason. The owner believes New Orleans and Chicago jazz somehow reached the western frontier. So the music's OK, even amid hollow wood cowboys and injuns. I took the G&T graciously from a zombie behind chipped teak.

Paranoia is setting in. When Desk Johnny said 'Are we speaking of the dead?' and 'I'm sure I'll see you round' that could be off-the-cuff. Daily banter. But how far into Gründgens' subterranea was Paperclip? What did he know, or maybe not know but I'd dig a hole in his flippancy.

There was one pair of eyes I trusted. I twirled my empty with ice, trying to melt more whisky from water. Lange. I can give no physical explanation for this, just I know he's trustworthy. Above ignominy.

I stood in pants and mote-flecked sun, thinking about Paps' paperwork in his office, locked up or in a tall sheaf on his table.

I was in KaDeWe department store and saw Fuchsia White. If I haven't explained this wondrous number, she is very pale black (hence the name) with russet, almost ginger hair and freckles.

"What goes along, Fuchsia?"

She hugged me without fuss. A warm matronly thing for one so slim. "I was so sorry to hear about Albert. Any news?" She looked at me with a sideways flick; so I guessed she figured he'd blown Berlin over debts. "I mean," she added, "the place is gone to shit. Don't come by. This morning a guy was taking down, you know, the big sign. Only once it was down you could still see the lettering behind, clear as day. I mean *do* come by, but... you know."

"Well now Fuchsia, I do plan to, in my own time."

Her eyes narrowed searchingly.

"What you're thinking is correct Fuchsia. A load of daisies needed pushing up."

"Oh my honey, don't be brave," I got squished again. "You have to come and stay with me and Gloria. We won't take no for one."

"Kind of you Madam Blanche. Truly, but I've stuff on."

"Dinner at least?"

"Well. Yes." I smiled. Our little net had unwound and I wanted it resewn. But I was a big boy now and kept some big boy decorum. She was a fox mind. In another life.

I'd watch the *Palast* sometimes. Feel its new ebb and flow. Hahn had a habit of taking a beer in the *Griechisch* after ten. Maybe to watch the footfall into his money-pit, or gauge what customers headed over from Roman's. No doubt with an eye to squeezing Roman out. Roman remained licenced but it was more coffee and cake now, directly in the eyeline of departing pissheads. I left a message with him for Gerhard. To meet on Thursday at 8pm.

We can't be trusted, can we, to organise our society. Look at us knocking each other off - slitting, shooting - and running for the cover of politics when we're ashamed and vulnerable. You know that phrase 'divide and conquer'? I'm not saying we do it deliberately, or that *we* do it at all. God's seen our patchwork federation and said: right, you lot are pinko; you lot stay walrus-chopped reactionaries with pointy hats; and you lot, well... God rubs his hands with glee... *you lot* can stoke a white-hot furnace of racial hatred. God admires his canvas: no, these brushes are too broad. Let's have some vengeance on Reds. Bit of anti-globalism. Non-anti-Semitic staunch imperialists over here. What about anti-democracy, ah, that's with pointy hats. Chuck in repugnance at Roma and horror at homos. Aghh, I forgot new women! Intellectuals can discuss those; and sexologists. (Shit, where's the clergy?) Man, these schisms are widening, like ice cracking on a pond and rendering the shallowness more opaque.

There was a scrapyard in the Neukölln-Treptow borders. *Hahn & Kloss Salvage*. It was believed Hahn used this for 'disposal', though that might as easily be for its location on the bank of the schiffahrtskanal, as its own ability to conceal. And I expect he'd want to sell the scrap free of bilious green flesh. ...Reason I mention it is: guess who skipped out together one sun-tinselled December morning? Gründgens and Hahn. Not just a burial ground for the unlucky, but a place to secrete alliances too. A VIP, gangland corporate suite if you will.

I slipped into a fire escape and snapped the Leica. If Hartmann's pics were bullshit, these wouldn't be. As they got dangerously near, I heard the dull click that said: end of roll.

My life's sham; fake in every way. Fakir at fifteen. I feel turned inside out. Disintegrating. I won't claim there are voices in my head, but there kind of *are*. My own is strongest. It's a logical voice - in both corollary and justice - except nothing that works in my head, plays *out*.

Winter insists I have not banished homosexuality, so what did Paps pay him for? I attend my KPD rallies and wallop youngsters. Stroll a river and chop a bumpkin. Advise Paps not to spend hookies and lay my own. I'm standoffish with Ray because he ought to straighten, but I get skewiff on his gear and wrestle him at night. I'm in love with Missy but *Missy's gone* (and doesn't like Chekhov). I bump Carlin, which I can only assume got Paps killed (patricide?). Lange and Gründgens sniff each death - I mean every bloody *one* - and entice me to the station on half-baked (but in the oven) evidence.

Detty my love,

I'm now home, well not far. From New York to Hattiesburg took two days, but the skies, the slow wide rivers. You must come and wash the grit from your hair, burn the grey from your skin. Our skies are forever.

Your letter - that message to 'decipher' - it worried me. What's happened? I hope you aren't getting involved, leave justice to the police. You've already been stupid and naive about what citizen-boy can do in the big bad world. Stay out (and be careful if you're round my father, he has dealings. Decipher that.). I've decided not to dwell on bad things and people, focus on what I control. You understand Baby-Man?

Fat Bess chirrups about Mama with that Orangeman, gallivaintin Europe while her daughter's in trouble with tears and hospital checks. You'll guess things didn't work with auditions. Should of listened to your jabber.

Wanna know what Mississippi and Alabama look like? I'll describe you a dream photo, so's you know. The trees are dark, like that crinkly veg that's good for you? Sunsets are coral pink through chocolate orange, no, maybe roast beef. Fish leap at sundown - snapping insects probably - it's calming. Whole days under a tree forgetting I ain't earning. All sinks away, you know?

My school sweetheart works at the abattoir and the foreman's got a blind eye, so I get offcuts. Bess can't say I ain't tossin' in.

Days are long and I'm trim, just in case, you know. It's nice here you can forget it. But, your face appears in the sky. Horsehead Detty, Deutsche boy. Is it possible to feel romantic about concrete and rain, and your hideous language?

Write me soonest.

Missy

✗

An addled rake's arse.

He bends and the towel falls, he catches it, but not before the crevasse I once idolised reveals sinking bone and flesh.

Missy, come home. Why does she write to this empty vessel? She took her clanging coal scuttle away when I was in love, and now writes me like it's easy mileage. Negotiable. Maybe she's right, but ember feelings shouldn't be poked from afar.

I don't see you like you expect (high contrast: bright teeth and dark skin in a roast beef dusk), no you're a nymph of the swamps, through mosquitos doors, curved like bas relief. I know you keep trim, you are a god of motion; how couldn't you?

~

"I need to speak with your husband, please. Captain Lehane."

"Yeah I know who my husband is. He's with company. I can dish you up some goat, if you like?"

"Frau Lehane, it's urgent. May I ask who the company is? Please, Davione?"

She gave me a look that was half chin withdrawal, half frown. "You can ask. What's this about honey?"

"Just that...' I pointed to a kitchen chair; she nodded and I sat. "We had discussed some provisional... plans, to ensure certain justices were seen to be delivered, in regard... to, er, ...I think I should just speak to Captain Lehane. Events have overtaken themselves."

She wiped her hands and cleared her throat. "I'd better announce you, so you don't overhear stuff."

"This is Aloysius Kapuze."

I nodded respectfully but then my mouth opened: "I was in the barber shop when you unleashed on Sharonstraße."

"Kuhn's?"

"Yes."

"I'm sorry, I read about it."

"I wasn't suggesting--"

Kapuze lifted a hand. "You have every right to call me out, and I do regret it. One day, there'll be no need. No need. But it's not yet. When I hear my boys took out any one... any one... of the Hahn crew I don't feel much. Only when..." he gestured at me, "innocents get hit."

"Which is bad for business, Aloysius."

"You're right Cap. But otherwise it went like a dream. Hence..." and he raised the fingers, rubbing them together.

"Look, er" Captain Lehane got up and ushered me to a seat. "I don't think we have any secrets. We can talk frankly in front of the boy. Davione sings to herself so she's hears very little."

"Quite the psychopath."

"Pardon me?"

Kapuze nodded at me. "Word from my boy is Detlef planned, staked and executed his hit with a singular relish."

I cleared my throat. "No, sir. You're wrong. It was Carlin who was like that. He was whistling on the way to a killing. I just doled my payback and left very quickly."

"Well it's rather skewed our agreement, Captain?"

"Undercut is the word you're after," Declan smiled. It was the first smile I'd seen on him. Dark.

Aloysius didn't find that funny, and grunted.

"I'm in credit," Declan said.

We both looked at him.

"Sure I am. You got your oxyacetylene. I'm owed a Hahn."

I left the Captain's house. Heading through Wedding over Luxembourg and Schul for the station, I looked right and saw a seam of ragged fire. There was a chaos of rubbish and makeshift blockades and the occasional exploding bottle, spewing fire on the ground or arcing the night.

It's getting too close, I thought. The Lehanes are three streets north. And us Fritz Bolshies can't fight for toffee. I mean blood and nails, ear-ripping, yank the crown jewels, win at all costs. Nor can I really, but I'm learning in the thug-dust.

Militias don't have rules because militias don't exist, except in fevered imaginings and fast-working tailors; they're answerable to belief. Pinch, kick and if a bollock splits, wear it.

Red steam rising I head in, see which side's got their backs to me on an east front.

Comrades behind tyres and wrenched signs, yanked bits of tram and parked auto. Many were kids, but an old fella was propping a Bergmann MP-18 that had clearly seen service; a fucking machine gun. But almost in them in my half-crouch I suddenly thought: you've got work to do, stop pissing around. Lehane's twang in my head agreed: *keep an eye out, I'll be busy.*

Promises. Obligations. A bullet up my arse.

I paused on my haunches. Stood and walked back to the crossing, turning for the station home, feeling good about my decision.

'Oh for god's sake.' ...Walking the pavement towards me was a bunch of *Jugendbund SA* products, perhaps oblivious they were the wrong end of 'The Battle for Luxembourg Straße' (not our finest campaign). And they'd soon split and encircled me.

"How can I help you boys?" I said.

"You can't, *roter* scum," said one holding a billy club, and looked at his entourage. "Help yourself?"

I said nothing, just stood staring. The seat of my pants was heavy with my tool. The speaker stepped closer.

"Now listen," I said, recalling a certain gent with a Bergmann at the barricade. "I'll strike you a bargain deal. I get on my way and you hurry on down Luxembourg Straße, just on the left there. There's a bunch of Red kids ripping posters and defacing your gauleiter."

This kid-man breathing in my face now looked up the street to where the buildings broke.

"Yeah? That was dumb. You've told us, but we haven't let you go."

"If you're quick, it's a field day."

He turned back grinning, slightly dazed or high though he couldn't be. "Oh, we'll be quick." Suddenly his arm was back and smashing my nose.

Through streaming eyes another - a Bavarian goblin - ran, jumped and launched the top of his head like a shot-put at my mouth. My tongue split and I could taste iron.

I was backing up now, feeling in my pleats. Out it came, I flipped the handle in my palm, spinning the head, and as goblin came at me I claw-hammered his cheek. It paused the others. As I yanked it out through the side of his lips they all shrank a little.

"Move," I said indicating a path through their ranks and headed for the two kids blocking my route. They parted, thank god, and I kept walking steadily. I could hear shuffling behind me, and finally looked back. They were heading for

Luxembourg. I spat some blood in the gutter and felt a sheet of wetness on my chin. Beside me a poster bemoaning Locarno (a gorilla in Wehrmacht fatigues overstriding the Ruhr), was hanging off the wall. I pulled it down to wipe my chin. As I headed for the station - hoping to wash in a public toilet - two things happened. Ray appeared like a rakish mirage. He faltered a little rounding the corner, then regained his stride with a beam. And back on Luxembourg, I distinctly heard machine gun fire. *Oops! Was that a little underhand, getting teenagers massacred?*

"Ray, are you following me? You're way off piste."

"God. Look at your face."

"Well dear Chorister, that's what I get for my principles. ...So?"

"What?"

"Why are you in Mitte?"

"A talk. I suppose a rally really. You know, redistribution of wealth, all that. Peaceful, indoors. I'm trying to take an interest, like you said."

I melted a bit. "Clean?"

"Sure man."

"My Ray, every day, better in every way."

"Sounds like a bullshit pamphlet."

"Probably is."

"Take you home? You look like a bad day at the Somme."

"Like you'd know." But it was all getting gentler. Maybe the stuffing from my gob or the rainbow egg on my forehead brought out his matriarch.

With scurrilous glances either way, he came and pushed the hair from my eyes to look at the damage. I'd never seen his eyes so clear and close; not really. By which I mean I'd never seen his unselfish eyes (like Mama's). We can all fake clarity in dissolution but he was properly boring in.

"Detty, there seems to be a hammer in your hand."

Shit, I'd simply hid it behind my leg. Not thought that through.

"If I had a gun it'd be a gun. We defend with what we have."

"Honey you frighten me."

"I'd rather be frightened of than walked on like an unknown grave."

~

I was starting to take risks; well, complacencies. I sat in *Cafe Wien* wearing my best guess at Austrian student clothes: waistcoat but no tie, off-white mac and felt trilby.

Gus Schuster the Palast owner was three tables away, talking to an intense man who seemed to have mistakenly oiled his face rather than his hair. His body was runty and civilian; that of a true nobody, the concave physique accentuated by double-breasted lapels. But his face gave away all that was needed. He wasn't smiling, and I imagined when he flipped on the smooth smarm, it could as easily give way to wiry vengeance.

Of their dynamic - over an effeminate silver pot of coffee - Schuster seemed the servile, the beta, with the other collecting his pantomimes like sea shells. I knew this man; had seen his photograph in the press. 'Gauleiter' of Berlin, Dr. Joseph Goebbels. Can you do that? Just make up titles? Bureaucratic offices that suit your inexorable shiftings of national scenery?

If so, from now on I am Beschützer Obliegt of Neukölln; and you shall call me as such.

I couldn't hear much, so decided to sit at the counter on a stool.

"...Herr Schuster, I am a man of culture myself, I know its power to impassion and enrage, as well as entertain by more squalid means."

Schuster shrugged and sat back: "We strike a balance between what the workers want and what we want to give the workers. You understand."

"That's well summarised but no, I don't understand. You may not know that you're a tool. Of the NSDAP. Or you would do well to be. To be on the correct side."

"I don't follow."

"You do. There's a man who has recently come into Brüning Theatrical Holdings. The industrious Gerhard Hahn."

"Oh, he's industrious for sure. Threatened me with menaces to keep the lease. He's converting it into Hahn's Bavarian Beer Cellar. It's not even a cellar, it's above ground."

"Yes."

Silence.

"Yes what?"

"That will happen."

"We are a cultural centre, Dr. Goebbels."

And so began the slow crescendo that would become this besuited slug's calling card: "Are you a Communist?"

"Entrepreneur."

"A Jew then."

"I'm an entrepreneur and property owner." Schuster's shoulders slumped.

"You are in one of the last bastions of staunch Communism in all Germany. Our party is winning votes all over the country. It is a matter of months before we reach this red maggot pit. On all sides you have enemies: the NSDAP ...your future Reich... the police, the respected Hahn Security Holdings who happen to hate socialism, and our own well-drilled SA to influence those sitting on the fence. How do you think the Palast will fair under such conditions, wheeling out half-naked negroes and ...ha!.. moronic satire while Germany pushes into the future."

"Well..." Schuster straightened his curly blond hair. "I hadn't--"

"Hahn will get the lease. All art commissioned in the gallery will be vetted. The renovation works start Thursday week with a view to opening 1st of March. I will personally give a speech, a rally, and there will be incentives to attend."

The iced-cave stare, low slung ears and downturned mouth, the cot-death body. Schuster said and did nothing. No nod, no shrug, no yes, no no. Though I knew inside he growled as a defeated cat might in sunken subservience to a victor.

"Speak of the devil, here's your new leaseholder and security expert. You two should meet again, amicably."

And there it was in the *Morgenpost*.

Daring bank raid nets over 900,000 RM from Berlin discount bank

198

Ha! Oxyacetylene courtesy of the British Army on the Rhine and a very long night drive. Price owing? One Hahn.

I stared at the Rotbart at night, after closing. What crowds might've been had melted. The wind-down had a pall (Gerhard kept the box office ticking over while he organised). The chorus girls were in mystery over the change of bosses and being told: 'just get on'. Except, between shows, the auditorium was changing.

I was wearing coal-black attire under St. Fridolin's, and pushed off to slip up the fire escape. Night creaked and echoed as I crowbarred the fire door into the backstage warren. Paint came away with the door: not really a fire exit, more sealed legislation. Nothing'd changed: Paps' womb-red velour obviously aligned with Hahn taste.

I smelled the corridor's lipstick and hot filaments - womens' detritus on unmoving air - and couldn't help going into the dressing room.

Paps' office was now the Lair of Hahn. Little change bar the brute builders' wall gouges of a couple of recessed cabinets and Paps' desk gone in favour of a larger, marble-topped one. There were dark oil-painted horses beneath ready to be remounted when the skirting and trim was repainted. I walked past his desk, wondering if the old key safe remained; Paps' cheap repro of Degas' *Dancer* covering it still was. Now was the time: I took off the picture. Bollocks. A dial.

I kicked in the desk from beneath - á la Cafe Wien - to pack what I could. Paused a moment: 'B. Mitte. 9 Raumerstraße, Helmholtzplatz. Mint.'

Balthazar?

I was leaving when I got a *fuck you* sensation. I went back to the girl's room and grabbed a thick lipstick, and in the wall wrote: 'Need to sort out your security.' I turned to go as the bag was heavy, but then went back, crossed out 'sort out' and wrote above 'address'. I looked at the wall, and it seemed too weak. So I added: 'Best regards. Your brother's executioner. And yours.'

"What is it now? Is there a channel I can report harassment? Some official form?"

"I want you to help me."

"I do. But then you come up with these vague signposts make me seem like I attract news."

"How d'you mean?"

"Like I'm the epicentre every time you have a press-quake."

Lange nodded. "Yes, yes you are."

"Where's Gründgens anyway? I haven't seen him in ages."

"Dealing with the press, public relations. That kind of thing."

"The great unwashed need answers!"

"I want you to help me, so that I don't have to keep traipsing through evidence."

"What's in it for me?"

Lange spanned his temples with finger and thumb, breathing deeply. "Detlef, you're a cheeky bugger now and you're what, sixteen? Will you be insufferable as an adult?"

I beamed him. "The future only knows."

"I believe you know quite a bit. Bear in mind the harder and longer I have to work to form a case against... a witness as opposed to, say, that witness aiding enquiries, the heavier the courts come down. Are you with me? That witness, should he cooperate..."

"Or she."

"...He or she cooperate, you're not only aiding justice, but making life easier for yourself."

"Define witness."

"Someone with information, who may or not also be accused. Accused and thereafter Defendant are subsets of witness. Witness keeps things suitably vague."

"But that's why I like you Inspector Lange, you're so precise."

There was a pause; a long one where I felt the sun through unclean windows heat my face, pleasantly, as though I were a cat.

"Where do you think you're father went? It's not some ruse so we can't read your rights is it?"

I looked down with a gulp. "I suppose he skipped town. Didn't leave me any message. Unless..."

"I'm sorry Detlef. You're having a rough time lately."

I sat straighter. "Anyway, we both know nothing meaningful comes from these meetings."

"I'll tell you where we are. You can decide if you'll help."

I shrugged, though Lange must have caught something as my gaze dropped.

"Do you think your father is OK?"

I shrugged again. At some point, I need to ask Lange about Declan Lehane.

~

"Let's go to that enormous thing."

"What thing?"

"In Leipzig."

"OK."

Raymund put on sandals and a burnt-rust linen shirt, packed untidy sandwiches, chilled fruit, wine, three potential swimming outfits, a blanket and two books, then we left for the Leipzig train. Oh no, wait - I hung on the door, swung heavily on its hinge - a cardigan against the German wind, some sunglasses, further nibbles, an umbrella, a change of 'town shoes', soap...

"Soap?"

"You imagine Leipzig lavatories have soap?"

"Go in nature." I raised a brow at his stooped back, the swan-like moled neck. ...Then we got the train, in whose compartment every Berliner'd realised Leipzig needed them today. We slapped Südfriedhof, past the angels with spread palms.

"Wow."

"Biggest monstrosity in Europe." I looked up at the solemn faces staring down. A breeze rolled my face lifting city clag. I unfolded the blanket and lay with hot feet.

Raymund picked his toes. "Blisters."

I laughed at him as I chomped bread. "So which costume will you wear, to stand ankle-deep in that ornamental pond."

"Get away from me," he shunted closer; all rectilinear and criss-crossed with grass.

I stretched out, but couldn't get out of the stern knights' gaze. I shut my eyes. Dozing off, Raymund popped a cork. "Funny isn't it..."

He was attempting to stay upright with his legs folded out the side.

"...How do they decide who gets these? Will I get one?"

"You'd have to do something huge."

"I *am* huge. In all senses."

"Have you slaughtered any French?"

"No. Aunt Odette's French."

"Crimeans?"

"Who are they? Don't sound very above board."

The grass's clipped glitter. Photons. I waved a finger at the unused tumbler and Raymund poured Pinot Blanc. "You have to be the spirit of an idea." I fingered a blade off my tongue.

"Eh?"

"A totality of struggles, all similar in nature."

"What are you talking about?"

"Go paddle, cloth-head."

"Cloth-head?" Ray got up on hands and knees and softly butted me. "Who is it probes you, with thematic depth and girth."

"Your flaccid ramifications?"

He launched up. "Come on, let's go in it."

"What?"

"See all the Titans and Behemoths, are they a thing? Huns and whatnot."

"Huns were fourteen hundred years ago. And not us. We'd hardly commemorate them. I'm happy here."

"Balls." He sauntered into its shadow.

I couldn't. Not with Ray. Soon I was dozing, a winter's afternoon with Missy, all chic and flappy, staring at our gods with disdain. My hands were in her pockets and her neck smelled of *Molinard*. She was right: these were not progressive people. The deserted crypt just scuttled leaves round our thighs. Then something happened. My sun-warmed retina was splicing blood in. Slash and split and the tinny clap of Carlin's gun. Ripped leg flying against wall. Concave thorax. Missy's choke under the knife in an alley. My face and Missy's dripped. I wiped red sheets off as quickly as they appeared.

No, no wait, now I carry the hamper from Detmold, sunlight splitting trees like a cockscomb - the branches furl and scrape. A deer leans its face from bracken but as Missy points, it looks at her ventriloquist mouth and darts off in a muscled flurry.

It is not progressive, perhaps, to take pride in a fatal clubbing when one's would-be lover walks in trust, gentle and easy beside, occasionally plucking a cowslip.

Karmic, mind. A thousand blades once threatened us, in our greased skin and beards. We knew their tactics - Arminius had studied them - but plumped for clubs and javelins instead. It is crucial to remain Barbarian in slaughter, *isn't that so Missy*?

"It's so beautiful here."

"Yes."

The zig-zag splits and to the right's a bog. I steer left using her ribs. In a slanted glade splitting chicken from the hamper the deer reappears, suffering us for walnut salad.

"Think you'll stay put? For a while?" I say casually, but my eyes and nose meet in fury.

She smooths her plus fours. "In Germany? It's not so bad when the sun's out."

"I meant at the Rotbart but..."

"Matilda keeps telling me I could do better now, and I like her keeping on telling me that," she grins. "Yeah, maybe the Rottie. Maybe Berlin."

"I suppose there'd be people you'd miss."

"Ah, we've world enough and time."

Nice firm 'we'. I stretch out under the dual gazes.

I'm an interstice between huge things; some copper-tinted reprieve. I'll lie here on Strandbad Grünau, toes in the cool Dahme, watch kingfishers lance their ochre.

Wait, where am I?

The only disturbance is a child in the distance, meadow-deep, brought up short by my hatted presence at his favourite swing. I am too large and too small for the times. I am the yellow ray of wisdom, illumination and constancy.

"You are?"

Jophiel has reappeared, uncanoned gender; my virile harvest. A buxom shadow on my shoulder in wide-brimmed straw, gathering her skirts at the waist; she cuts the muggy river with Parisian tang. I close my notebook on Missy's gaze. "Stop nosing, woman. It's dialogue".

"You didn't bring marmalade."

It's a deeper voice, a thinner shadow. Fucking Ray.

"Who eats marmalade for lunch?"

We got the train in petalled dusk. "Read about that Furtwanger feller?" Raymund murmured. "They found more kids."

"More masks?"

"Half-ones. The ones they give veterans. Sick fuck."

~

"I'm sorry to drop by unannounced."

"Albert's son. Dieter."

"Detlef."

"What can I do for you? I followed your father's advice for weeks, no further news."

"Oh. That's all fine. The machine is with the idiot."

"And if we change currency again? There's talk the Rentenmark needs to be… stabilised."

"Paps couldn't give away your whereabouts if he tried. He's dead."

For some odd reason Balthazar looked at his watch, then back at me; confused and shocked.

"Well… I, I… I'm sorry… Albert? He's dead?"

"Very much so."

"Are you OK?"

"I can't not be, can I. It's happened."

"Come in. Keeping you on the doorstep. My god, Albert."

"Yes," I felt his soft furnishings as I passed. "If you don't mind confidentials, he's lying in Carlin Hahn's embrace."

Balthazar looked at me with mixed faces. "Confidentials?"

"Nobody's supposed to know. The sod on Paps' head was meant for Carlin Hahn."

"I read he was dead."

"Sure he's dead. And nicely buried, with Paps in with him."

"You're going too fast. Sit down and have a drink."

"But how much do you want to know? As tensions stand, I'd advise against *any* information."

Balthazar fumbled some crystal glasses and filled them. "Albert's death is unknown."

"Correct."

"OK. Before you spill the lot tell me why you're here. Not that I object."

"Birth certificates."

"Yes."

"You do them."

"I did once."

"Still?"

"*Once* like for a friend, not once upon a time."

"I need one."

Balthazar was foxed. "What for? You're..." Then the merest glimmer of comprehension."Oh, maybe I see."

"You do?"

"Social care. Albert's affairs. That kind of thing?"

Christ, he had a quick mind.

~

Kapuze the Younger sat in a green wing-chair, incongruous I assume, with the handful of military, leather bound books Declan Lehane had collected since becoming an older gentleman. (I checked the spines mind, and they weren't your usual; make your teeth quake: *Home Rule & Infiltrating Terrorism: A Cookbook*; or *Two Centuries of Sovereign Rule: Our Legacy*.).

What would you say about Kapuze? ...He was young, dark and dashing; modelled on Stalin's early work. Nobody much knew about his brother - maybe intentionally - but rumour was the pair, though not twins, looked much the same.

He nodded in my direction. Still unhappy with my presence.

"The boy has vested interests," Lehane batted away. "If anything more so than me. Is that fair to say?" He looked at me.

I nodded.

"Your funeral," Kapuze held up his hands. "It's all set."

"Good."

"I need a favour," I said, clearing my throat and saying it again louder. This humility wasn't suiting me: I'd shoot Kapuze as soon as his back was turned; probably not Declan.

"Seems to be favour day, ask away," Kapuze said.

"I need something from Gerhard before... you know."

"Something you can't get from a corpse?"

"I assume a man like him is swimming in lawyers, and--"

"Hark at him!" Kapuze grinned.

"Hear him out," Declan refused to smile. Perhaps his 'avenues of enquiry' had led him over the earth of my life.

"--and now he owns Paps' theatre. Soon as he's dead it probably gets passed on. I need to release it."

"Any plan?"

"I'll think of something."

"Knee-pants psychos," Kapuze chuckled. "Wanna join our outfit?"

"Well, Mr Kapuze I hear you're a generous and equable employer, but violent robbery isn't a career I want to pursue."

"Bless your little face! Actually it's not so little. Like a Jew fucked a horse."

My eyes shone in anger, but lowered.

Kapuze must have found my serious face amusing, but serious talk deserves gravitas, no? I shoved my jaw into my spangled glass like it was blackcurrant juice and slurped, felt the burn of the neat island whisky on my chest.

When Kapuze was going and me too, Lehane ushered me back. I hung in the lounge with my coat.

"Sit down."

I did as bid.

"Another?" his nails tapped his empty.

"I'm alright."

"Yes."

I sat, as Lehane refilled slowly, came over and sat. After a while:

"There are avenues."

"I'm gonna end up working for them, aren't I."

"No no. Avenues. People, families."

"I'm not with you."

"Sorry, I can be a bit... well Davione says I go round the houses a bit. Waffle."

I shrugged with a tilted head.

"The point is that no bastard, however criminal, is an island."

"Agreed."

"All men have ties to the innocent."

I was about to repeat, but stayed quiet.

"I'm exploring," he said. "...I'm thinking we'll be able to return your father's stake. Upon the same logic, the same abuse of innocence, on which so much has been taken."

"OK," I finally took his meaning. "Would you let me know how and when I should act."

"For sure."

Which I took to mean Ulster techniques and methods. I feel sorry for Lange. He's trying to do right in a painfully wrong world. A place getting wronger by the year.

~

"What the hell is this?"

"Some leaflet. Came through the door."

"Why is it here?"

"I don't know. Ask the person who posted it."

"I mean, why isn't it in the bin?"

"I was reading it."

"When you'd finished, why didn't you *then* put it in the bin?"

"It's interesting. I may find out more."

"You're serious?"

"Yes. Have you read it?"

"I can summarise it, my dear Chorister, in the same way you can summarise the sweat and tears of playwrights." Raymund just shrugged. So I launched: "My kind are holding Germany to ransom."

"Playwrights?"

"Jews. Foreign debt stops Germany being great. Separatists must be imprisoned. The Treaty of Versailles doesn't exist. The October Criminals must be whipped. Oh, and communists are parasites. Have I missed anything?"

"Yes actually, clever little Detlef has missed the crucial point. We have no national pride, because the rug is constantly pulled from under us."

"Who by? The Kaiser? Calvin Coolidge? Scheming Kikes? Look out!" I shouted. Raymund jumped. He was very jittery these days.

"What the hell are you shouting about?"

"There was an invisible Jew behind you with his hand in your pocket."

"Don't play martyr. Obviously I don't agree with that."

"Because you're sleeping with that."

"It's the principle. Germans should take back control of our country."

"It's scapegoating, Ray. Are you stupid and blind also?"

"I just said, didn't I. I don't agree with who they call enemies. I agree we need self-determination back."

"It's scapegoating, Ray. Are you stupid and blind also?"

"I'm not a stuck record."

"If each time you stand up you fall on your arse, who's fault is that?"

"Gravity's."

"And if each time you try to walk you trip over, who do you blame?"

"Badly laid carpets. Uneven paving. Poor civic maintenance."

"Stop being a frivolous bastard, Raymund." I screwed up the leaflet and threw it at him but it veered and dropped short. "That stuff's toxic."

"Frivolous bastard, eh?" He gave me bad eyes. Deep eyes. I suddenly felt very sorry for him. He was trying so hard and having a shaky time. You can be clean twenty-three hours, fifty nine minutes a day. It's just that one minute slip. He was trying so hard. I walked to him and grasped him firmly in my arms. He returned the embrace, but it was so much softer and tremblier than Raymund of old.

"Appropriate authorisation."

"Yes."

"Where would I get this authorisation."

"The courts."

"Authorisation from the courts."

"How long has he been missing?"

"About three weeks."

"Ah. You'll have to wait ninety days."

"And then I can access his affairs."

"No, you'll have to make an application to the courts."

"How long will that take?"

"That I cannot say sir."

"Roughly."

"If Albert Brüning is missing, and I've no reason to doubt you, you'll need confirmation from the police that this is his status, and then make your application to the court, along with identification you are his son and over the age of majority. All being well, you can then act as Power of Attorney, until or unless instructed otherwise."

"What if he were dead."

"If he were dead, perish the thought, a death certificate, unless the executor of his will instructed the courts otherwise, would suffice. However, they would need confirmation, and visibility of his will in that instance."

"So if he isn't dead, but his will instructs someone else to execute his affairs in the event of his death, then what?"

"In that instance, confirmation of his status as missing person would probably be enough for you to execute his affairs temporarily."

"What if I buggered up his affairs?"

"That's up to you sir."

"What if he doesn't have a will?"

"The courts will confirm your eligibility."

"Thanks for your help."

"Sir," said my new pal. But he said nothing more, and primed me a thin one. I left the bank. Should have implied more strongly that Paps wasn't dead to Lange. How can I ask Lange to confirm he's missing if he suspects he's dead?

~

What's the fate of gangsters? Historically I think only three: get away with it and live among loose women and sparkly drinks on yachts; get caught and imprisoned (on release rejoining same), or...

You listen to Captain Lehane studiously when he says 'he'll be busy', because what Captain Lehane doesn't do, is blow hot air.

Yes, the third fate is it gets sorted out starkly, bleakly, away from the police's nostrils.

I mean it was revolting. I only went for a catch-up, tete-a-tete, some light Irish or Grenadine cuisine. Pleasantries, catching up on Missy's news (none), retiring to the lounge, the poured cognac. The smiling but distant face. I was drawing the cognac deep when the tobacco tin landed in my lap.

"Take it or leave it."

I looked up. "I'm alright for now."

"It's not tobacco."

I opened the tin and saw a finger. With a ring on. And the drying gouts around its base. I wondered if I was going to vomit. I certainly wasn't going to pick it up, though such connoisseurism might be expected.

"We laid off the Chicago spray so you could get your dues."

Dues came out like *dyoo-ez*. I felt like a bat'd got too fat and sat in the senior cave. All I could say was: "She's your daughter."

"That's not her finger."

"Yes, obviously. I mean…"

"His wife will still love him one finger the less. And if she doesn't… he'll have to grow a new one."

"Who?"

"Jonas Hahn. A shipping merchant in Bremen. Keeps his nose clean," and he nodded at the tin. "Married with kids."

I had to hurry to catch up with events, in my head. A third Hahn, apparently legit, settled in matrimony and Bremen's salty air, fingers to the tune of nine.

"Sir, you--"

"You don't have to call me Sir. We might one day be relatives, no?"

That also took me aback. It wasn't said like a threat to ask for her hand. It was more like... gruff omniscience. Dismissive even. I got the spooky feeling, in Declan's low-lit teaky lair, that he knew all and had God on his side. Which you'll agree is both helpful and terrifying.

I spoke slowly, phrasing carefully. "I post, or personally take Gerhard Hahn his brother's finger. An innocent... caught in the crossfire as it were."

Declan didn't move; he'd drawn back the curtain and was looking over our shitheap nation, the best bits anyway. "Keep on."

"Which I use as leverage to sign back the theatre."

"We'll do our bit."

"How d'you mean?"

"Protection. A presence."

"Kapuze's lot?"

Declan must've been getting tired of his own curtness. He sat down with a sigh. "There is a convergence of events and feelings. You know? Which has landed with us. Kapuze, the Neukolln constab--"

"Lange."

"Indeed. A weight of feeling wants all Hahns below ground."

I nodded, looked at the tin in my lap. "And poor old Jonas Hahn loses a finger."

A smouldering look ignited; I could almost hear the flame. I'd angered god. "Don't you's fucken dare."

"What?"

"My daughter's face."

"I'm sorry sir. I can do retaliation, a... a... as you know."

After a while, his black wrath began to dissipate. He got up again and paced, uncomfortable with something. "You're a good kid. I'll say that."

I said nothing. He wasn't good at warmth.

"There will come a time..." *here we go* "when water will be thicker than blood. You may think that's a good thing."

He looked at me significantly with the clear, tiger-stripe irises; a stare I had to assume was over my Red tendencies.

I shrugged.

"It's not. It's an illusion. But right now blood is just about thicker than water, and there'll be justice."

~

I looked at the scrumpled sheaf of leaflet on the floor. I went and slowly uncurled it.

"That's why you were in Wedding."

"What?"

"Not communism or social cohesion. And it certainly wasn't a fucking coincidence."

"What you talking about? I helped you home, remember?"

"The enemy. That must have stung. Couldn't have looked good with the cub scouts. Going all bumboy on a Red."

"Fuck off Detty. You're delusional. You should cut back on the drink."

"You rat. You fucking sewer-dweller."

"Yes. Well. *My* latest pursuits tend to be non-violent, eh?" If he'd had a drink, he'd have twirled it winningly at my face. Then Raymund made - I can only assume - a last attempt at aloof and far-flung dismissal.

"What are we doing about dinner?"

"You don't have the fortitude. You fucking snake."

"No, not for a brand new argument. If that's what you want."

"You're still not denying it."

"Fucking hell. You're giving me the shakes. No I don't have much fortitude." The statuesque face was pinched and inverted. "Not now."

"So when then lover? I'll hang around. All agog to see this new Ray when he emerges. So long as he doesn't arrive in rural uniform."

"You're a bitch Dets. You're just being a bitch."

I held up the offending leaflet.

"Leave me alone," he said, and disappeared into the ocean of our bedroom. Once the door'd closed, he shouted: "I'm taking an interest! Forgive any egregious errors I make along the way."

Pfaah! I thought, and bounced around the lounge.

~

"We were a bit concerned." Ernst Bebel's face sparkled in his home; less pallid than daylight. His roaring fire lit contours of affluence. "With all this happening."

"You mean Papa?"

"The papers. Do you have any idea what happened?"

I dipped my eyes, and concentrated on the Georgian beef soup. It was delicious, and Ernst's new wife Rilla seemed intent on it. She'd cooked it. And her flame-red hair curled beautifully round a heart face. Her chest was flushed. All I knew about her was reputation; a firebrand Trotskyite when penning ink but apparently not so in person. In her quietness I felt entropy; attrition. Hot blood.

She threw her cutlery down when a new voice emerged from the darkness behind our lamps and fire.

"That's Otto. Our newest."

"Not our fucking newest, Ernst. *Our* only," floated back gaily through the lounge.

Ernst flapped silverware back at her. "Rilla's quite right. I talk like you're the same, don't I Günter? You and Otto are quite different. À Chacun Son Goût."

(Christ. You've got your work cut out, Ernst.)

"Listen," said Günter. "This is interesting."

"What?"

I was watching dying embers. This house was like some vast geometric bird-hide of sheet glass and timber, wedged against the sky. Ernst and Rilla were arguing over dishes but it died to a bicker; some smoochy grumble. Günter sat on the sofa, splayed in his entirety, with a magazine splashed on his knees.

"What you said?"

"I haven't said anything."

"Carbon monoxide poisoning."

"What?"

"It leaves a body pink. Red even."

"Politics can do that."

"Eh?"

I turned back to look at him. He wasn't amused; now or ever. "I was just saying, politics can turn a man red."

"I'm talking about *women*. Dead bodies. You're like Vati. Ignore what I'm *saying*."

I'd a glass in my hand, swilled. "Go on. Carbymoxide turns women pink."

"*Car*bon Mon*ox*ide. Remember you said your mother was full of blood even though she was drained of blood."

"I don't want to talk about my mother."

"Yes but--"

"Please Günts. I've had a great evening. Let's not dredge up my mother."

"Shut case."

I looked at the fire, dying embers, feeling it was time to go. Ernst and Rilla returned. She wore silk and skin, affected disaffection as she gazed boredly at some cornice. Man, architecture, that's the way forward. That gets you nice shit.

~

I found Paps' will in his home paperwork. Mama's death prompted it, and the whole estate (ha!) is mine on reaching majority. Which I almost have. So damn the bank and Mr. Signature with his brass sleeve clips.

Just need to force Gerhard's hand holding a fountain pen, with a notary present who definitely oughtn't to see any severed fingers. Tricky.

Maybe joining the adult RFB wasn't my best idea. We met in north-central Berlin and, in early mist, I felt the camaraderie of cold men in wool with tempers on a long fuse.

Mine wasn't. You wouldn't choose me for your team.

I hopped off the train at Putlitzstraße, a grassroots worker and African district (Fuchsia's feller worked a crane on Westhafen). I was in violent clothing; frankly insurrectionist. I mean look at me. Black canvas. Balaclava in pocket. I refuse to wear an armband but I'm a short hop from a gas mask. Each day - if days matter to you - is a clash.

Ignore that my membership card reads *Rote Jungfront*. I've a vaster understanding of activism than the acne kids.

We'd a meeting in a theatrical hall near Moabit prison. All sorts of harvest-crazed ruralists got wind, because smashing *Rot-Berlin* is the only activity worth getting the train in for. Bavarian Separatists. Silesian Nationalists. These were lost people, descending on a city with splintering brains. The ones to watch were the NSDAP who, like goat-herders or border control, penned the confused into an armband and doctrine they didn't get, then prodded them toward street skirmishes.

In our own ranks dissent came from Reichsbanner Republicans: a nonsense Menshevik club for lawful parliament manoeuvres.

K✮mrade Riker Keller's voice was rising to its wobbling glissando, when the NSDAP in beige shirts and red accoutrements came in the entrance with bats. One - only one - had a gun, and fired into the roof.

Everyone dived to the floor including Komrade Keller, who managed to crawl to the side fire door, open it, and watch the diaspora. The guy with the gun must have been propaganda - he fired no more. The NSDAP moved out the church entrance to head off the side door with bats.

I was reading my *Examiner* in a rhombus of sun, which contrasted with an altogether chilly Raymund behind... Dear me, Gründgens sprawls on a public pin. This I'd failed to notice.

"It's all very well struggling with addiction, Ray, lying there like a pale young man, but one must always be *about* something. Or one may as well be French."

(Rest without industry, industry without rest: it's how the drugs get hold.) He just smoked with long brattish fingers, as though the taste annoyed him. "C'est moi."

And what the hell is a comparison microscope? I don't like the sound of that. Though Lange could hardly harass me more, with such pressure, might there be a temptation to fidget evidence?

Calls for Neukölln Police Chief to Resign

Yesterday at a press conference received with unprecedented anger, Hauptkommisar Gründgens was called to account over the staggering level of violence erupting in Neukölln.

In defiant tone *BZ am Mittag*'s reporter asked: 'Do you have undeclared business interests in the borough with certain brothers? I know who's responsible for the shootings. My wife knows. Her ninety year old father Griswald knows. All Neukölln knows. Why are you not making arrests?'

'We are employing the latest ballistic and forensic techniques. Charges require evidence, and we have had a comparison microscope shipped from California to put that together.'

When questioned about the string of female murders linked to the Oranienstraße killing, Detective Inspector Grundgens stated: 'Our investigation proceeds as fast as possible without risking error. While press and public become impatient for arrests, it would be worse to draw hasty conclusions and file erroneous charges. This would tarnish the Kriminalpolizei's reputation and raise further risk to the public if the killer remains at large.'

He was greeted with sarcastic laughter and catcalls: But the killer is at large! ...What the hell are you doing? ...Resign Grundgens! ...Hand in your badge.'

~

"Someone to see you sir."

Lange looked up. "Detlef. Come in."

"Sorry to pitch up unannounced."

"Oh it's my honour," Lange actually smiled and dipped a mock-bow. "No summons."

I didn't say anything, and the silence grew old.

"What can I do for you? Sit, please."

"I'll help you as best I can," I said. I'd figured out a lot last night blinking in the dark, and on the way here, but I'd tread carefully.

"Where to start? As you've probably read, Neukölln's running riot over our enquiries."

"I read Gründgens drubbing by the press, yes."

"His problem," Lange said quite dismissively.

"Not a fan?"

"We're off topic."

"Mm."

I looked at the proferred chair in its pool of sunlight, swirling dust specks up as I sat. "This is delicate. I'm in a dangerous position, you understand."

"No, I don't understand because you've said nothing."

"What I mean is--"

"What you mean is you want confidentiality, and I can't promise it."

My eyes flicking back at the door betrayed me. I was close to getting up and getting out.

"However, I'm aware that in your bereavement the cases we're looking at may be distressing, and that you're a minor. I can't guarantee confidentiality, but I've no wish to cause distress."

"We need to help each other. You'll understand why when I'm finished."

"I'm an officer of the law." Lange spread his hands out.

I breathed deep. "My father was killed by Gerhard Hahn."

I let this sink in, as Lange's face nosedived into shock. "Your father's dead?"

"I saw it happen at Carlin's funeral. Just before it, Gründgens was graveside in civvies, batting away cameras. I don't know if he knew, because the congregation moved away before it happened. But... I kind of think he must've."

"Carlin's funeral?"

"Yes."

Lange was deeply confused. "You were at the funeral, witnessing your father's murder?"

"No. Well yes. I was there but hidden in the, like... shrubs. Nobody knows I saw it."

"You reported him missing two weeks ago."

"Because I'm stuck. If I tell you where the body is, it's a matter of days before Hahn gets hauled in, at least for questioning. But unless he's a missing person I can't execute his affairs."

"You can't anyway, you're too young."

"Mm."

"What's that mean?"

"I need to execute his affairs."

"Whoa. You realise there are repercussions here. You're an orphaned minor."

"That's why I'm appealing to your better nature."

"My dereliction you mean?"

"I'm not asking for dereliction."

"You are."

"I'm asking for trust, man to man."

"Officer to minor."

I huffed and flipped out my hands. My hopes had backfired.

"I thought you were coming to help with the damned Oranienstraße stuff. And you spring me another one."

I looked up, I supposed, like a wounded animal.

"Forgive me, that was unprofessional. I'm dreadfully sorry Detlef."

"It's OK. The shock passed quite quickly, the whole thing was so sudden. But... I mentioned his affairs because I think he signed over his assets before he was killed. That's why I asked you to keep this to yourself."

Lange's eyes narrowed. "This is nothing like the whole story is it." He sighed and got up, disconcerted. "You picked a great place to tell me. Shall we get out of here? If I'm entering dereliction, might as well do it in style."

In the foyer Lange signed me out, "I'll drive him home."

He pulled up his dark green Daimler in the street beside Cafe Pushkin.

At the chipped round table I laughed nervously. "I guess you're relaxed here, can speak freely."

"I guess I can."

"Among friends."

Lange looked over my shoulder. A waiter hovered.

"Pushkin's waiters are famously discreet. Isn't that so Maria."

"Afternoon Herr Lange. Are you well?"

"I'll be the better for a beer, and you Detlef?"

"Er, Cassis."

Maria disappeared.

Lange frowned at the front window absently. There was a terrace for fashionable nobodies to receive sunshine with their coffees.

"See that guy," he pointed at the back of someone's head through the big stencilled glass. "That's who I have to deal with."

I turned and looked. Couldn't really see anyone Lange-related and turned back. "Deal with? What, an informant?"

Lange laughed. "Hell no. That's Gründgens' boss. Well technically mine too. Comes here 5:30 on the dot every day. Stares across the plaza on his own."

"Do you have to deal with him?"

"If Gründgens plays up. The guy's retiring soon. When I go in his office it's like some drooling nursing home. Losing his marbles. Shouldn't be allowed."

"What's a comparison microscope?"

"There's a clue in the name," Lange eyeballed a menu.

"Thanks."

"It's ballistics. Well, forensics too. I asked some boffins in California to ship one."

"You'll have to enlighten me."

"Forensics is like, crime-scene investigation. Some people are claiming... well, leave that for now... but ballistics is trajectories of bullets, barrel signatures, that kind of thing. Why?"

"I figured it was to do with bullets. That's why I asked for discretion, or dereliction. How would it help you if I could pull all the guns from Hahn's arsenal... *before* you disinterred Paps."

'Thanks,' Lange nodded at the waiter and took a slow sip. Seemed he liked to mull things. "So your father was shot."

I nodded.

"You'd have to get all the guns. Hypothetically. If I allowed you to do that."

"I can narrow the weapon down. Stubby, high-pitched."

"Yeah, that's the Hahn's preferred Mauser."

"Really?" I scoffed. "Tell that to Kühn the barber. He got perforated with daylight."

"I want to talk about your mother."

"You do?"

"Seeing as we're man to man, for a little while."

"Sure."

"I think my superior wants to frame either you or your fa... late father, as the Neukölln serial killer."

He let that sink in, but sink in it had long ago.

"Explains his diligent inspection of our fire equipment."

"The man's a lunatic in civil clothing. I can't abide him, and he can't abide your race."

"Judaism isn't a race. And I'm Catholic. I mean I'm not, but you see what I mean."

Lange was amused. "He who is without sin casts the first stone."

"Hell does that mean?"

He eyed me seriously. "I know it was probably self-defence. On the Havel."

"Are you off duty?"

Lange toyed his glass, himself glassy. "What can I say? I can't unknow what I know."

"You could if you were drunk. Right," I took another deep breath. "We went on a stroll. A bunch of hicks threw rocks at Missy. She got one in the head. I'm not talking about pebbles. It was a biblical stoning man. Rocks. They stoned her for being a coon. She ended up face-down in the river. I'd taken to carrying a too--"

"Yes? A tool?"

"Whatever I could," I opened out my palms like, *come on*. "So I went in. Initially it was self-defence but..."

"Stop there."

I did for a bit. Got another tumbler of glittery booze. The place filled a little: family outings, lone drunks, tatty reds with scurrilous eyes and of course, Gründgens' drooling boss greenhousing the sun.

As I've said Neukölln is odd. Austrian Adolf calls it Redkölln. Which it isn't. Not really. People want relief. I told you earlier about the cops. How the police are divided and confused: they like established order, but far-righters blame everyone left of themselves for 1919, including the police. The directive from above (supported by imperial magistrates) is to punish Commies. Half the police are sick of arresting starving Reds for robbery or underpaying or fighting, and sympathise with socialism. See?

"They're like mamas to me."

"Who?"

"The girls, those drama queens. If some bastard on the street can shoot in the name of greed or politics, I can protect my own."

Lange gave a middle-distance laugh that was more a huff. "I was hoping you'd help me with Oranienstraße."

On that note I was getting miffed. "Look, I know nothing about bloody Oranienstraße. Forget about me and The Grand. I've come to talk about what I *have* been involved in."

"Alright. But you're still appended to that enquiry."

"Edsel Richter should be in prison for Mama's murder, 'cept he's in a mental asylum. So please don't ask about *similarities.*"

Lange produced a pack of cigarettes - unsuited to his face - and toothed one. "My boss isn't bright. That's the first thing you should know. The second thing... " Lange leant back, flapped smoke and shook his head. "Jesus... discussing police business with a boy."

I took it, but couldn't take the blousy brasserie tone. "Except you haven't."

"I'll corner Gründgens. Get him out. I need to prove he's taking money."

"Which I suppose, brings us to Michael Hartmann."

"Correct."

"You trust him, or is it money?"

"There are benefits in going to the highest bidder. For me."

"Unless you're outbid. But then, Gründgens would have to know something was for sale."

Lange laughed. "Shouldn't you be at school?"

Chinwag concluded we parted ways. I looked at old tonsured Gründgens' boss from the front. It was the very still man from the *Wien*; Pickelhauber. Is that what getting old means? An endless impervious stare, on your own.

"Ray, can you put your foul socks in the basket? You wear them for days."

"I don't."

"You do. I've seen you putting yesterday's on in the morning."

"So's I don't soil a new pair before I've washed."

"You can't be that dirty."

"Ergo, neither can my socks."

"Just put your fucking laundry down."

Too much whiskey and the unclear brunt of morning (and a rather active night judging by my gait). The only route out of still-drunkness was air and salty schnitzel. So I left Raymund dribbling, headed to Potsdamer.

I'd picked up my letter to post on the way out, thumbing her name, hesitating in the hall until the ground floor flat opened and its owner mistily ogled me.

My Missy of the South,

I've become dislocated from the youth you see in those photos. It's hard to explain and I have a confession...

Cowardly to confess in handwriting, but this way I get the honesty of distance; the honesty of composition.

I was indeed with that 'beautiful wreck' while we were together. I hesitate to say I swing both ways because I've not, before or since, been attracted to another man. (And those psychoanalysis sessions I was going to? They were supposed to *cure* me!).

The reason I feel so ripped up and splintered is because I loved both of you for different reasons; yours was the realer.

After you left, I pulled Raymund in from the streets, into *your* flat. He was in a bad way - skinny as a loungeroom manta ray and taking morphine and cocaine for breakfast; the one to calm, the other to awaken: I mean, where can that reasonably end?

I realised it was an act of charity, not desire, which was a healthy conclusion (no?).

He made great efforts to clean up. And succeeded. But as each temple is demolished, another takes its place. We have to worship somewhere, and Raymund was showing disastrous affiliations to the far-right. It was, I suppose, mere filler for the vacuum. But I was at a Communist rally in Moabit and turned a corner to walk slap bang into Ray during street riots, bad clashes. (Tempting to announce to his brown-shirted coterie he's a bumboy. They'd be thrilled).

We had a showdown: a confrontation. Shortly after that he lapsed and dived back into junk.

So, why am I telling you this. Perhaps I am evading another piece of news - one which I cannot write, I feel too paranoid and raw to put it in ink. There was another death. A violent one. Someone we have strong ties to. Me in blood (ever evaporating), and you in the theatre work and accidental revenge he put your way.

What I said is true. I do love you and miss you. And I wish you'd come back to Berlin to ground me in your life. To laugh at my pretention. To ignore my idiocy and furrow me in your body. You are the ground I would have swallow me up.

Always in highest regard,

Detlef.

~

"I understand Inspector Lange is all over you. Both of them, in fact."

"And you're a man of great understanding. Piss off Michael."

"No need for that."

"No?"

I was in a bad mood. I'd waited until Gerhard the Killer went for his 10pm krug and office lights were out, and leveraging the Rotbart fire escape, I claw-hammered his door hinges and cabinet, establishing that Gerhard's gun stash was empty - either all in use or he'd moved it. And it didn't escape me that for every indiscreet break-in, Gerhard might write off any previous murders as mistaken foes.

"Let me buy you a drink."

"Can't you get what you need from the dailies?"

"That puts me beyond use."

"You have one?"

"I'll buy you that drink."

"Fine."

They arrived, little pockets of amber, and Hartmann made great fuss with cardboard mats. "All that garbage I wrote about your mother and Oranienstraße. It sells. But its not what I'm interested in."

"How noble. Putting my family in the spotlight while the public clamour for an arrest."

"Alibis tight?"

"God," I couldn't help but laugh. "You're very hard to like Michael. Which is a shame. In another life eh?"

"Well... I'm just buying you a drink. Is all."

"You don't have your notebook out."

"No."

"I suppose you've dug out that I'm gay."

"Not really."

"Well half."

"You were dating the queen of Neukölln."

"Jeez man. You make me uncomfortable."

"She *is* a beauty."

I had to stare hard, because I didn't know what was in that. "So what are you interested in?"

"Your Papa."

"OK," I rounded on the stool. "Why don't you say what you want. Maybe I'll spill. But I'll decide once you're straight."

"Sure," Hartmann waved stifling air with the back of his hand. "Every faint track becomes a bridleway, which joins a road that leads back to the people you've killed."

"I'd advise you keep your voice down."

"Advise away."

Hartmann's company was now spiky and invasive.

I spoke in a gabble: "The hammer that killed Lorenz Beck killed Carlin, who slashed Missy and whose death caused my father's."

"What?"

"Nothing." I sat at my teak, swilling.

"What did you say."

"How's about I send you a manuscript. That's what you like."

"Deal. I need to ask you something."

"No more questions."

We sat hunched and cold a while, tapping our glasses.

"Just about Missy's fa--"

"Like I say, you'll get a manuscript."

~

"Are you's a racist, Mr. Kapuze?"

"If you want to discuss German purity, I'm the wrong man. Though I do wonder."

"What?"

"Where it can go?"

"Well that's obvious. Wealth and opportunity. At least on *that* we agree, no?"

"How long do these golden eggs get laid for? I'll grant you there's a fad. A novelty in all this..." he pushed away the air, "...Yankee glitz."

"Perhaps we're leaning out of different pulpits, Mr Kapuze. As a safe breaker, a wholesale robber, I'd've thought you also had a grip on economics."

A sideways tilt, mirrored by his hand, confirmed that was perhaps true.

"And economics respects no borders, nations or races. In that regard it's truly unprejudiced."

"As I said, there's a shelf life."

"To what? Again I'll ask you are you a racist Mr. Kapuze?"

Kapuze grinned. "I'm Italian. Of course I am."

"My daughter is a beautiful Mulatto. Well she was. Now the best money she can make is here, in Berlin, the Große. She wants to come back. But the minute she squirrels away enough to live comfortably, I'll ship her home again."

There was no trace of mirth. The captain's tone becoming menacing.

"That's how economics sets foot in your Germany. I'm afraid that runt Austrian is correct. The world will exploit you. No-one's above it."

And Berlin just hunkers ignoring our confusion: the stuff that might one day rattle it.

Ray was kind. No really, talked in my ear on the screechy trains. He was coming on in bounds with that 'what do other people do' schtick. I respected it, to the point I forgot about an unopened letter from Missy at the flat.

I picked it up the following evening and it read:

Hey my lover,
    Truth to say I got all heartache at your photo and reading your awful news. I splashed many. I know what you meant by 'someone we have close ties to is

236

gone'. Took me a while (accounting for my late reply). You must be in shock. I'm so sorry. What happens to the Rottie? And living arrangements. Any arrangements? I wish I was there.

Now I gotta say, I knew all along about Raymund. Which doesn't mean you can move him in, charity or not!

But I ain't addressing these sordids before I say mine. I'm in turmoil 'cause Matilda's *still* trying to get me into the Große. I'm overseas for G**'s sake but she doesn't get that, because what's maybe is definite in her head.

Mom and Pops are near you. Are they OK? I ask them, but I get skaty crap like 'xx sends love' or 'hope it's working out back home'. It ain't news and it *ain't news*.

What's happening. I'm falling apart. That river I told you about, with the orange sunsets and dancing flies, sometimes it seems like a storm-drain or sewer. Yeah I know.

But I read into Pops' letters - or his inserts in Mom's - like: 'until the coast's clear'. Is that just my wanderlust or is that the scene?

I mean if it's true I'll just ready my bags. I miss you horsehead nebula. Miss my family and the chattering girls. I miss the lights and lies.

And in regards us.

Well, what are we?

When I retire to bed and Bessie is snoring (fully-clothed downstairs), your face appears, maybe a moon. Maybe a guardian.

Far lover.

Missy.

Ray was all hands and I couldn't stand it. I got up and sat naked on a chair - not quite, I still had socks on - with a whisky the size of Belgium.

I looked on flickering Berlin like maybe Berlin was the imposter, the illusion. A city jutting in civilian confidence, believing itself above Germany, which now corrupts from the sticks inwards. From Prussia and the south our edges burn with bigotry.

"What you doing Dets?"

"Go back to sleep Ray."

I need more. I'm a pre-Raphaelite; a Nazarine outrun. I need more than Proserpine's fateful fruit; these polemic seasons...

He raised himself on an elbow. "Want to talk?"

"Go to sleep."

...Details on what exactly *is* above and below us. I need evidence, damn it, that we're more than this daily mess.

Missy's letters, perhaps unwittingly, draw her back through time. (I lock them safely, her composed scrawl). Sometimes when she looks at me I see all womankind. The direct gaze, the ripe skin and binge and giggle. Maybe she's my higher, my Ceres. My spirit and my Proserpine.

Ray lapsed. The opium pipe came out - a bamboo thing with pewter attachments, or the little stained ivory one - then after a while he counteracted it (while still using it) with cocaine in his wine. Eventually he was smoking heroin again and not eating. The decline was not swift, but with an inner drive I couldn't distinguish between delusion or heavy purpose.

I would look on, not judgmentally, just in my own torpor: realising man's will is not his own. Least, not when you know the breadth of your options. And you can string out fucking-yourself-up for quite a while.

When he was most receptive I'd give him yoghurt and peaches, or whatever fruit we had. Stupidly thinking a shot of vitamins would have him bounding with the joys of spring. I began to drink heavily. He might have thought it was sympatico but it was actually a means to talk and act as recklessly as him.

Usually I chose what I said carefully, but one of alcohol's wondrous effects is a disregard for, and use of, bits of truth.

~

"We still meeting like this?"

"When officialdom is required." He wasn't smiling; no trace.

"I couldn't get the pieces. They tightened up."

"Least of your worries."

"Has something happened? I thought--"

Lange was troubled, and kept darting glances at me as he paced.

"My... superior will be officially questioning you and your father. Well, the latter in absentia."

"For what?"

"The Oranienstraße murder and... that of your mother."

"Pardon me?"

"Gründgens has... concluded from the evidence, that the *marks* in the deceased's bones are the same. From the same weapon. From the same hand."

"What marks?"

"Striations in the bone, same blade, same cutter's tools. Each edge leaves a signature."

"Balony. What are you talking about? Is this more microscope rot? That's for bullets."

"We have bone samples."

"Lucky you. Chopping up victims on a slab. What a life you lead."

"And what a life *you* lead, Detlef. Cross-sections indicate the same weapon, through identical imperfections in the whetting, and your prints are all over the weapon."

"What *whetting*? And where is he? If I'm accused of matricide by that lunkhead I'd like him in the room."

"Would you now. I'm afraid," Lange pressed his head at the window. "The evidence is in his favour."

"Am I under arrest?"

"Unless you give me a blinding reason not to."

"We've an arrangement," I heard myself weakly announce.

Lange's face was livid and scared. "You've dug a hole Detlef. It's not just the bloody Hahns who dig our graves is it."

I recalled Günter in firelight. "Maybe I can."

"Can lie? Screw my career? Give me a reason?"

"A reason not to arrest me, yes," I said calmly. "You'll have to let me go."

"I tried that."

"Try again."

~

And then I came in one day and his bag was packed. His little leather suitcase, as thin and unstuffed as himself. And just as battered and distressed.

"What are you doing?"

"I've got to go home."

"Why?"

"Because I'll die. If I don't."

"Ray, if you die it's by your own hand. It doesn't have to be like this."

"I can't help it. I need to go home. It's the only way."

He looked so miserable; so truly beaten. Time had taken and shaken him. Time had nurtured and coaxed the little sapling only to turn on it like a howling gale in adulthood. It had lured him with promises and poisoned him in an alley. Fucking time. Fucking Raymund.

"Maybe it's best," I said softly. "Hannover, right?"

He nodded.

"How are you getting there?"

"Train."

"Have you got a ticket?"

"I was going to sell crystals at the station."

"Christ Ray. Wait. I might have enough."

I rummaged in a tin. "Come on, we'll take the Stadtbahn together."

"Thanks Dets."

I walk with Raymond down the street: rickety Adonis on a pole of calcium; Lothario undone.

Self Portrait with Turmoil

Redkölln '27

Who should be accompanying Lange in the corridor but Michael Hartmann, publisher of 'investigative fiction', and now apparently a sleuth.

"It's far-fetched," said Hartmann. "It would take a level of skill and research I doubt anyone but you has in this den."

"The hell does that mean. I'm trying to solve the bloody thing not implicate myself. "

Hartmann shrugged.

"I checked the samples. There was no similarity."

"And now there is." Hartmann's face opened like a pair of arms, as if to say QED.

And the desk officer cleared his throat loudly to indicate me and Günter sitting, swinging our legs waiting, in this strangely dead precinct.

"That's opportune," said Hartmann, "We were discussing you."

Lange glared at Hartmann, which I took to mean *you're sharing?* "Only very indirectly," Hartmann backtracked.

"What's up Michael, you want exclusive pulp? "

"I should probably clear something up between the thre... Who's the boy. Is he with you?"

Günter slid off the chair still clutching my rolled up *Forensics Quarterly*, grown sweaty and creased in his palm.

"Günter Bebel. Aspiring forensician... is that a word? "

"Maybe. In time. "

"We, er..." I wagged my finger between the pair of us; our bizarre duo. "...Günter may have some pertinent info."

"Confidential police info?" Lange flung a look at Hartmann.

"Confidential in that I'd want Plague Town here to hop it, or sign a non-disclosure."

"In which regard. Which case?"

"Well. You can judge. "

"I apprehend, I don't ju--"

"You're so literal Lange. And a better man for it."

Following Lange into the guts of his establishment one got the feeling everyone awaited the footfall of Gründgens. Like some enraged tyrant or unruly god.

"Come on then silver-spoon, Bebel Junior, what have you got for us?"

Günter rose to no bait. Either oblivious or above it; it was hard to tell from his businesslike face. "Well on a side note, the Rottie fire axe has nothing to do with Oranienstraße. I've had it in my possession for nearly a year. Detlef spotted it when he was at ours."

"Doesn't rule out Zelda Brüning. Or you as the murderer, little man, come to that," Lange gave an amiable grin.

Günter's head drew back like Lange was an imbecile. "No-oo." Günter looked around, "So to business, do you have any photos of the Zelda Brüning crime scene?"

Lange's eyes flicked briefly at me. "Somewhere around."

"Would you fetch them?"

Lange spluttered. "Fetch them?"

"Find them, if you can, and bring them out. Also any issues of *Forensics Quarterly* you may keep hold of."

"I've a private subscription, at home."

"Hmm," Günter tapped his lip. "Then I'll explain my thinking and you can corroborate in your own time."

Lange shot a curious grin at me.

"You see, Detlef said the most memorable oddity at his mother's death was that though she was bisected and dismembered, she remained a flushed pink. Which you'd hardly expect from a half-drained corpse. Hence I asked for the FQ issues to illustrate."

"Many of our crime scene photographs would back that up."

"Carbon monoxide poisoning."

"Eh?"

"It leaves the body a flushed red permanently. She was dead from CO poisoning before an axe went near her. Because you couldn't get CO into her blood unless she was respiring. And we know the pair argued and drank copiously, in... in the absence of Detlef and his papa. Cooked on the stove."

"We do?" --Lange's eyes crimped.

I waved at him like an ignored ghost. "I lived there?"

Günter pushed his glasses up with fat thumbs. "Uncooked food on the hob from the previous evening and plenty of empty bottles."

"Mm," said Lange. "All this we knew, of course."

"Convinced?" I chirped. "*And* Richter's schizophrenic."

"That's a mechanism," Lange said. "What about motive? And the small matter of cutting her to pieces."

"Oh come on."

"What."

"He *thought* he'd killed her, so he disposed of her. Got interrupted and it looked like a psychopath's work." I glanced between Lange and sleuth Bebel. "I mean, a normal psychopath."

~

Nothing had changed when the respectful gravedigger had outlined and dug away from flesh. Papa lay with his pale face confused and angry, hugging Carlin's coffin like an enraged fan.

The birches and poplars rattled pale leaves. Steam punctuated our heads like terrible ideas. The digger's shovel, each time, made the same sound as my hammer in Carlin's neck, like penance or a chain gang; 'chok, lift, slump, chok, lift, slump'.

Maybe Hahn & Kloss scrapyard wasn't Gerhard's preferred burial site, nor the shipping canal. Maybe this was. What better place to inter hundreds of misdeeds than a cemetary, where the people lie undisturbed and a congregation is expected, complicit in concealment.

"Well it's not proof," Lange said, "but I can make Gerhard's life miserable until it is."

I stared at Paps unfocused, a little swimmingly in the dusk. "When you've done what you need to, can you put him on ice? Keep the press out? I don't know what I'll do about a resting place. If it gets out, I'm in social care."

Lange weighed this. "While I can."

The digger's shovel hit something metal. He peered into the earth. Then more delicately dug around whatever he'd hit.

Lange went over to the gravedigger in his suitably earthy clothes. I heard: "Service charge," and a banknote passed. "Your time's appreciated."

Digger doffed a cap. "You should take a closer look, sir."

Lange's face creased, but then he looked into the earth. "You may be in luck Detlef."

I walked across, and the digger gingerly stepped into the grave with a rake to pick out a gun by its trigger-guard; a Mauser.

"Ha!" I shouted. "He wasn't waving. He was tossing."

Lange stared at me.

"The fool threw the gun in after the body. I thought he was just waving some curse at Paps."

"Please tell me," said Lange, "he wasn't wearing gloves."

My shoulders slumped. "I think he was."

Lange turned back to the digger. "Listen, you don't speak to anyone. If I see any headlines, if Gerhard Hahn acts strange," he turned and pointed at the red building behind, "if any frocks in there find out, anyone at all, I'll arrest you for obstructing justice. There's an enquiry on and I need silence."

Queen of the Boards,

It's three a.m. and the streets are quiet, and I feel you are still my lover and altar; my angel and redeemer.

Raymund has disappeared. He plumbed new smack depths and relinquished all will. One morning (I was not haranguing him or making life difficult: I was supportive and his chef too) he looked up from despair and said he was going home. Home for Raymund is Hannover. He has wealthy and remote parents in the suburbs there.

He never arrived. I called the number I'd prised from him a week ago to see how his clean-up was going, but his parents' were clueless. 'What homecoming? We haven't seen him in over a year.'

I don't know if you follow German prattle, but a predator in Hannover - don't laugh, he's dubbed the Butcher of Hannover and subsequently 'Wolf' and 'Vampire' due to certain methods - was arrested and faces twenty-seven charges of murder. This beast - Fritz Haarman - has been picking up rentboys and Bohos, musicians and down-at-heel runaways at Hannover station, before the unspeakable...

I am worried. He's disappeared and he fits the bill.

I cannot bury my father properly, partly lack of money, and for other reasons I can't go into.

Violence is all around me, or that's what it feels like. Do you wish to associate with me? These constant shocks build up, and it seems my culture is a neat paving stone to be lifted and watch the seething ants beneath.

I'm not going to dissuade you from coming. Of the three people who want you back in our theatres, two have cast a vote in favour, and you are undecided. That makes 2.5 out of 3. Come home!

Until you do, I will describe your face in the stars on clear nights.

Love ever after,

Dets.

I did consider visiting Hannover to pay condolences to Raymund's folks, but that extinguishes all hope doesn't it - or accelerates its fall - and anyway I'd never met them. What use is a stranger saying "sorry to hear".

Opposite the Pharussäle in Wedding I stood like a gawping child, skint and, I realised, aimless now. I was quite far back from a militant throng around the steps. A banner above proclaimed: "The Collapse of the Bourgeois Class State", with a gentle breeze flapping it. My rent was due in three weeks and I had a measly thousand Rentens to my name.

I felt a firm grasp around my bicep. I looked up, sleepy and compliant: I was being picked up by the KriPo's comedy assistants, the keystone LaPo in uniform.

"Hands where we can see them. Don't want you hammering anyone."

"Thor Junior," said a laughing voice I couldn't see.

"What are you arresting me for?"

"Well I'd prefer to arrest your father, but he's gone walkabout."

I recognised that voice.

Police and the back row of Nazis were looking at me. It seemed to me that civilians also stopped and stood behind their ranks. I don't mean they were blocked by the crowd, I *think* I mean they were supporting the cordon. Tacitly.

"Walkabout, you serious?"

"Serious as a corpse trail."

"You don't know?"

"Know what? If you want to shop your father and save your skin, just let me know where he is."

"You *don't* know. Christ. You're not so deep in their pockets. Aaaagh," a twisted arm shut me up.

"Yeah, well. Let's get this one packed away."

"Where's Lange?"

"Never you mind. New policies."

And behind that cordon of brown, melting into workshirts and brogues and shopkeepers' aprons, I saw Herr Defeats, his face ghostly milk-white. Perhaps - if I didn't get locked in a cell - I'd attend school next week, ask him all about it. Except... he was Herr Defeats, so if he threw his weight into your cause - I giggled as I was shoved in the van - the outcome was surely foregone.

~

My block-headed mule,

Your news of Raymund is frightening. I dip my head in prayer (you hear them in Berlin?). I'll say I'd have liked to meet him. Minus the junk. Sounds like he had more than he gave.

250

But don't jump to conclusions, maybe he arrived and thought better, went wandering, holed up somewhere to cold turkey... Could be anything.

I am coiled like a spring with news.

I'm coming back, if you'll welcome me? Will you have me? Passenger. Tourist. Matilda has secured me a part, a gig at the Große, and better still a few months' residence. Rehearsals have already started so there's a blank spot - or maybe an understudy? - til I get there. She said I'd be letting her down and her name would be mud if I didn't show.

I worry about you Detlef. You're a magnet for the worst of Berlin. I cannot speak of your father, as I don't know or understand your circumstances.

And with me coming back and all. I have to write short and quick, as I am frantically arranging my travel. Will it make you feel good to know... I am not buying my return ticket yet?

I hope so.

Please ensure all linen is washed and fresh towels are available, and then you may retire. I breakfast at ten o'clock.

Until the 26th then,

✗

Missy.

Being thrust shamefully through the front foyer, I saw Hartmann, off stage in the wings, in a glossy corridor looking in; to the drama of my life. Michael bloody Hartmann.

Lange was around. And it didn't take long with Gründgens' face in my own before he arrived. 'Cept now he was as quiet as a shrew.

"So."

"So what?"

"Comparisons. Bone samples."

"I don't need to know the inner workings of your lurid profession."

"Unless you *are* the inner workings."

"Officer Lange." I cast about. "You're a proper cop. Can he just haul me in and make cryptic comments? Is that due process?"

Gründgens himself sarcastically agreed. "Yes comrade Lange, is this acceptable to you? I'd love to know your exciting liberal views."

Lange wasn't in my corner. "You should probably hear the Chief out."

"Excellent," Gründgens turned back to me. "Now I have a mandate from a junior officer to do my job."

"It's not technically your--"

"Enough!"

And Lange didn't look comfortable, not with two obedient juniors in the room probably also on a payroll.

"Has my colleague provided any information on the evidence we'll be holding you on?"

"No. How could he?"

"So. We've taken bone samples, thigh bones, from Oranienstraße and your mother's murder, and both match the murder weapon."

"How on *earth* can you deduce that? Why are you carving up my Mama! What bollocks. I think you might be taking this forensics gimmick too far."

"We already had the samples. ...Striations. Whetting tools. They align."

"Do they. Officer Lange, can I have a cigarette?"

The pair of opposed officers looked at each other, appeared to agree, and Lange left for some. Gründgens shouted: "Bring the photostats."

Minus his 'evidence' Gründgens seemed a bit unanchored.

I ventured: "Lot of pressure on you."

His eye peered.

"I read the papers man. You said yourself, locking up the wrong guy twice would reflect badly."

Gründgens grinned. "Oh, no no, we've got our guy." He looked at his accompaniment in the room. Quiet, stolid. Cheats and liars. "You see, forensics can shape itself around the accused."

I looked at my shoes. All seemed lost without Lange in attendance. Well. Also with Paps gone, Mama gone, Carlin gone, Lorenz gone; and Missy expected shortly for an arrested boyfriend. I saw Lange's head returning, bobbing behind glass.

"Officer Lange has the evidence we'll charge you with."

"Not quite. Sir," Lange announced at the door.

"What d'you mean?"

"There's strong indications that the Oranienstraße body was tampered with. Samples were replaced. It's rather alarming. It not only casts doubt on the Oranienstraße murder, but our general procedures and practice. Our overall security. Diligence."

"You shit. You pile of shit."

"Does that mean my application for Governance is rejected?"

"You're no better than me." Gründgens' face looked sourer than I'd ever seen. "All louses."

"Lice," replied Lange.

~

I was walking home and saw a shape, shivering in February rain. It had put on a little weight, but its head still darted about sharply. Beside it was an unmistakable hatbox and a round-cornered floral suitcase.

I was crossing the street and she clocked me.

"What the hell?" I yelled. "You're a day early. I was gonna--"

"I changed my ticket. Got a headwind. Your country's an icicle, get the bloody kettle on the hob and put me to bed."

She'd almost beaten her own letter.

"When I've seen to that Ma'am, may I retire for the evening."

Her widened mouth allowed the broadest of grins, and she jumped on me, heavy with Southern food; I staggered.

"If I'm happy with your work yes, you may retire."

"Jesus girl. We need to get you back in the practice rooms."

"What are you suggesting?" But she was all big-cat nuzzles; bitey.

She stayed over that night, and the fuzz of her nethers pressed with trans-Atlantic absence. Throughout she murmured *baby-child*, and I guessed I'd never outgrow that; unless she meant something quite different.

Following morning she announced she wanted to spend a few days with Mama, until her crates came. I should give her a bell when they did, or just come over.

To a surprise that shamed me, Missy immediately had work. I don't know why I doubt her and live so pessimistically. That girl laughs more than I do.

It's clear that theatre directors are getting squitty over the commandeering of art by the masses. (Movies, radio, all this cheap new tat.) Any Fritz with one shoe, no job and a broken hat can 'do art', so plays have hit the doldrums. Missy's role, poached by the *Großes* artistic director Erik Charell, was in *The Stuffed Shirt and the Bolshevik*.

A commie has an affair with a general's bored wife. He also has another mistress, a shrewish homebody played by a Missy totally miscast. The only decent aspect is she gets to sing a sad song. After much to-ing and fro-ing that makes no sense, the General shoots his wife and the commie. It left a sour taste, close to home. The dead commie has gangster friends who work hand in hand with the police to bring the General to justice, to draw parallels between gangsterism and the constabulary, you catch me? Christ...

General
Who are you to arrest me with your *new republic?* You serve us and we instruct you. We make law and rid the Fatherland of

vermin. Do you want communism in your life and home?

Officer

Never tried it. I suppose it tastes like boiled cabbage. Anyway you can't just shoot who you fancy or I'd shoot half of Berlin.

General

You're no better than the tick who held me 'til you arrived. This administration cannot last, remember that, it is built on swamp.

Officer

Well the subsidence should make your escape easier.

Court proceedings are projected on a screen behind, a white-bearded papier mache head sits among pistons and a conveyor belt with flat-capped workers walking in line past it, the other end of the stage Missy sits behind a sewing machine looking demure, while the dead lovers' ghosts dance in white.

We walked through the lobby.

"Your part was awful."

"Thanks Hon."

"No, obviously you were wonderful. But the role."

Apart from the queasy murder scene, most of my brain thought: this makes no bloody sense. The Bolshevik's amoral, the General's fighting a losing battle with the present, there is *literally* a god in the machine and the women are thick and servile (well done). The officers and gangsters are nothing like each other though a long passage has them nodding sagely and saying "are we so very different" (yes). I've no idea what the writer was saying, but the Republic banned his radio adaptation. If I were a censor, I wouldn't know what I was banning.

"Yeah well. It buys more discs and vodka, and that pasta and sausage we like."

I sighed. "You're better than this."

"I'm no better than my wages."

That last made something sink - perhaps for always. I got that feeling so hard to describe and harder to bear: between hunger, yearning, sadness and a feeling all has passed and is lost. As though you've been put in a glass cube and can see the world but never touch or know it.

"Die Nibelungen is showing at the Universum?"

"Ain't that fantastical trash?"

I raised an eyebrow. "Sorry, what have I just sat through?"

"No, I want a new sparkly dress. We'll go to Wertheim."

~

The Berlin Examiner

VOL. XIX., NO. 118.   Tuesday 24 October

Palast Theatre impresario disinterred from Luisenstadt grave of gangster Carlin Hahn

I realised it all didn't matter much. There was no recognisable future or safety. I could no more protect Missy or Raymund from the deals of harm - the new brutalities - than I could my Mama or Paps.

But I was proud of one goon.

"Honey I've done your laundry."

"You left some stuff."

"It'll go in the next lot."

Missy came out in a towel. I had to get up.

"Go write your play." Her face shone, and maybe the scars perked.

"I'll get to it."

She looked pleasantly surprised; the prod. "Ooh, so grown up."

"Wasn't I?"

"Always, honey-child."

"Shall I put the phono on?"

"You flip. I'll uncork."

She padded to the kitchen. I watched her lean into untidy bottles. No safety; only the present.

~

Ever briefly think you're a seer? It can probably happen to anyone: a loop of sight. For instance, I know there will be a man in the future who questions the linearity of time and solidity of atoms. I don't know why or how I know this, or its significance. Sometimes I witness my own angers as seeds of a terrible future, burgeoning from the most casual days. The slap of the letterbox brings a leaflet. The rattle of a machine gun brings a dead *Stahlhelm*, in time a martyr.

My police interrogators are split neatly between a lazy Jew-hating pension-featherer, and a quite diligent (and I think humane) deputy. Who, in this terrible game, takes control of intent. We are fragile, forging ourselves.

Jeez I'm disintegrating. And I've got Ray falling apart in my flat, within sight, while I splinter in my own disgrace.

I didn't want to go home; sat on a bench dedicated to the fallen, soaking photons. Lange's green Daimler passed, stopped, reversed to the kerb, winding the window. "Hey kid."

"Kerb crawling is illegal." I leant in.

"So's hammering people in the face."

"Well, how did it go?"

"I was given access, and the dates and payments roughly match to Hartmann's statement and photos. Until an enquiry is concluded, he's out of service. He certainly won't be doing any press."

~

Cap Lehane and Kapuze were on hand at the *Palast* for my singular delivery. But I planned to shuffle Gerhard to Cafe *Wien*, negotiate on less hallowed ground.

It hadn't escaped me that in the elapsed time (not doing great things to the finger), news may have short-circuited from Bremen to Berlin of Jonas' luck. But that's OK. If nobody expects an occupying Ulster Rifleman to dismember citizens, it's difficult to pin.

At the door of the renamed *Bavarian Beer Cellar*, I was stopped.

"You don't look the age."

"I need to speak to the boss. I have something he'll want to see, believe me. And there's them of course." I nodded back into the bright foyer.

My oaf-in-a-coat looked at another oaf-in-a-coat beyond the fountain. The first had Italian inflection and manner. Stood with the gripped wrist out front, just like my interlocutor.

"And him."

Doorman Oaf looked the other side of the fountain at someone much scarier than Paulo the Wop. All I could see was hay-bailers, hoods, canals and silence. Tom Quigley. A large, dull-looking man with receding auburn hair and pale lips in a baggy face. Everything about this man might sag or wobble, but not his eyes. Which turned in my direction at that moment. *I* was terrified and he was protecting me.

"I'll speak to the boss," the doorman offered. "What you want me to tell 'im."

"Tell him..." I pondered, "Tell him... His broader family is in immediate danger."

"Immediate... danger," he echoed. A minute later, he appeared in half-shade with a beckoning hand. I slung my head at my coterie.

"Not them."

"Yes them."

Gerhard sat at the centre of the blood-red web stolen from my father, with his unsmiling focus gathered in like the legs of a compact spider.

"The sprat surfaces."

I didn't know what gambit to make (this isn't my scene) so simply said: "I killed your brother."

Gerhard looked slightly off guard but rectified quickly. "In which case those thugs shouldn't have killed your father. You should be underground."

"You killed my father, I watched you. "

"You're all getting a bit problematic."

"Brünings or Jews in general? Here. Deposit on the return sale of the theatre," I said and tossed the tobacco tin onto his desk, only it clattered and bounced open, the ringed finger falling onto the green leather.

He looked a little shaken. "You."

"Not entirely."

"He's an innocent man you fucking idiot. A legal businessman."

"As was Papa. And Missy."

"You could have left Berlin."

"Why?"

"So who's backing this adventure of yours. This excursion?"

"If you don't know, why would I tell you. "

"I hope you enjoyed breathing while you could."

I shrugged. "I'm no fool Hahn."

"And what do you think is going to happen?"

"I just need you to sign this back. Brüning Theatrical Holdings, which, by the way, is now a misnomer."

"Miss-what?"

I rolled my eyes in the leather-punched room. There was a clatter below, but not of an expectant audience, least not our type; any singing would gain its momentum off-stage, on the sand and grit spewn floors now furbishing my home.

"And you can start by taking that tawdry brawler down." I nodded at the painting of a boxer over the safe.

"Let's get this over with." Quite fleet of foot, Gerhard sprang up and pulled open the gun cabinet. "You fucking fool" he muttered. "Little boys in a new world."

"The place is crawling, Hahn. People who'd put you in the ground. Including the constabulary."

"And you come in here with your short pants, empty-handed. "

"I'd advise against going outside unless its with me and my blessing. "

"Kapuze with you?"

"You're not needed Hahn. Not liked. All Berlin wants your scalp, not just Kapuze. Gone, or underground, either is fine."

He laughed at that. "We've never been liked and it's never mattered. If push comes to shove little Brüning, I'll unload this gun through your face."

"And your brother?" I nodded at the slightly blackening finger on his desk.

He grinned nastily at me. "You think I love him? He knew the risks of being born a Hahn. Just know that you're cornering a rat. This is *my* joint."

"Out you go then. Into the big bad world. My psychiatrist tells me I'm not psychotic."

Gerhard looked at me strangely then. I don't know why I said it, but it seemed to unnerve him.

Paulo was restlessly quiet in the corridor; Gerhard's goons had disarmed by numbers it seemed. With no compunction to talk, Paulo didn't talk; nor break gaze.

Now what have I undertaken? I can't know can I, so I plough the present, hoping the plough's blade doesn't slice my foot and maybe treasure turns up. You think me cocky maybe, but I'm not; I've always given the world the deference it demands.

I walked down the stairs unsure whose gun may go off. The one in my back, Paulo's and Tom's aimed at Gerhard (only a few centimetres clear of my cheeks), or a cacophony in the lobby if panic twitched their itchy fingers.

I know the outcome of this; this escort off the premises. People don't know what they're doing anymore. Captain Lehane has an acuity, but where it'll lead I can't say. Kapuze's bunch have their Sherwood Forest loyalism and bank hauls. Kapuze himself (whichever one it is) has a cult of personality in grub street ink. And Gerhard has shrunk whatever first drove his neighbourhood brutalism, to a mere refusal to lose.

The Palast lobby clipped and bustled, a little shorter now of Bohos. Seeing glinting muzzles and ratty eyes, space began to clear around us.

The proprietor Schuster caught up with Fartleiter Goebbels at the tarpauline'd Jonah by the entrance, grasped his arm and pointed up to St. Fridolin's vaulted roof. I followed his finger. Something sparked in sun, and again. A shape could be made out; erect and still. Fartleiter took control and hurried out into the plaza, down an alley in the low sun. He came out looking satisfied, as I remained prodded with Gerhard's Tommy muzzle. Odd situation: here's me hostage in my own raid where us raiders know the destination to take the hostage-taker (Gerhard) but he doesn't, and the hostage holds a tin with his own hostage-taker's brother's finger.

At the entrance, Tom Quigley appeared, to shepherd our chain of eye-for-eye, finger-for-theatre avengers up the street to Cafe *Wien*. Paulo had moved ahead into the plaza.

Two meat-wagons from our same district station were parked far and remote from each other ogling the other suspiciously. Lange in one, Gründgens in the other. How did Gründgens even know about today?

Oddest of all - and I could be mistaken but I wasn't - was the soft sound of a silenced gun, overhead on the breeze, followed by a slump and crack. Which just left Dr. Goebbels the crippled mollusc skulking with Schuster, evaluating his theatre of bigotry: not in itself criminal.

Behind the curtain of Cafe *Wien*, Kapuze's own jacket potatoes were having fun with Hahn crew flesh, rope puzzles and chairs, Kapuze sat on emperor Gerhard's throne with his courtly lawyer Gennady Chaban in attendance: a Russian tailored in fine grey with floppy black hair and a scowl. (If you wanna get right-wing about who to let in, we could do without these. All that training thrown to the highest bidder. Like God spending the sabbath in a whorehouse.)

I stood in the back room, usually with smoke eddies and full of moon faces and meteors with toy cards in pork pie hands.

"What's that?"

"Your majority shareholding. Your stock, Herr Hahn. We've added a page for you to sign it back."

"To who, you? Or the dead impresario? Or the kid with my gun in his back?"

"If anything happens to the kid, Frau Sophie Hahn's a widow, and all your merry men - as currently held - will fill Kirchhof to capacity."

"So what now, Samaritan Kapuze?"

Lawyer Chaban answered: "Just sign and we'll be out of your way."

"If I don't?"

Chaban: "Well, that's when I'd have to leave the room."

The door opened, and Lange walked in bearing more cold steel. He closed the door softly and said nothing. Just kept his gun handy.

Hahn looked around, chewing his mouth. He wasn't on a winner; wouldn't make a killing. In fact, it could all get worse. "Why all the cops and Irishmen?"

"Irishmen?"

"The Ultach hopping rooves."

Lange said quietly, "Oh, he'd say street justice."

"We're looking to the future," Kapuze added, "Done our homework. You should try. Mutual interest."

"All this," Gerhard wrenched a smile. "To hand over a beer hall to a gay boy for flopping plays. What's underneath, a diamond mine?"

"There'll be more opportunities for you to release stock, at similar prices. Or learn to shoot straight."

I'm angling all this: what's afoot; what's *weak* here. Time's a premium obviously: time is blossoming like sunk blood, and I'm just the favour, right? A perilous beneficent in this. This equation could lose *me*. Lange could lose me, with his entrapping snaps and intrinsic forensics and Kapuze confabs. Where the hell's Declan? The Cap. Gave me the finger and exited... Me. Shivering like static; twisting kaleidoscopes and head fuzz. The zoetrope's run down and all the stencilled demons are posing. Any moment it'll move again and what I don't know mayn't then matter.

...Gerhard. What's there, now, in his frozen moment. He's got Gründgens but Lange's nailing Gründgens also. Gerhard knows diddly about internal grievances. What does he think *I'm* playing at except the obvious: my damned theatre. ...And what am I doing with a finger? He can only associate me and this finger - technically his finger - with Kapuze. Maybe the Cap. Only Gerhard doesn't know about the Cap. Or nothing incriminating, not down here; in crime, where criminals are.

So I'll be Gerhard edging out, spotting angles and moving ...alive and lithe... out of this... fluid. Where's the weakness in this membrane?

Maybe I'm the weakness.

Lange got shunted by the opening door. Gründgens barged in with Michael Hartmann, loaded and flashed. Judas.

"I'll take over from here," said Gründgens. He sounded confident; his voice had a little boom in it.

"Sir, you're not up to speed on this... incident. Perhaps you'll help with the arrests outside? Loading the vans."

I felt the muzzle that had dug in my back depart.

Hahn came round the front of me, said "as we mean to go on" and shot me in the foot.

Aaagh*aaaow*. ...My foot's smoking. He fucking shot me. Pain like a train to a tunnel, sudden compression. And Gerhard searches faces while my loafer pours out sticky me;

just as I was fanning faces in my mind. Pulsing, reddening. I daren't lift the crumpling leather foot, lest it fall apart. Never notice our bits till they break; till bone shatters. Till... blood. Pools. On the floor.

Outside I could hear a commotion. Italian, Irish, German, guns - maybe warning shots, maybe a corridor war - who knew.

Hahn dangled his gun loosely. Kapuze wasn't holding and nor was Gründgens. Leaving Lange in charge of bullets. Hartmann got busy snapping.

"Oh dear Lange," said Gründgens. "Was that accidental, did your gun go off through nerves? Or deliberate, pre-planned when you brokered a deal with scum Kapuze? Entrapping and shooting a minor."

"What!" hissed Lange.

Spinning lights. I noticed Hartmann was photographing at strange angles, and seemed relaxed. Where initially he was sure to get both my injury and Lange with his gun in frame, plus the theatre documentation for the record, the angles began to change a little. *Throb, wump.*

Finally Kapuze spoke. He was looking at Judas. "You done yet?"

"Sure," Hartmann replied. He smiled.

Kapuze pulled a gun and pointed it at Hahn. "Don't move. Gun on the floor". He shouted to the corridor. "Everything alright out there?"

A muffled but definite "All sewn up," floated back.

Lange turned his gun on boss Gründgens.

"Now that," Gründgens said, and it was distinctly a growl, "is not going to help your case."

"Your case," Lange said quietly, and pulled some cuffs. Once he'd cuffed his boss, he turned and did the same to Hahn.

"Hey," I said. I picked up the contract and rustled it loudly in the air.

"Bring it to the station."

A slow procession with me confused, spangled and limping in the middle - like a useless King chess piece in protection, the *weakness* - out of the cafe. Of three uniformed officers, one was bound and one of the other two had a gun pointing at him. I began to think I'd an idea what had happened - but Gerhard was still just too blasé about all this; too... unruffled.

In clangs, jangles and slit tin windows I chewed my lip, wrapping police lint round my foot as Berlin glittered by. Sliding and sparking in electric trouble.

Then we were flashed down by a soft-topped grey BMW which - for a civilian car - seemed highly determined to waylay the police; arms out the windows jabbing at the kerb.

"What's this?" I said to Lange. "Why have you stopped?"

"It's a strange day."

With both vehicles halted, out hopped the polio doctor of literature Joseph Goebbels. He went round to Lange's window.

"It seems your stupid Ulsterman, your middleman Lehane... is dead."

I went cold. Brain and spine suddenly as cold as my foot. Oh me. Oh my.

"He was on the roof of St. Fridolin's, a concealed threat to my talk this evening, you see?... Or so the Palast security assure me. A few hours ago. I thought I'd let you know in front of loverboy here, that his sliced mongrel's father is passed on. For everything else, I think you and I should take a walk."

Lange looked hard at me. I swallowed. Lange got out of the wagon.

As they walked off Goebbels said: "Do you deal with lawyers much, Inspector?" But he didn't wait for an answer, carried on talking and the only word I caught was "...circumstantial".

I sat there beside Lange's deputy, his Thompson across his lap, finger over the trigger-guard, ogling the BMW's occupants. After a while he murmured "Gaulieter. What the fuck is a Gaulieter anyway?"

Hahn sat cuffed in the back. *Oh my god. Jesus H.* My head was threshing. How the hell would I break the news to Missy before someone else or the press did. Turmoil; an oil painting of Bedlam.

"I mean, it's like me announcing I'm the king of Spain and you having to go along with it."

"What?"

"Gauleiter."

I could see Lange and Goebbels standing twenty yards away. For all Lange's controlled protestation, Goebbels' body language began hunched and menacing but would become jabbing and accusatory as his body uncoiled.

But I saw something else too. Deep in the shadows of the Merc, faint and crumpled, sunk in upholstery and a grey overcoat, sat Pickelhaube.

They returned to the van and the back door wrenched and clanged.

"Out Hahn," Lange said simply. We were in East Central Berlin so it wouldn't be a shooting party.

Hahn grinned in the dimness, opened his mouth as if to say something scathing, but didn't bother. He got out.

I sat with the nameless deputy in front and heard keys jangle, saw the partial shapes of Lange and Hahn locked in the act of liberation, and then Gründgens piped up:

"Hurry up. These cuffs dig in."

Goebbels fixed him with an icy searchlight. "No. You can stay with your wolves. They look lean and hungry, don't you think? I've heard hunger turns wolves on themselves."

And rubbing his wrists Gerhard Hahn started moving, then swaggering off into the evening while Goebbels went back to his hefty BMW.

~

I stood outside the Lehane front door staring at it for quite a while. Inside I heard Missy's voice shout from room to room: "Where's Pops? I'm starving!"

It was a few moments before a muffled response came back, as though from a room full of laundry or soft materials. "Said he had some business, wouldn't be late."

I sensed Missy huff. Didn't take much for a huff. I clenched my teeth and rang the bell. As feet shuffled to the door I swiped my cap off my head, suddenly self-conscious of it; leant my crutch against the wall. Missy opened the door. "Jeepers, that was quick."

"What?" I said.

"My crates." She looked down at my heavily-bandaged oversize foot.

I shook my head.

"What's happened?"

"Can we go and sit down? And you'd better get Frau Lehane."

"You call her Davione. You always do." Missy looked at my cap, screwed and wrung in my hands. "You're scaring me, what's the matter Babes."

I nodded at the interior and she let the door back, eyes rather wide. "Go get Frau..." I began in a hoarse whisper, "Davione."

She stared at me a few moments then quickly walked to the muffled room. A little chatter and they both appeared.

"I have distressing news. Better sit down. "

Neither did.

"I'm afraid Declan was shot this afternoon."

"He's alive?" Davione said immediately. Missy just stared, her mouth peeling apart.

"No." I said. "It seems either Gaulieter Goebbels or his men, or Palast security, shot him on the roof of St. Fridolin's. By the account of... members of Sonnenallee police station he was an armed threat. Mistaken for a fanatic."

The way Missy was staring at me, slack-mouthed, eyes brimming with fear, was like I was a phono she could will to spin backwards and the words reenter my mouth.

Davione began nodding, and finally said: "Get out of my home."

My cap was now damp with sweat, my head dizzy with exhaustion. My club foot throbbed in its soaked bandage.

"Don't come near my daughter. Not you. Not any Brüning."

I nodded. "I'm sorry," and I started for the door. Paused. "There are no other Brünings. Except my senile grandpap in a home. Someone will need to identify the Captain." I continued to leave.

"Wait, " said Davione. "Did you not understand when your own parents were killed? Or when Missy was used as a bargaining chip for debts? Or when you were shot at for passing fake money?"

"We both wanted the same, like everyone in Neukölln. But we weren't the ones to do it. My own father was none too bright and made some terrible mistakes."

"Leave now."

As I closed their front door I saw Missy stumble, no stagger, to a chair.

Morning sun pools me from the corridor end window. I shake my head in bafflement as I lock the flat's door and leave (Missy doesn't want me home when she picks up her things). I'm a true fucking moron. I'd assumed the way she spoke of Declan and *to* him indicated a cold distance of estrangement.

Couldn't have been more wrong. She disapproved of him, how he acted, the bad and shady expedience, his reserve with his own daughter. And she blasted him over life as a Rifleman, an occupier, a unionist and beyond. But only a certified cretin couldn't see it covered a deep and angry love.

Here's me wanting to be a dramatist, and I couldn't figure that out. Tailor's dummy Raymund was brighter than me, even with an arm full of junk and no books on his shelf.

~

"They rob banks! You're a policeman and I thought you were straight. How do I trust a straight cop who's bent."

"The same way you trusted your father who counterfeits money. Trust has districts."

"Not in your position."

"I protect the innocent. Banks are insured. I wanted Hahn and Gründgens out of Neukölln."

"And the Kapuzes?"

He looked away and muttered, "They respect the common man."

"So it's merely a question of quality?"

Lange curled his mouth. "They don't squeeze a margin for fuck all. Kapuze stabilises Friedrichschain while Hahn will turn the good workers of Neukölln over to worse poverty and the right-wing. Hahn is a bad insurance company without paperwork, guarantee or trade description. A vicious illusion."

Lange raised a significant brow at me.

"The Kapuzes' time will come; they're too powerful, but it's not now."

"Really. And what about Gerhard? The fotze with the guardian angel."

~

I made an appointment to see Dr. Winter again, with my own cash this time. But he wasn't quite the same.

"Do sit down Detlef."

I did. "How's tricks Doc?"

"Life creeps on in its petty pace."

I looked at him. "Are you OK?"

"As much as one can be."

"This is a bad time," I gripped the rests of the chair to get up.

"No worse than any other."

"Doc, I was hoping you could help me a little. A little further."

"You want *me* to help *you*."

"Well, yes." I looked around his office. "I mean, you're still practising, right?"

"Technically."

I did then notice a box beside his desk, into which some of the books from his shelves must've jumped.

"Well, shall I begin?"

"Why not."

"It's a good thing I don't have depression, isn't it."

"How so?"

"Coming to visit you. Right ray of sunshine today."

"I'm sorry. I'll be a more professional. So is this still about your hankering for boys?"

"I told you before, it was one boy. I now believe it may have been just aesthetic, you know? Like Plato?"

"Did you interfere with each others' chaps?"

"Yes."

"Then it's homosexual."

"Come on Doc. I was younger. It's easy for feelings to get confused. Hero worship, all that."

"Phallocentrism."

"Pardon?"

"Worship of the penis."

"I don't worship at that altar, thank you. I merely sip the font water."

"OK, if you think it was... Platonic and you're happy with that, why have you come to see me?"

"To ask your views."

"On?"

"Psychosis."

He seemed to perk in a flash of being valued; the relevance that pulls one from solipsism.

"What kind?"

"Well, you know these new-fangled Nazis they have now."

That immediately put him back behind his cloud. He nodded.

"And, they had a youth section. Train young, bend minds, you know?... but then that all got banned."

"Well. Not any more."

"Correct, not any more. Anyway, while they were banned, they kind of still existed and everyone knew it."

He nodded again.

"So, I was at a demo and it got rowdy, and I came out a bit, black and blue. Look..." I showed him the inside of my lip, which was still lumpy and suckable.

"An NSDAP rally? Dear me. Do you..." his eyes went rather gaunt and haunted. "...follow that stuff?"

"No, I was the other side. K Marx. Anyway, I found one alone and I laid in, with a view to doing real damage. I floored him. Had a hammer with me, but we won't go into that. So I had him at my mercy and I nearly killed him. It was in my head. I felt I was actually going to kill him, even though it was nothing like… you could never argue, it was self-defence. What do you make of that?"

"But you didn't?"

"No. I stopped myself."

"Why?"

"It didn't feel right."

"I see. A hammer?"

"That's circumstantial."

"On your way to a carpenters' convention?"

I sighed. "My family got into trouble with the neighbourhood top men. I was in the habit of carrying it. The hammer isn't the point."

"Nasty," Dr. Winter murmured. He then looked away, gazing out the window, apparently permanently, because he didn't speak again.

"Are you alright Doc. You really don't seem yourself today."

"Yes."

"So, in psychosis terms, where does that put me?"

"You were in your right mind."

"Yes."

"And you stopped yourself."

"Yes."

"I would say you're *not* psychotic."

"What if it happened again and I didn't?"

"Mmm," he started to shift back to gazy, non-talk mode and I had to literally click my fingers at him. "Doc, doc! I was really hoping you'd help."

"Help? How can I help. How can anyone help anyone. Hell is round the corner, can't you feel it?"

"No, well maybe a little, sometimes, but that's just... I dunno, resistance to change isn't it?"

"Ha!" He'd totally lost the plot now. "A great reckoning will come upon us, can't you see?"

"Jesus Christ. I'll let your secretary know to bring in some sedatives." I got out of the chair and stormed out of the room.

~

New evidence in 1922 Zelda Dönitz murder trial.
Review of Wittenau patient Edsel Richter to commence

I saw Weiß the other day. His black eye-slit looked faked like shoeshine; his nostril was ripped from its moorings; a scuffed and bloody graze below his eye became purple bruising on his jaw under his ear. He walked with a limp and clutched ribs.

I didn't say hello: he didn't look talkative, and anyway he'd pulled the rug from Paps.

Time can pull the rug from all our feet. Fads of temperament, the money-weather, regulations, peculiar whims of trade delegates.

Economics used to step out proud and sure, with a sharp briefcase full of unassailable rules, like armour. Like a lawyer might swat an assailant with his case notes. But money will give us another trouncing before the NSDAP do.

In Weiß's case though, he'd lately been over-sparkly. Time and its peoples hadn't waited for semi-reasonable instruction.

All the excuses they needed were before their eyes. Where a tasteful wristwatch had sat in vintage tarnish, now multi-dialled platinum swelled the ranks of shiny objects on his fingers. Where he'd once alternated two fedoras, now each morning brought a brand new, increasingly garish felt contraption. His trousers grew in brightness and if his rain mac got wet he'd buy a new one and have the wet delivered home for maintenance.

Yes, what they had was a fat, wealthy, gay Jewish American investor, walking alone. Even I might have stuck the boot in.

I also saw - my initial joy fading to regret - Raymund. He was alive. He'd been no Hannover Wolf victim, maybe had never left. I was walking aimlessly through the grimed greens of Hebrewland and Raymund got into a polizei car at Gesundbrunnen S-Bahn. He sat in the passenger seat, chatted at length, before scanning the streets and hopping out again.

~

I was in a cafe at the end of Sharonstraße, far from Cafe *Wien* and the *Palast*, waiting to see if Missy'd show. Either find a solution or begin the dissolution. I was the dartboard for their anger, even though Declan would always have done what he did, what he chose, my ideas in his ear or not. He was rough justice and what'd I to do with that? Lehane sold blowtorches in exchange for murder.

Outside, our brash sun and hurrying hats and bobs reassured, but Berlin looked like what it was becoming: uncertain. Nearer the *Palast*, stupid, sweating Germans headed for the beer hall.

I gazed, and out of leftfield walked Ernst Bebel in a blue sports jacket, with stormy Günter on one side, and lovely Rilla on the other with a buggy pram. She looked happy and he pensive as though, scaffolded by circumstance, he wasn't sure what he thought, but there it was. In the buggy was their new amendment, Otto Bebel, asleep, behaving; usefully quiet. What might have been a footnote in Herr Bebel's life was now a crawling narrative.

In fairness, Ernst tried to turn down Gerhard over reconstructing the *Rottie*, but Gerhard Hahn manhandles; he has persuasion. More so since most of Kapuze's mob drifted off, and Kapuze concentrates solely on banks now. Thereby famous.

An hour and a half passed and Missy didn't show. I took another dug-out sweep of Sharonstraße.

Dawn invades my table lamp and my play's done. It concerns an angel who commits a terrible crime and is banished to hell. The angel bargains with god and is allowed out on probation, but must agree to be supervised by the other angels. They'll mentor his activities, manage his finances and provide a weekly stipend, reporting back to God.

Over a short period of time, the angel becomes saintly - the envy of other angels - supervising great charities and exhibitions and progress in human tolerance and the sciences. So saintly in fact, that a delegation of priests petition God to have him canonised. This provokes in the already jealous supervising angels, such all-consuming envy and rage they lynch the angel, ripping him apart. They are ashamed of their bloodlust, as is God, who banishes them all. Beyond heaven they set upon each other and there is a period of great darkness as God sits alone in Heaven and his angels commit savage acts.

I think it'll work, but casting's crucial. The fallen angel must have large, supplicant eyes and a bald head to illustrate newborn innocence. Only a thin moustache will denote adulthood. He will dress in starchy high collars, tie and waistcoat. A medium-sized angel with a paunch.

Plus I wrote a novel anonymously, wrapped in paper to give Michael, on which I'll place his Leica 35 with a new film. Whether it'll see *Hartmann & Schwartz* daylight I can't say, but Hartmann has extracted his pulp-pound. It concerns a Raskolnikov type who has a blinding vision he must eradicate from his sphere all heinous and misguided people.

My bags are by the door, the heavy stuff sent already to a tiny studio in Hamburg's docks. I sling a holdall strap on my shoulder, lift my suitcase, and grab the Hartmann parcels from the table. A last look at my nest and the door jangles locked behind me.

The street is leafy but once again there's distant noise. I've come to think of this clamour as barbarians at the gate: let's go see.

A bobbing brigade coming south-east down Sonnenallee. Over there - in the mottled overhang of buildings, the shop-skirts - Landespoizei bucket-heads are wrapped in floor-length carpets, their helmets designed for idiocy. The only thing undermining this idiocy is the odd lowered Thompson, and lining the avenues are Rotfront, half-asleep and unsure.

I grasp a bystander's arm. "What gives? Who organised this?"

"Who do you think? He's sitting in that open-top."

Dr. Goebbels has sent his damp-pitted brownshirts into Neukölln. Poor workers' Redkölln! Now that's provocative. That... is sticking your fucking neck out.

People dart about on rooftops. Just dark streaks in the corner of my eye, or a glint of metal. But there's further complexity in this pending car-crash: the damned clergy. A frocked Protestant - one of these baffled Puritans - in the middle of the street, in line for a barrage of goosesteps. His disciples have opted for the pavement.

"Who's up on the roof?"

"Oh," this bag-eyed bystander dropped his eyes to my gripped *Shwayder* case. "I'd guess it's SA and maybe some Hahns for local know-how. Security and such."

"Sheesh," I became self-conscious of my luggage. "That's the last thing they need, proper organisation."

This man didn't look well. He had the malnourishment of belief, his left arm tight against his coat; probably a shiv or blade. "You a shouter or a scalper, Comrade?"

"I hadn't decided."

"Shouters are no use to me."

"And what are *you*?"

"The Soviet wasn't built in the Duma, was it? Bullets and blood my friend."

"But this is Germany."

He snorted. "Is it."

And here's *Kuhn's*. I lug my trunk to the door. His son Elias does it now, clipping keratin with gritted teeth - at least the new severe style keeps him in business. He looks up.

I ask a favour... *being the last kid to see his father alive and all, could I leave my bag here for an hour, and...*

...Well, I know his Paps used to keep his, *ahem*, service issue upstairs. *Could I?* I point up the shadows.

It's a while, but Elias shrugs; I've no idea what's in the shrug. The electric handles continue over a teenage parade ground.

I jangle from Kuhn's, head south-east, and as Kottbusser Damm joins me, so does a spray of freckles.

"What goes along?" Fuchsia asked, her face so untouched, as if Berlin's grime just ignored her cocoa-froth sheen. "You getting out?"

I looked at my holdall, but she was quietly concealing her own luggage as I glanced down, behind a long Holeproof'd leg. Since I'd seen her, old Catch-All had got some bad amnesia, it was said. A fight too many - a slugged bone connection took out all his history. She came home one night to a perfect stranger; couldn't remember her at all.

"I guess. Not much here except you, petal." --I wondered if news was in about Declan, and mine and Missy's run-in.

"You'll be back, Dets? Stay in touch?"

I squinted at her paisley bag and hatbox, swinging behind in little clasped fingers. I was puzzled and out-of-joint; my jaw hinged at her.

"Well, I'd better get back to my own turf. My kingdom." She was shifting her weight from foot to foot. "Gloria's paranoid about bailiffs. Empty house."

I thought she'd say more but her eyes moved on. I watched her cross the street, with hair so copper for a Caribbean girl, almost flaxen, seemed to trap the sun like curled glass.

It's one last thing. I'll strive like Furtwanger to commit something bigger than myself: an echo in the print chamber.

Gründgens, you see, is treading a new beat. Probably with a bad back, but no lesser spring - no less gaiety - for that.

Tallow faces flicker, capped heads - caught expressions in the transient impression; what's that a montage? There's crowds from Wilhelm, dispersed out of Bülow but - I'm revulsed - there's laughter and smiles too as if showing up, having a day out, will do.

Königgrätzer Straße, Gründgens' tread is less muffled by crowds, enough to conceal but allow me an exit.

How he plods. Everyman with his finger in the jar, with his everyman hates and crisp evening paper, his boiled broccoli. Tonight he'll sit scratching his neck, ruminative in a favoured wingback, considering his preservation; a job well done, a retirement cushioned in iffy satin.

And me - ridiculous, these fingers should be holding the pen of Jophiel, not curling a Glock's worn butt.

On Königgrätzer he's paused by an advert post - an islet - reading the last tidbit of his *Morgen*, then dumping it at a kiosk for a *Tageblatt*.

He walks on past the new trammelled Phoebus Palast, towards an awkward spot where scaffolders have built out into the avenue, leaving a shadowed underpass.

I look around. Of course there are eyes - bored, scrutinous, on a salary - if anything, Gründgens' status has improved.

Now!

I run in his wake as he dips into shade, the Glock rises, but he's hearing and turning - I see his open lips smile and mouthing maybe it's Kike, maybe it's strike, but it opens his mouth and I push the muzzle in and fire.

There are white sparks flicked and spattered red across the scaffold.

And the ring - the muffled underwater throb and ear blood - subsides and the noise of the street returns. Sharp lines and hats and posters; the sound of running boots.

I pick up speed, exit the scaffold and turn back for the Phoebus but the sun's bright, like armour. Plunging the alley's shade there's no handle on the side doors, and the fire stairs are blocked with wire. I clamber the rail and bolt to the second floor. A window's open, an office, calm shirtsleeves within reach.

I hear my name but don't turn.

Almost reach the cool sill...

The boots echo and congeal. Firing starts and shouting. Cement cracks in dust around me. Then the sting hits the back of my thigh thudding my knee into the wall. Another, and the leg holding me gives. The world's on a spindle, the sky whips over the rooves and it's blurred brick.

Crushing, rending jolt.

There's a pale hand on my forehead, another cradling my matted auburn. Conscious in red eddies and blackish pain, I'm all broken like a vase beside children.

"Oh Detty... what have you done? You'll hang for it."

"Ray..." I'm slipping, my mouth is wind-blown petals, "it's just a blot. On my copybook."